THE DEMON'S WATCH

www.davidficklingbooks.co.uk

THE DEMON'S WATCH

CONRAD MASON

OXFORD · NEW YORK

31 Beaumont Street
Oxford OX1 2NP, UK

THE DEMON'S WATCH
A DAVID FICKLING BOOK 978 0 857 56031 5

First published in Great Britain by David Fickling Books,
a division of Random House Children's Publishers UK
A Random House Group Company

Hardback edition published 2012
Paperback edition published 2013

1 3 5 7 9 10 8 6 4 2

Set in Berling

DAVID FICKLING BOOKS
31 Beaumont Street, Oxford, OX1 2NP

www.**randomhousechildrens**.co.uk
www.**totallyrandombooks**.co.uk
www.**randomhouse**.co.uk

Addresses for companies within The Random House Group Limited can be found at: www.randomhouse.co.uk/offices.htm

THE RANDOM HOUSE GROUP Limited Reg. No. 954009

A CIP catalogue record for this book is available from the British Library.

Printed and bound in Great Britain by CPI Group (UK) Ltd,
Croydon, CR0 4YY

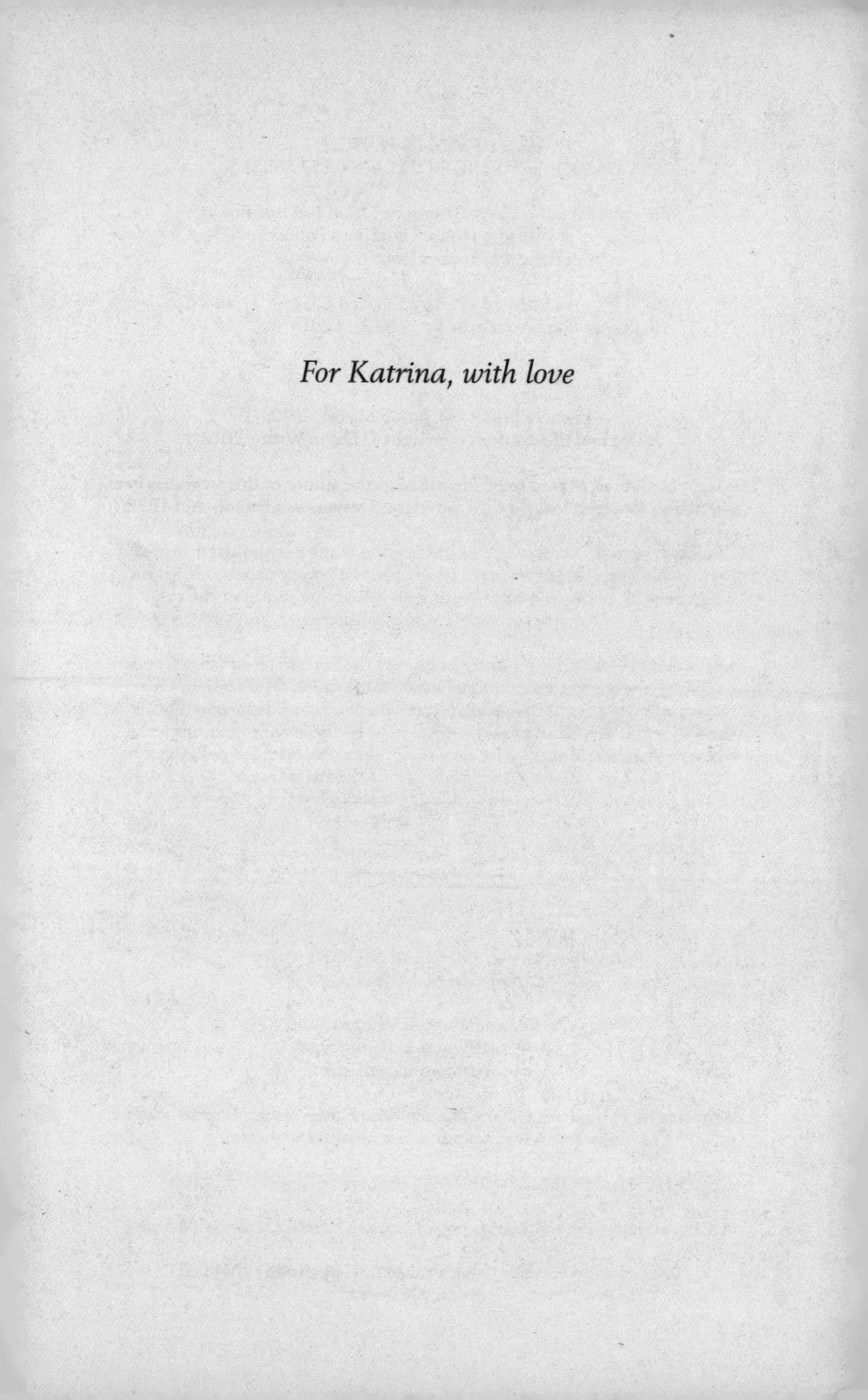

For Katrina, with love

N
E
S
W
HEL
THE NORTHERN WASTES
THE EBONY OCEAN
YSILAND
THE OLD WORLD
THE FLATLAND DUCHIES
THE LONELY ISLE
THE FARIAN TRENCH
LAST SIGHTING OF THALIN THE NAVIGATOR
SCRIMPORT
FAYT
AZURMOUTH
THE MIDDLE ISLANDS
DUCHY OF GARRAN
RENNETH
To THE NEW WORLD
THE KING'S ROCK

PORT FAYT
WYRMWOOD MANOR
LIGHTHOUSE
THE LEGLESS MERMAID
DOCKSIDE
MARLINSPIKE QUARTER
CROSSTREE QUARTER
BOOTLES' PIE SHOP
FLAGSTAFF QUARTER
THALIN SQUARE

The old woman smiles into the darkness.

Her cloak is already drenched, but still the rain beats at her back, drips from her hood and streams over her hands, where they cling onto the cold tiles of the rooftop.

Port Fayt. At last.

She closes her eyes and breathes in deep, savouring the familiar tang of salt, sweat and rotten fish that haunts every twisting, cobbled street.

Ten years. Can it really have been so long?

Port Fayt.

A flash of lightning reveals the town to her. The

bobbing mass of masts in the bay, where galleons rock beside wavecutters, hobgoblin junks and dhows, half-scaled for crews of imps. The clutter of buildings sprawling out from the harbour, clinging to the headlands on either side, their skyline a jumble of red-tiled roofs, chimneys and wooden cranes. In the midst of it all, the grey dome and spire of the town hall in Thalin Square, and high up on the cliff top, the lighthouse, striped red and white like a child's lollipop.

The wind howls, and the rain batters the tiles. And still the old woman smiles.

Port Fayt.

The jewel of the Middle Islands, they call it. A safe haven in the vastness of the Ebony Ocean. Each day, more creatures dare the long voyage here from the Old World, and every one of them can be sure of a welcome. Human or troll. Imp or elf. Here they are all just Fayters. Here they are all equal – or as equal as their wits can make them.

Port Fayt.

Crouched on the rooftop, the old woman drinks it in, recalling every detail. She remembers the chatter of the fairy market in the Marlinspike Quarter, the bragging of the merchants in the town hall and the bustle of Mer Way, Port Fayt's main artery, snaking more than a mile from the docks to Thalin Square. She licks a drop of rain-water from her lips, and still she smiles.

How she hates it.

Port Fayt.

She has come for it, at last.

PART ONE
Contraband

Chapter One

Balancing a clattering pile of dirty dishes in one hand and a tray of empty tankards in the other, Joseph Grubb tried to navigate through the midday tide of drunken sailors. He dodged a staggering dwarf, ducked as a plate went flying over his head and stooped to pick up a fallen tankard, nodding at a one-legged man who, judging by the skull embroidered on his eye patch, probably wasn't an honest fisherman.

It was business as usual in the Legless Mermaid, refuge of the lowliest crooks, scoundrels and rogues in Port Fayt. Not that Grubb was complaining. As his uncle Mr Lightly, the landlord, liked to remind him, he was no better than the customers.

Joseph Grubb was a half-and-half. Not quite goblin and not quite human. It meant he was small and quick enough to weave through the Mermaid at its busiest. But it also meant having mottled grey-pink skin and pointed ears, and Fayters yelling 'mongrel' at him every day.

Then again, according to Mr Lightly, Grubb was lucky to get any work at all – especially in an establishment as fine as the Legless Mermaid.

Someone grabbed hold of Grubb's apron and nearly dragged him off his feet.

'More grog here, matey,' slurred the customer. He was a plump man sitting on his own at a corner table, with long, greasy hair, a gold earring and a lazy eye – although that might have had something to do with the grog he'd been drinking. There wasn't an inch of his table that didn't have a drained tankard on it.

Grubb wrinkled his nose, trying not to breathe in.

'Yes, sir. More grog, on its way.'

'And a nice big plate o' steamed eels.'

'Got it.'

Grubb sighed, and pushed his way back into the crowd. It was at times like these that he wondered about slipping out one night and never coming back. But, as his uncle would have told him, he was just being stupid. Where could he go? He was a mongrel, with no parents and no friends. He didn't like to admit it, but Mr Lightly was right. He was lucky to work here.

'Tankard of grog, Uncle,' he said, reaching up to set his load on the bar. 'And a plate of eels for the gentleman in the corner.'

Mr Lightly was a burly, red-faced human who never, ever called his nephew by his first name. He poured the drink, handed it to Grubb and hit him hard on the ear.

'How many times do I have to tell you, mongrel? You don't call me Uncle. Especially not in public.'

'Yes, Mr Lightly. Sorry, sir.'

'Your mother might have been a goblin lover, but I stinking well ain't. Got it?'

Grubb didn't trust himself to reply. He nodded, rubbing his head for the fourth or fifth time that day, and zigzagged back through the crowd to deliver the grog.

The man with the lazy eye snatched it and slurped away, dripping most of it onto his filthy coat. Within seconds, the tankard came down with a bang and the man let out a long, gurgling burp.

'Ahhhh, that's better. Thank yer kindly, matey.'

'You're welcome,' said Grubb, faintly disgusted. He turned to go, but the man was holding onto his apron again.

'Hold on there, lad. What's the rush, eh? Sit down.'

'Umm . . . I'm not . . .'

'Never mind that. You seem like a decent sort, matey. Won't yer help out a cove who's new in town?'

'Well, I . . .'

'Hear tell there's to be a party tonight, out on the docks. What's that in aid of, eh?'

Grubb looked around. No one seemed to need him, and he was desperate to rest his aching feet. Besides, Mr Lightly was always telling him to keep the customers happy. They loved to talk, once they'd got a few of Lightly's Finest Bowelbusters inside them. The stuff loosened tongues as well as bladders. Loosened just about everything, in fact.

'You mean the Grand Party?' he said.

'That's the one, matey.'

Grubb sat down and tried to explain.

'The Grand Party is . . . well, er, it's just a big party, really. Everyone in Port Fayt is invited, and it's all paid for by the governor. We have it once a year, to celebrate the first day of the festival, and it's—'

'Slow down, lad. Festival? What festival?'

Grubb did his best not to look surprised. The man clearly knew nothing about Port Fayt.

'The Festival of the Sea. It lasts four days, starting today. At the end there's a huge pageant, and everyone wears fancy dress and parades through the town. It's all because of Thalin the Navigator. Sort of to thank him.' Grubb realized that he was enjoying himself. It felt good, being able to help out this stranger. 'He was an explorer from the Old World. It was him who first discovered the Middle Islands and founded Port Fayt. It was supposed to be a safe place for everyone. You know, humans, trolls, elves and so on . . . All living together in peace.'

The man frowned and peered around at the other customers, as if he was only just noticing them. There was a gang of stevedores by the bar – humans, a few dwarves and a large green troll, drinking and arm-wrestling. The troll won every time, of course, but they were all enjoying themselves too much to mind. At the table next to them, an impish sailor was chattering away to an elf – tall and slender, with ghostly white skin. She was seated and bent low over the table, but the imp still had to stand on tiptoes to talk to her. His nostrils quivered with excitement as he told his story.

'Seems to work, eh, matey?' said the man at last. 'Maybe this Thalin o' yours was on to something, mixing everyone up. Never seen the like, back in the Old World. Folks keep themselves to themselves back there.'

Grubb shrugged. It did work. More or less. Unless you happened to be a mongrel. He looked down at his hands, grey-pink with long bony fingers, and sighed.

'So, this cove, Thalin the Navigator,' said the man. 'What happened to him?'

'They say he was, er . . . eaten. By a sea demon called the Maw.'

The man thought about that for a few moments, then snorted.

'Sounds like a load of old bilge to me, matey.'

Grubb chuckled. He was starting to like the stranger. He seemed honest and straightforward, which was unheard of in the Mermaid. And besides, being called matey was a lot better than being called mongrel.

'So will you be going to the party?' he asked.

The man gave a sly smile, checked his tankard was empty and belched.

'Oh, I reckon I'll be there, lad. Got a spot of business to take care of. Got to keep yer appointments, ain't yer?'

'I suppose so,' Grubb agreed, though he had no idea what the man was talking about.

'What's yer name?' asked the man, holding out a hand.

'Grubb,' said Grubb. He shook the hand. 'Pleased to meet you.'

'Aye, and you too, matey. I'm Captain Phineus Clagg.'

Grubb felt his ears twitch.

'Captain?'

'That's right. Captain of the *Sharkbane* – fastest ship in the Ebony Ocean. She's a wavecutter, like o' which you've never seen. Ain't nothing like standing at her prow, feeling the salt spray on yer cheeks. That's the life, matey. Tell yer what, you should join us. Always room for a smart lad on board.'

Mr Lightly appeared with a steaming plate of eels, dumped it on the table and belted Grubb round the head.

'Enough chit-chat, mongrel,' he wheezed, heading back to the bar. 'Get to work.'

Clagg pulled a penknife from his pocket and began to eat, slicing off chunks of eel, spearing them with the knife and stuffing them into his mouth. The conversation was obviously over.

'Oi, mongrel!' yelled someone from the other side of the tavern.

Grubb hurried off, rubbing his head for the fifth or sixth time that day. His heart was racing. It wasn't every day you met a ship's captain in the Legless

Mermaid. He had to talk to him again. Could there really be room for a mongrel in his crew? Grubb was sick to death of the Mermaid, and he was pretty sure Mr Lightly wouldn't be sorry to see him go.

He tried to imagine himself as a seafaring adventurer aboard a wavecutter, just like Thalin the Navigator. It didn't seem that likely. But then, Phineus Clagg hadn't seemed like much of a captain himself. Funny, what he'd said about an appointment at the Grand Party. What did he—

CRRRRRASH!

Grubb spun round.

Phineus Clagg's table was lying on its side, several feet from where it had been before. The captain himself lay dazed beside it, his chair broken beneath him and his eels spilled all over his shirt.

Grubb caught his breath. Standing over the fallen man was a gigantic figure, taller than anyone else in the tavern. His shaved head brushed the ceiling. His muscled torso was bare, the dark brown skin covered in intricate, swirling black tattoos. And his massive fist held a massive cutlass.

'Surprise,' said the ogre.

The cutlass blade hovered inches above Clagg's neck.

The Legless Mermaid had gone very quiet. Ogres

weren't exactly common, even in Port Fayt, and Grubb had never seen one as big as this before.

'Captain Phineus Clagg, if I don't mistake,' said the ogre. He spoke with a harsh foreign accent that Grubb didn't recognize. 'You coming with me.'

'Well, well,' said Phineus Clagg, from the floor. His eyes were searching round the room, looking for any chance of escape. 'If it ain't my, er . . . my dear old friend Tuck? Now look here, matey, as it happens I'm right in the middle of lunch, so this ain't what you'd call a convenient moment.'

'You no worry,' said Tuck. 'Plenty more eels where you going.'

'Where's that?' asked Clagg, brightening a little.

'Bottom of sea.'

The ogre chuckled – a guttural, roaring sound that made several customers flinch.

'Now, now, gents,' said Mr Lightly nervously, from behind the bar. 'There's no need for any violence. Er, not in here, at least.'

BANG!

Grubb jumped. The ogre was clutching at his ankle, howling like a harpooned walrus, and Phineus Clagg was on his feet. He dropped a tiny smoking pistol and vaulted the overturned table, coat-tails flying, his eyes fixed on the door. Too slow. Tuck swung his cutlass sideways and Clagg tried to dodge; he tripped, staggered, turned it into a roll to one side and sprang up into a crouch. The ogre was still between him and the door. Clagg licked his lips and tugged a short curved cutlass from his belt.

There was a scraping of chairs and tables as customers scrambled to get out of the way, clearing a space around the two fighters. Grubb was jostled backwards, staring at the pair of them. Drunken brawls broke out every day in the Legless Mermaid, but a real fight, with real weapons . . . He didn't exactly want to watch, but he couldn't help himself.

Tuck lifted his hand from his ankle and shook it, spattering the flagstones with spots of blood, so dark it was almost black.

'You . . .' he growled. 'You make me bleed.'

His face twisted into a scowl and he lunged forward, hacking and slashing, his blade spinning like an iron windmill. Clagg stepped back, parrying desperately. He almost tripped over an empty bottle, then scraped past a table, snatched a stool and tried to fend the ogre off with it. But the ogre's cutlass chopped into the legs, tore the stool out of Clagg's hand and sent it clattering to the floor.

Grubb was shoved in all directions at once. Some people were laughing and cheering on the fighters.

Others were drawing their own weapons and wading in. Several heavily armed, overexcited crooks surged towards him, and he dived under the nearest table. He would be safe there. No one was going to care about the tavern mongrel at a time like this.

The table shattered, and Captain Phineus Clagg came crashing down on top of him.

'*Aaaughh!*' yelped Grubb.

'Sorry, matey,' croaked Clagg.

'Get out my way, bilge rats,' yelled Tuck. 'GET OUT MY WAY!'

But the place was in chaos, and there was no way through. Phineus Clagg leaped to his feet and shoved through the crowd. Grubb sat up just in time to see him dive through a window, taking most of the glass with him. Cursing, the ogre elbowed his way to the door, and was gone.

It was a long time before Mr Lightly managed to restore order.

'Settle down, everyone,' he was puffing. 'It's quite safe now. YOU! Put that down.'

A young troll sheepishly lowered the chair he was about to break over his friend's head.

Mr Lightly's eyes fell on Grubb, sitting in a daze amid the wreckage of the table he'd hidden under, rubbing his head for the sixth or seventh time that day.

'Maw's teeth, mongrel!' he snapped. 'Don't just sit around like some ugly brain-dead sea slug. Sort out this mess.'

Grubb nodded, fetched a broom and began sweeping up broken shards of table. Like all the furniture at the Legless Mermaid, it had been cobbled together out of driftwood gathered from the beach. No wonder it had fallen apart so easily.

His foot brushed against something on the floor, and he bent down to pick it up.

A thin package, wrapped in fancy black velvet and tied up with a silver cord. It was no wider or longer than his forearm, and weighed almost nothing. He tried shaking the package, but it made no sound. Captain Clagg must have dropped it when he fell.

Grubb looked round. His uncle was facing away from him, apologizing to some customers and herding others out of the tavern. He only had a second or two. Quickly, he lifted up his shirt and stuffed the package into his belt, out of sight.

His ears were tingling and his heart was racing all over again. Whatever it was, it looked like something valuable, all wrapped up like that.

Maybe Clagg would escape from the ogre and come back for it.

Maybe he'd be delighted that Grubb had found it for him.

Maybe he'd ask how he could ever repay him, and Grubb would ask to join his crew, and he'd set sail aboard the *Sharkbane*, off into the sunset, in search of adventure . . .

Probably not.

But *maybe*.

Chapter Two

Captain Newton's boots thudded on the cobblestones, still wet from last night's rain.

It was lunch time, and Fayters thronged the quayside. Stevedores rolled barrels down gangplanks, heaved wooden crates, argued with harassed revenue officials. Traders haggled, shook hands, tried to fleece one another. Food sellers ducked and weaved among the crowds, hawking greasy paper bags of shellfish, slices of fried octopus and flagons of grog, and yelling curses at the messenger fairies who whirred through the air, running errands for their masters. Out in the bay, sailors clambered over rigging. Sails were unfurled, anchors weighed, orders bellowed.

If Fayters were the town's life-blood, then the harbour was its beating heart.

Newton nodded. It was a beautiful day, all right. Damp air, clear blue sky and a nice breeze. Just the way he liked it. His own messenger fairy, Slik, fluttered just ahead of him, pale sunshine glinting off his tiny wings.

'Morning, Newt,' called a fisherman.

'Jonas. Fish biting?'

'Aye, plenty.'

Yes. Today was going to be a good day.

As busy as they were, Fayters took care to keep out of his way. Captain Newton was a human, but as big as a troll. His head was shaved and scarred, and on his right cheek he wore a blue shark tattoo – the mark of the Demon's Watch: protectors of Port Fayt, friends to all honest townsfolk and enemies to any thief, smuggler or pirate who crossed their path.

In short, picking a fight with Captain Newton was a seriously bad idea, and it didn't take a magician to see that.

Newton stopped at a run-down wooden food stall beside a pier, and bought a pastry. It was hot and sweet, and he munched it appreciatively. Slik folded away his wings and settled on the edge of the counter, leaning back against a pepper pot and swinging his legs over the side.

'How do you like it, Mr Newton?' asked the food seller, a young elf, tall and slender and almost as pale as his white apron.

Newton nodded slowly, stuck a finger in his mouth and picked at his teeth.

'Not bad. Not bad at all.'

'I made it specially for you, see?'

'Hmmmm.' That didn't seem very likely.

'Special ingredients, Mr Newton. For a special customer.'

Newton broke off a small piece and handed it to Slik.

'What do you reckon?'

The fairy crammed the pastry into his mouth, chewed it for a few seconds, then spat it out and made a face.

'Horrible. What's it made of – mouldy leather?'

'Excuse my fairy,' said Newton, giving Slik a look. 'It's delicious.'

The elf sniffed and began wiping down the counter meaningfully. Slik took the hint and leaped into the air, hovering and landing lightly on Newton's shoulder.

'Well, it'd better be, that's all,' said the food seller.

'It's for the Grand Party tonight, see? Special order from the Cockatrice Company. Gotta make three hundred by this evening. I'm going up in the world, see, Mr Newton?'

'Congratulations,' said Newton. He brushed pastry crumbs from his lips, fished around in a pocket of his battered blue coat and laid a half-ducat coin on the counter. 'The company'll be pleased.'

'How about you, Mr Newton?' said the elf, tucking the coin away in his apron and hunting for change. 'Is the Watch busy these days?'

Newton had just opened his mouth to reply when there was an angry shout from the far end of the pier.

'*We had a deal, you lazy good-fer-nothing!*'

Newton recognized that voice. He grinned at the elf.

'Looks like we're going to be. Enjoy the party. And keep the change.'

At the end of the pier, a small goblin was shaking with rage and bellowing at a troll captain more than twice his height. Newton had never seen the troll before, but he knew the goblin all right.

Jeb the Snitch.

There was a saying on the harbour front: *What the Snitch don't know ain't worth knowing*. Jeb was always a little vague about how he got his information, but the Demon's Watch had made enough arrests with his help that Newton was prepared to overlook the details.

After his knowledge of Port Fayt's criminal underworld, Jeb the Snitch was best known for his outfits. This morning he was got up in an orange waistcoat and a purple jacket with diamond buttons – both slightly too big for him, as if they'd been made for a human. Gold rings flashed on his pointed ears. Newton didn't know much about the latest fashions, but he could see that the Snitch looked like a mad parrot.

The troll was grumbling as Newton strolled up.

'Look, a tormenta ain't exactly my fault, is it? There ain't no sailing in a flaming *magical storm*, Jeb. You know that.'

'Oh yeah? Well, in case you hadn't noticed, knucklehead, the tormenta was last night, and today's today if I ain't mistaken, and you promised you'd get my griffin bile out *before* the festival, didn't yer?'

The troll shrugged.

'Ain't been a tormenta in years, Jeb. And on the eve of the festival and all. Bad omen that is, sure as the sea.'

'Oh, omens, is it? You've been listening to too many old wives' tales. Next you'll be telling me it means that the Maw is angry and stirring in the depths and blah blah blinking blah. And this from a grown troll.'

Newton came up behind Jeb and laid a hand on his shoulder. The goblin flinched and turned his grey face towards Newton, his small, pale eyes darting round nervously. In Jeb's line of work, it paid to be a little paranoid.

'Oh, it's you. Morning, Newt.'

'Jeb.'

The troll took his chance, and slipped away.

'What a load o' walrus dung,' muttered Jeb. 'Talk about gullible. Omens!'

'Got any leads for me today, Jeb?'

The goblin licked his lips and made a big show of looking over both shoulders before leaning in.

'Funny you should ask actually, 'cos it just so happens I do. Got something very tasty indeed, if I say so myself.'

'Go on.'

'Whoa, not so fast, mate. Let's talk price, eh?' He grinned.

'The usual. Plus the usual bonus if we catch some-one. Same as always.'

'Come on, Newt. Here's me, trying to make an honest living . . .'

Newton raised an eyebrow.

'All right, all right, if that's the way it is. But we can't talk here, see? Gotta go somewhere a bit more private.'

Two minutes later, they had found a quiet table in Spottington's Velvethouse. The sweet smell of velvetbean hung heavy in the air, mingling with the smoke from customers' pipes. Spottington's was one of the oldest and most respectable velvethouses in Port Fayt. The tablecloths were clean. The waiters were polite. The customers were few, elderly and mostly half asleep. It was a safe place to talk.

They sat, Jeb patting down his coat and rearranging the cuffs. Up close, Newton noticed that the goblin's diamond buttons were fake, and that the earrings he wore weren't gold after all, but polished brass. The rest of his clothing was still just as alarming, though.

'You know you look like a mad parrot?' said Slik, from Newton's shoulder. For someone so small he had a very loud voice.

'Tell your fairy to keep his gob shut.'

'You heard him, Slik,' said Newton sternly. 'Watch it.'

Slik muttered something under his breath, yawned

and fluttered down to the tablecloth for a nap.

A waiter bustled over with two steaming cups of velvetbean.

'How about that tormenta last night, gents?' he said cheerily. 'Bad omen, that is, and no mistake.'

The Snitch rolled his eyes.

'So, Jeb,' said Newton, hoping to cut the goblin off before he launched into another rant. 'How's the griffin-bile business?'

'Bad,' said Jeb, when he was sure the waiter had gone. 'Very bad. Can't shift it out of the Middle Islands these days. And it ain't just bile, neither. Indigo merchants are going out of business. Zephyrum's rare as cockatrice teeth. Saw a warehouse yesterday, stuffed to the rafters with sacks of velvetbeans just sitting there, and what ain't being stolen by fairies is just rotting away. It were a sad sight, Newt, I can tell yer. Trade with the Old World's drying up, thanks to the League.'

'Hm.'

'Word is they've got their grubby mitts on most of the mainland now, and they don't want to do business with us Fayters. Anyone who ain't human is just scum to them.'

'Aye.'

'Worse than scum. Creatures of darkness.

Demonspawn. All that bilge. Maw's teeth, the Old World's gone crazy, Newt. Almost makes you—'

'Right,' cut in Newton, more gruffly than he'd intended.

Jeb shut up at once.

Newton frowned, and massaged the red, blistered marks that ran around his wrists. *The League of the Light*. It had been twenty years since the League's men had given him those scars. But the memories were still fresh.

He sipped his drink, wiped away a velvetbean moustache and changed the subject.

'Let's have this lead then, eh?'

'Down to business, is it? Right you are.'

The Snitch leaned forward, his eyes scanning round the room, checking that no one was listening.

'Word is, there's a new smuggler in town. Came in last night with a cargo, something big . . . *right in the middle of the tormenta*.'

Newton raised an eyebrow. It was a good lead. Superstition or no superstition, smuggling in the midst of a magical storm was about as safe as playing kiss chase with a shark. That meant this smuggler was either very stupid, or very clever indeed.

'Any idea where to find him?'

Jeb grinned, revealing his pointed goblin teeth.

'He'll be at the Grand Party tonight. Whatever the cargo is, it's going to be handed over after sundown, below decks on the *Wraith's Revenge*. You can nab the smuggler and 'is customer at the same time. Kill two dragons with one fireball, see?'

Newton nodded. Smugglers. Always picking the most inconvenient times to do their dirty work. Of course, that was to be expected. But even at the Grand Party, the Demon's Watch would be ready and waiting.

'All right,' he said. 'C'mon, Slik.'

He gave the snoozing fairy a gentle prod.

'*Whassammmfff leemealone . . .*'

'Wake up.'

'*Mmmff no, no, the blue one . . . with the lacy bits.*'

'I said, wake up.'

Slik sat up and rubbed his eyes.

'Oi! I was asleep, you big oaf.'

'Too bad. Round up the Watch and have them meet me here at dusk, armed and ready for the Grand Party. We've got a smuggler to catch.'

'What about a bit of sugar then? I haven't had a granule in three days.'

Newton pulled a chunk from his coat pocket and broke off a piece for the fairy. 'Don't eat it all at once.

You remember what happened last time.' The vomit stains still hadn't washed out.

Grumbling, Slik tucked the tiny sugar lump into a tiny knapsack, flapped his wings and set off through Spottington's haze of tobacco and velvetbean. Newton watched him go.

'That fairy,' he muttered. 'Cost me eight ducats and gives me nothing but trouble.'

'Ah, he ain't so bad, Newt. Now, what about my payment, eh?'

Newton replaced the sugar and brought out his money pouch. 'One last thing. This smuggler. Has he got a name?'

'Thought you'd never ask. He's a podgy old soak, with a crazy left eye and not much use for baths. Goes by the name of Clagg. Captain Phineus Clagg.'

Chapter Three

Grubb hummed as he washed the dishes. Mr Lightly didn't like him to sing, so he ran through the words in his head:

Scrub the dishes, scrub them clean,
Cleaner than you've ever seen.

It was something his mother used to sing, a long, long time ago, in their little house with the green front door. Grubb tried to go through it at least once every day. After all, there was no one else to remember it for him, and it felt good to have something of hers. Even if it wasn't an actual, real thing.

They'd all worked together to do the dishes in those days, Grubb bringing the plates from the table, Mother washing, and Father drying with a tatty old dishcloth. Mother always tied her long brown hair back, and as she sang, Father would lean in to kiss her on the cheek . . .

Grubb sighed, set aside the plate and looked at the mountain that still remained, towering over him. He'd already been going for half an hour, and it looked the same as when he'd started. *Just focus on cleaning one thing at a time* – that was the way to do it.

'Mongrel? MONGREL?'

Grubb shook water from his hands, smeared them dry on his apron and scurried out of the tiny kitchen into the bar, as quickly as he could. He had learned long ago not to keep Mr Lightly waiting.

His uncle was staggering down the stairs, stinking of perfume, dressed in dirty white breeches, a filthy red waistcoat and a golden jacket that had seen better days. The clothes looked like they'd been made for someone a lot smaller, and a lot more graceful.

'Where in all the bleeding blue sea is my blasted wig?' roared Mr Lightly. 'You know I can't go to the Grand Party without it.'

'I don't know, Unc— Mr Lightly, sir.'

His uncle crossed the floor in three giant strides,

lifted him up by his apron strings and shoved him back against the wall.

'Don't lie to me, boy.'

Grubb's feet scrabbled against the plaster behind him.

'Maybe . . . Maybe it's in your closet, sir?'

Mr Lightly dropped him.

'You think I didn't look there already? You think I'm stupid, mongrel?'

Grubb scampered round behind the bar. He didn't like the colour of his uncle's face. It was always the best way to tell what mood he was in. Pink, and you were safe. Red, stay out of his way. Right now, Mr Lightly wasn't too far from purple. Grubb tried to work out what he could say to make him calm down, knowing it was hopeless.

'I'll help you look,' he offered.

Mr Lightly's eyes narrowed until they were barely visible in his fleshy face.

'You goblins arc all the same,' he snarled. 'I told Eleanor that, before she married your father. But would she listen? Thieves, the lot of you. I must be the kindest innkeeper in the whole of Port Fayt, taking on a snivelling, sneaking, wretched runt of a greyskin like you. What have you done with my wig, mongrel? Answer me!'

'I . . .'

Mr Lightly lurched forward.

'You sack of scum! You've lived with me for six years, and every single day you've been a disappointment. Now for the last time, WHERE IS MY—'

He stopped, distracted by something beyond the bar. Grubb turned to see what it was, silently thanking Thalin for the interruption.

The tavern door was open, and standing there in the frame was the silhouetted figure of a slim young man. He was freckled, ginger-haired and dressed in a smart, dark green jacket. Something about him gave the impression of a gentleman – although of course no real gentleman would come within a mile of the Legless Mermaid.

Grubb's relief ebbed away. He could have sworn that he'd locked that door, and now Mr Lightly was going to be furious with him for forgetting. He *had* locked it though. Hadn't he?

'We're closed,' said Mr Lightly.

'I am aware of it,' said the man, with a hint of an Old World accent. He reached into his coat pocket, drew out a leather money bag and dangled it by its strings, jingling it meaningfully.

Within seconds Mr Lightly's colour went from

purple to red, and then back to his usual deep pink. He pinched the point of Grubb's right ear between finger and thumb, steering him towards a barrel of Finest Bowelbuster.

'And what can we do for you, sir? A mug of grog?'

'No grog,' said the stranger. He moved closer, his footsteps making no noise at all. No wonder they hadn't heard him come in.

'I'm looking for something that belongs to me. Something that I lost. It's valuable, and I want it back.'

His eyes glinted in the gloom, and Grubb saw with a shock that they weren't blue or brown like a normal human's eyes. They were yellow.

'Well, yes,' said Mr Lightly. 'Naturally, naturally. Mongr— Er, boy, bring out some of the best firewater for our friend here.'

'I dropped it here earlier today,' said the stranger, as Grubb headed for the pantry. 'A small black velvet package, tied with a silver cord.'

Grubb froze. *A black package with a silver cord.* A moment passed before he managed to recover and start walking again as if nothing was wrong. As soon as he was out of sight round the corner he stopped, breathing deeply. He felt for the package, hidden under his shirt. Yes, it was still there.

The man was lying. It was Phineus Clagg who'd

dropped it. So that meant this man was . . . he was . . .

Trying to steal it.

'Black velvet, eh?' said Mr Lightly. He'd put on an exaggerated accent which he probably thought made him sound refined. 'That doesn't ring any bells, unfortunately. Here, let me check our lost property box.' There was a brief sound of rummaging. 'No,' he said at last. 'It's not here. Just a moment.'

Grubb backed further into the passageway, blood pounding in his ears. There was no telling what Mr Lightly would do if he found out that his nephew had kept the package hidden from him.

He started off towards the storeroom. But he'd taken no more than three paces when a hand fell on his shoulder, and he turned to find Mr Lightly looming over him, his face hidden in shadow so that Grubb couldn't tell what colour it was. That was probably for the best.

'Mongrel. Small black velvet package. Belongs to a customer. Have you seen it?'

Grubb shook his head.

'No, sir.'

Mr Lightly leaned in closer, and Grubb saw that his eyes were narrowed and his face was halfway between pink and red. The stench of perfume was overpowering.

'Are you sure?'

He had no choice. He'd already told a lie. Now he had to stand by it.

'I'm sure, sir.'

'You cleared up after that fight, boy. If this gentleman dropped something, you should've found it. So I'm asking you again, have you seen a black velvet package?'

Grubb swallowed hard.

'Maybe . . . Maybe someone took it?'

There was a long silence. Mr Lightly glared at him, hands resting heavy on his shoulders, and Grubb became very aware of the soft feel of the velvet against his skin.

'We're going to talk more about this, mongrel,' said his uncle, at last. 'Don't you worry. I never trusted a goblin before, and sure as the sea I'm not starting now. Wait here.'

Grubb stood, shaking, as Mr Lightly returned to the bar.

He was dead.

He couldn't hide the package. Mr Lightly knew every inch of the tavern. He would find it. And when it was discovered . . .

No, don't panic. Stay calm. He closed his eyes, took a deep breath, and counted to ten.

He wasn't dead. Not yet, anyway.

There was a way out of this.

He turned and scurried on towards the pantry, slipped through the door and closed it behind him. Casting around in the cramped, gloomy space, he found a large barrel that was almost empty, then heaved at it, pushing it towards the door, the firewater sloshing inside it. His goblin muscles weren't up to much, and his arms felt as though they might snap at any moment. Finally, though, he managed to get it under the door handle. It wouldn't keep the door blocked for long, but with luck he wouldn't need more than a few moments. And Mr Lightly was busy anyway, talking to the man with the yellow eyes.

Grubb felt like he was in some kind of mad dream. Every action felt unnatural, as if he was a bad actor in a street theatre show. But he carried on anyway. He clambered onto a keg of firewater, hopped up on a cask of pickled eels and hauled himself on top of a large barrel of grog. Above him was a tiny window – too small for a human to squeeze through, but big enough for a goblin boy like Grubb.

He paused for a moment. Could he really do this? If he did, he could never come back. That much he knew. His only hope was that he wouldn't need to. Captain Clagg had said there would be a space for him in his crew. *Always room for a smart lad on board.* And if Grubb brought him back his package, the captain would be sure to take him on. Wouldn't he?

'Mongrel?' came Mr Lightly's voice. 'Hurry up with that firewater.'

You snivelling, sneaking, wretched runt of a greyskin.

His hands shaking, Grubb lifted the catch and pushed the window open. He took a deep breath, spent a moment trying to decide whether to go forwards or backwards, and finally squeezed through, head first. It was the wrong decision. He tumbled out onto the cobbles below, only just managing to throw up his arms in time to protect his head, and turn the fall into a roll. He picked himself up, took off his apron and hurried along the alleyway to the front of the tavern.

Out of nowhere, Grubb was overcome by a surge of emotion. The Legless Mermaid was his home. Or at least, it had been for the last six years, ever since the blackcoats had brought him here, and Mr Lightly had agreed to take him. Ever since he'd left the house with the green front door.

Ever since the night his parents had died.

He paused, panting, at the corner. He took one last look back, through a window into the bar, and . . .

Grubb found himself staring straight into the eyes

of the ginger-haired man. The stranger was watching him, wearing an odd, hungry smile. He didn't seem surprised to see the tavern boy outside the tavern. It was almost as if he'd been expecting it. A strange thought came into Grubb's head – he felt like a mouse, looking into the yellow eyes of a cat.

'MONGREL!' came a howl from behind him.

Mr Lightly had managed to get into the storeroom, and now his head was squeezed through the window, his face blue, his eyes bulging.

'Get back here at ONCE,' he growled. 'Don't you DARE take another step. Don't you DARE!'

Grubb looked back at the man with the yellow eyes. Somehow, the man's smile grew even odder, and even hungrier. He winked.

A shiver ran through Grubb's body, and he turned and raced down the street, faster than he'd ever run in his life before.

Soon the Legless Mermaid was far behind him. But he kept running, his heart pounding, his fingers wrapped tightly around the black velvet package.

In a dusty old workshop on a peaceful street in the Crosstree Quarter, John Boggs holds his breath as he covers the last patch of bare wood with green paint. He sits back to admire his brushwork and sighs happily.

For four years in a row now, Boggs has won the prize for best float in the Pageant of the Sea. The way things are going, he is fully expecting to make it five. Yes, he thinks, allowing himself a little chuckle of pleasure. He can hardly lose.

This year, his centrepiece is a large model of the sea demon, the Maw, as a gigantic green octopus. It's made out of wood, wire, ropes and canvas, and is designed so that if you pull on a bit of string, it waves hinged tentacles up and down. Not for nothing is John Boggs known as one of the finest carpenters in Port Fayt.

'She really is a beauty,' sighs his apprentice, an imp called Will. He is standing back, hands on hips as he admires the sea demon. 'I think it's your best float yet, sir. Folks'll be terrified. It'll be just as if the Maw came out of the sea and ran through the streets.'

Boggs grunts. He isn't good with compliments.

'Town busy today?' he asks, taking bread and cheese from his lunch basket, and settling down on a stool.

'Yes, sir. Lot of folks arriving for the festival, I reckon. Mer Way's looking grand. They're hanging up them little flags on string. What do you call 'em?'

'Bunting,' supplies Boggs.

'Bunting, that's right.' Will sits cross-legged among the sawdust on the workshop floor. 'No one seems too bothered about that tormenta the other night, anyway.'

'Too right, lad,' says Boggs, passing his assistant a hunk of bread and a lump of cheese, and biting into his own portion. 'And that's the way it should be. Magical storms . . . You can't go getting upset at little things like that. Just superstition, in my book.'

'Is that right, Mr Boggs?' says someone who isn't Will.

Boggs is so surprised he drops his cheese and kicks over a flagon of water.

'Blimey,' he says, his voice a croak. 'I mean, good day, ma'am.'

He hadn't heard her come in. He hadn't the time before either, now that he thinks of it.

'Afternoon, ma'am,' says Will, scrambling to his feet.

The old woman ignores him. She stands motionless in the doorway, draped in the same grey hooded cloak she wore the first time she came to the workshop.

'Is it ready?'

She speaks precisely, sharply. And with a hint of an Old World accent, Boggs realizes. He nods, crosses the workshop floor and pulls a large dustsheet from the old woman's commission.

'I followed your instructions, ma'am,' he says. His voice is hoarse. 'And I added in the zephyrum rod, like you wanted.'

He doesn't know what it's for, this . . . thing *that the old woman wanted him to make. But he knows well enough that zephyrum is a magic metal. And in Port Fayt, the use of magic without a warrant is a serious crime.*

The woman approaches the contraption and examines it. She runs her fingers over the gleaming, polished zephyrum, and Boggs almost gasps in shock as he sees how shrivelled her hand is. It isn't the first time that he is glad of the hood she wears, so that he doesn't have to see her face or meet her eyes. He catches sight of Will watching curiously, and motions for him to stay quiet.

The old woman stands silent for a moment.

'Good,' she says.

Boggs realizes he has been holding his breath, and lets it out in a sigh of relief.

'Excellent,' he says, feeling much calmer already. 'We aim to please. Young Will here helped with some of the woodwork. A first-rate apprentice. Run and fetch my account book, eh, Will?'

The imp hurries out through a side door.

'Now, if we may discuss payment . . . I'm afraid I'll have to charge a little more than my original estimate. Zephyrum costs an arm and a leg these days, as I'm sure you understand. Because of the League's sanctions, of course. Old World politics, eh?'

Boggs talks a lot when he is nervous.

'You shall have your payment,' says the old woman.

She draws out a leather money pouch that looks almost as ancient as she does, takes out a ducat and holds it out for him. But as he reaches for it, she closes her fingers. Boggs is left, arm half extended, unsure what to do.

'It is strange,' she says dreamily. 'Strange how much you care for these useless scraps of metal. Can you eat a ducat?'

It is the most she has ever said to him, and it makes him feel uncomfortable again. He wishes Will would hurry up with the account book.

'Er, no, ma'am,' he says.

'Can you sleep on ducats? Can they keep you warm?'

He says nothing.

'These ducats have sapped your strength, Mr Boggs. Sucked away your willpower. They have blinded you.'

With a rustle of her robes, she tosses the coin, spinning, into the air. It rises almost to the roof, falls and stops. Hovering, level with the old woman's face.

Sweat breaks out on Boggs' brow. He feels dizzy.

'Oh Thalin. But you can't . . . I mean, do you have a warrant to use magic?'

'But you shall have your ducats,' says the old woman, as if she hasn't heard him. She is watching the coin, rotating lazily in nothingness. 'You shall have them all, Mr Boggs.'

The last thing Mr Boggs ever sees is the strange sight of coins rising from the pouch like a shoal of fish through water, some old and dull, some new and shiny, and then speeding towards him, fast, faster, faster . . .

Faster than musket balls.

Chapter Four

Thunk!

The knife slammed into the target, buried halfway to the hilt, just to the right of the bull's-eye.

Thunk!

Thunk!

Two more, forming a neat triangle with the first.

Tabitha Mandeville tied back her long blue hair, one eye closed, frowning at the target. She tossed her last knife up in the air, watched it turn, glittering like a minnow, and caught it by the blade. She spun like a dancer, once, twice, and let fly . . .

THUNK!

Bull's-eye. Tabitha nodded to herself, still frowning, and went to collect her weapons.

'Nicely done, Tabs,' said Frank.

'Aye,' said Paddy. 'Remind me not to nick your sandwiches again.'

The Demon's Watch were lounging in the shade outside Bootles' Pie Shop. The street was cosy, cobbled and quiet except for the occasional whine of a messenger fairy zipping past, the squeak of the pie-shop sign swinging in the breeze and the distant surge of the sea.

It was blissful, and Tabitha was bored out of her mind.

She sighed as she headed back to throw the knives again. The other watchmen seemed to be enjoying themselves all right. Frank and Paddy, the troll twins, were sitting round an old barrel with Hal, playing triominoes. The twins were mostly too busy telling jokes and punching each other to pay much attention to the game. Hal, on the other hand, was silent, studying his tiles so hard he barely blinked.

When Tabitha had first met him – a pale, mousy-haired, bespectacled young man – she hadn't been able to believe that someone so skinny and nervous-looking could be a watchman. That was before she'd seen his magic.

Old Jon the elf sat a little way apart from the youngsters, leaning against the wall with his long white hair spread over his bony shoulders like a shawl. He was smoking a pipe and staring into the distance.

'Got your costume sorted for the pageant, Tabs?' asked Paddy as she passed. He reached over to ruffle her hair with a heavy green hand.

Tabitha squirmed away. The twins knew how much the hair-ruffling annoyed her. Which was exactly why they kept doing it.

'Hands off,' she snapped. 'And no, I haven't.'

'Jon?' tried Paddy's brother, Frank. 'What about you?'

Old Jon smiled, shook his head, and went back to his smoking and staring. It took a lot more than that to get a word out of Old Jon.

Tabitha tried to ignore the twins and concentrate on the target. She hefted a knife, and sent it whistling through the air.

Thunk!

'How about you, Hal?' asked Paddy. 'I bet you've got something special up those magical sleeves of yours, eh?'

The magician frowned, took off his round spectacles and rubbed at them with a handkerchief.

'On the contrary, I doubt I will be dressing up at

all. It's a little . . . childish, don't you think? Not to mention undignified.'

Frank groaned and held his head in his hands.

'Well, aren't you lot a ray of sunshine? Maw's teeth! The pageant's in three days, so you'd better start coming up with some good fancy dress ideas. Maybe you should all go together as a big bunch of sour grapes.'

Tabitha rolled her eyes, and kept throwing.

Thunk!

Thunk!

Mrs Bootle, the twins' mother, bustled out of the doorway and set down a huge tray of crab sandwiches on a barrel.

'Don't want you starving,' she said.

Mrs Bootle was big, even for a troll, but she looked like an imp compared to her two towering sons.

'Thank you, Mrs Bootle.'

'Wait till you try these,' said Paddy. 'They'll blow your breeches off.'

'Ma makes the best crab sandwich in Port Fayt.'

'. . . in the Middle Islands!'

'. . . in the Ebony Ocean!'

'Stop it, you two,' chortled Mrs Bootle, obviously not wanting them to stop at all.

'What about *your* costumes then?' Tabitha asked

the twins, when Mrs Bootle had disappeared back inside. 'What have you got that's so great?'

The trolls looked at each other and tapped their bony green noses, mirror images of each other.

'It's a secret . . .'

'. . . but it's going to be brilliant.'

'Have a guess.'

Tabitha frowned in mock concentration, and threw her last knife.

THUNK!

'A pair of giant clowns?'

She dodged behind the crab sandwich barrel as Frank lunged for her. It was just a playful swipe, and he wasn't trying to hurt her, of course, but you had to be careful. After all, he was a troll, and at least twice as big as her.

'Ha ha, very funny,' said Paddy, picking out the largest of the sandwiches as Tabitha slumped down onto a spare stool. 'You won't be laughing when we win the prize for best costumes.'

Hal finished polishing his spectacles and laid down his last triomino.

'Again?' complained Frank. 'Are you cheating, Hal? You do know spells aren't allowed in triominoes?'

'Magicians never cheat.'

'Walrus dung.'

'Charming. Perhaps once you've spent five years at the Azurmouth Academy, studying how to manipulate natural laws with the power of the mind, we could discuss the correct usage of—'

'Why is nothing happening?' said Tabitha.

They all looked at her.

'I mean, you'd think something would be up. This is the Festival of the Sea, for Thalin's sake. What's wrong with these criminals? I'm fed up with watching you lot play triominoes. I want to catch some smugglers. Or some thieves, at least.'

She rubbed at the shark tattoo on her arm. It was fresh and blue, newly inked and still a little sore. The mark of the Demon's Watch. She'd lived with Newton for practically her whole life now, and she'd been at every Demon's Watch meeting since her fifth birthday. But now that she was finally a real member, with a tattoo and a blue coat of her own, it seemed like he was determined to give her the most boring jobs he could think of.

Besides, the most exciting thing they'd done in a month was arresting a toothless, hundred-year-old elf, fresh off a ship from the Old World, with fifty griffin feathers hidden in her knickers. The old bag hadn't even put up a fight.

Old Jon laid down his pipe.

'You'll get your chance, Tabitha,' he said, in his calm, deep voice. 'Soon enough.'

'You should be pleased, Tabs,' said Paddy, spraying out morsels of crab. 'No smugglers means we're doing our jobs right.'

'I know, but . . .'

'Anyway,' said Frank, 'Newt will sniff something out. He always does. Tell you what, how about we take a stroll down to the harbour, see if we can pick up any leads ourselves? Maybe there'll be some pickpockets we can—'

A tiny figure dropped out of the air and slammed into the triominoes, sending them clattering onto the cobblestones. Slik. He sat down on top of the barrel, amid the wreckage of the game, and giggled.

'Hey,' said Paddy. 'We hadn't finished.'

Slik blew a raspberry.

'Well, you shouldn't be sitting around playing stupid games all day anyway.'

'Where's Newton?' asked Tabitha.

'Who knows? He was at Spottington's Velvethouse when I left him.'

'Is there any news?'

'Course not. I've just come for your sparkling conversation.'

Paddy flicked a triomino tile at the fairy, forcing him to dodge out of the way.

'All right, all right! Captain Newton says you're to get dressed for the Grand Party, and meet him outside Spottington's at dusk. Armed.'

Frank punched Tabitha on the arm, a little harder than she would have liked.

'What did I tell you? Something's up, I can feel it.'

'Dusk,' said Paddy thoughtfully. 'That gives us more than enough time to show Hal how to really play this game.'

'Stupid ugly trolls,' Slik muttered, and took off before the Bootle twins could respond.

For the first time that day, Tabitha grinned. It was happening at last. Her first real adventure as a watchman. She picked up a crab sandwich and bit into it hungrily. Frank and Paddy were right. It was the best she had ever tasted.

Chapter Five

Grubb wandered the streets in a daze. He passed Fayters hanging up gold and purple bunting in Mer Way. He stood for a while in Thalin Square, watching the merchants coming and going from the town hall in their white wigs and fancy coats, wondering if one of them might help him, but knowing that they wouldn't. He asked a greengrocer if he could spare an apple, and the greengrocer told him to get lost before he called the blackcoats.

Once or twice he had a funny feeling that someone was watching him.

He walked back down Mer Way and into the Marlinspike Quarter, aiming for the street that his parents had lived on. He didn't know why. There would be a new family living there now, of course, in the house with the green front door. But before he got there he ran into a gang of goblin boys who were bigger and older than him, and laughed at his mottled skin, and chased him for three or four streets before giving up, shouting after him that mongrels weren't welcome down their way.

What would his father have done? Grubb didn't know. He could barely even remember his face.

He ducked into a side street, slumped down against a wall and brought out the black velvet package, peering at it and trying to guess what might be inside. A dragon's tooth, perhaps, or a bar of zephyrum. It had to be something valuable – otherwise why would it be wrapped up like that? And why would the ginger-haired man want to steal it? He toyed with the idea of opening the package, but even though he badly wanted to know what was inside, he decided against it. For some reason, he felt as if Captain Clagg wouldn't want him to.

Anyway, it didn't really matter. What mattered was that he was going to take it back to its owner. At the Grand Party, tonight. Captain Clagg had said he would be there. Grubb would find him and return the package, and in his gratitude, the captain would take him on and give him a place on board the *Sharkbane*. Then maybe, *maybe*, everything would be all right.

Of course, finding one particular person among the crowds at the party was going to be about as easy as finding one particular weevil in Mr Lightly's pantry. But there was always a chance that he'd be lucky. He felt like it was about time for a bit of luck to come his way.

And at least now, he had a plan.

He scrambled to his feet, thrust the package into his belt and headed back towards Mer Way, feeling hopeful for the first time since he'd left the Legless Mermaid.

The afternoon wore on and became dusk, and the streets began to fill with Fayters in their finest clothes, ready for the Grand Party. Grubb wandered amongst them, waist-high to most of the crowd, one hand clenched around the black velvet package. He longed for the hour when the festivities would begin.

But as the shadows lengthened and the streets grew darker, he began to worry. Mr Lightly would be at the party too, wigless, in his golden jacket and red waistcoat. He might have put the word out that his mongrel had gone missing. What if Grubb was spotted and taken back to the Legless Mermaid?

He had just turned back onto Mer Way for what felt like the hundredth time when someone barged into him from behind, sending him stumbling over the cobblestones.

'Watch where you're going,' slurred the stranger, barely stopping to look at him. It was a young imp, dressed up to the nines. He wore a powdered wig and tricorne hat, a red satin coat, a clean white shirt and breeches and a pair of large-heeled silver shoes which gave him a good few extra inches in height. He looked just like a fancy gentleman, except that his big, round eyes were crossed and he was having difficulty walking in a straight line. The bottle he was swigging from clearly wasn't helping.

An idea popped into Grubb's head. Take away the heels, and the imp was smaller than an adult goblin. Probably no bigger than a mongrel boy. He took a deep breath, and curled his fingers tighter around the package.

This was it. *A bit of luck, at last . . .*

Grubb waited until the stranger was a good ten paces away, then began to follow, as surreptitiously as he could. It wasn't hard. Years of avoiding Mr Lightly's attention had made him good at hiding in the shadows. Then again, he probably could have been a fire-breathing dragon and the imp wouldn't have noticed. There was no way he was going to get to the party in that state.

As he tottered along, the imp sang happily to himself:

'*Oh, I knew a fair young impish lass as fair as fair could be,*
Dum dum de dum dum, asked her to marry me . . .'

Grubb followed through lanes and back streets until, at last, the imp staggered to a halt in a deserted alleyway. He raised the bottle to his lips, promptly overbalanced and fell over backwards, his tricorne toppling onto the cobblestones. For a few moments he lay there on the ground, giggling. Then he muttered something revolting about someone called Betsey and rolled over onto his side, smacking his lips. Ten seconds later, he was snoring heavily, cradling the bottle to his chest like a newborn baby.

Grubb crept closer, half expecting the imp to open his eyes. Nothing. He was out cold. Trying not to breathe in the stench of firewater, Grubb prised the sleeper's pink fingers away from the bottle, spread his arms out wide and removed the red satin coat.

He held it up to himself, and breathed a sigh of relief. It was perfect.

First he took off his own coat and shirt, leaving them in a pile on the ground with Captain Clagg's package placed carefully on top. Then, keeping one eye on the package, he removed the imp's shirt and pulled it on himself. Last of all, he put on the wig and the red jacket.

The new clothing felt tight and stiff, and when he caught a glimpse of his reflection in a puddle he barely recognized himself. He looked just like a rich merchant's boy. Even if Mr Lightly saw him at the party, he probably wouldn't know who he was looking at.

Grubb took the imp by the arms and hauled him to the side of the alley, where he'd be less likely to be robbed by the first gang of drunkards who came this way. He would leave his own shirt and coat. That way, at least the imp would have something to wear when he woke up.

There was a movement in the shadows opposite.

Grubb let the imp slump and hurried back to stand guard over the package and his bundle of clothes. Was he seeing things? After everything that had happened so far today, it would be no big surprise if he'd gone crazy. No, it was probably just a rat. He was probably just being stupid. He adjusted his wig, and smoothed out his new jacket.

Something darted out of the shadows towards him.

He leaped forward, but not fast enough. A small, dark blur tore between his legs and came to a halt, silhouetted in the centre of the alley.

It was a ginger cat, and in its mouth it held the black velvet package.

Maybe he had gone crazy after all.

The cat was staring straight at him, and a strange thought came into his head – he felt like a mouse, looking into the yellow eyes of . . . well . . . of a cat.

The cat dropped the package between its front paws.

'Get lost, mongrel,' it said.

Chapter Six

It was dark in the alleyway, and the bangs and crackles of fireworks from the Grand Party sounded muffled and distant as the watchmen padded through the shadows.

For the hundredth time, Tabitha checked her throwing knives were all in place in the bandolier, and glanced over her shoulder. She could just make out the hulking troll shapes of the Bootle brothers. Behind them she caught the glint of Hal's spectacles, and Old Jon's tall, thin figure, bringing up the rear. Tonight they had exchanged their usual blue jackets for garish party clothes, but every one of them bore the shark tattoo of the Watch, and every one of them was armed. Every one except Hal, of course. Hal didn't need a weapon to defend himself.

Ahead of her strode Newton, tall and silent, his combat staff folded in three and hidden beneath a purple satin coat.

Tabitha's whole body was buzzing with excitement, but she forced herself to look as serious as possible. This had to go well. It was her chance to show Newton what she could do, at last.

A smuggler. They were going to catch a real, proper, possibly extremely dangerous *smuggler*.

She couldn't wait.

Thalin Square was deserted, except for a few small groups making their way to the Grand Party on the quayside. The vast marble town hall stood cold and empty. A breeze stirred a few scraps of rubbish over the cobblestones. Even the buskers were nowhere to be seen.

Newton stopped and gave a signal, and they all clustered round at the foot of the plinth that stood in the centre of the square. The bronze statue towering above them showed Thalin the Navigator – a rugged, handsome human, dressed in a simple tunic, long hair flying dramatically out in the wind. His sword was raised, ready to stab down at his foe, the Maw. The sea demon was almost comical; a winding serpent that coiled around Thalin's leg trying to bite his arm. Tabitha imagined the real thing would have been less . . . ridiculous. If it had ever even existed.

'So, everyone clear?' said Newton. 'Keep it quiet. No heroics, no showing off, no nothing.' He looked sternly at the hulking Bootle brothers. Both of them tried to look innocent, and failed. 'Quiet' wasn't usually their style.

'Aye, Captain.'

'Right y'are.'

'Good. Hal, you're with me. Once we're on board the *Wraith's Revenge*, we'll head for the hold, intercept the cargo handover and arrest Phineus Clagg and his customer, whoever that is. The rest of you, stay on the upper decks and keep an eye out for Clagg or his crew. Tabs, you're lookout. Understood?'

Tabitha felt like he'd tipped a bucket of bilge over her head.

Lookout?

She snorted in disgust. After all the excitement, she was going to be lookout again?

Newton noticed.

'Promise you'll stay out of trouble, Tabs? And keep those knives out of sight.'

She grunted and began to take off her jacket to rearrange the bandolier of throwing knives underneath. Her cheeks were burning. It wasn't fair, him speaking to her like that in front of everyone. She had the same tattoo as them, didn't she? It wasn't like she was actually his daughter. So what did she have to do to get him to treat her like a real person?

'Good plan, Newt,' Paddy was saying. 'And by the way, it's good to see you lot looking smart for a change.'

'I'm not sure about this green though,' said Frank, frowning down at his jacket. 'I reckon I'd suit a red one better. You know, with some nice long tails, and maybe some fancy gold bits? Hey, Hal, can you magic me something like that?'

Hal sighed, and pushed his glasses up his nose.

'I don't expect you to fully appreciate the intricacies of my craft, but please . . . "Magic me something like that"?'

Paddy chuckled, and thumped his brother on the arm.

'Don't worry, Frank, it wouldn't make any difference. Ain't no jacket in all the Old World that'll make our mugs any less ugly.'

Five minutes later, they were making their way through the crowds on the harbour front. Rockets burst high above the bay, staining the night sky with reds, blues and greens, which reflected off the black water below. The Grand Party had begun.

Tabitha's ears filled with chatter, laughter and music, and her mouth watered at the scent of barbecued meat and fish. The quayside was decked out with bunting, paper chains and coloured lanterns and rammed with Fayters, laughing, singing and jostling each other. Fire-eaters, jugglers and contortionists competed for attention and tips, but most Fayters were ignoring them, occupied with the more serious business of eating and drinking. A tiny, giggling elf girl dodged around Tabitha's legs, using them as cover from an even tinier goblin boy chasing after her. Tabitha grinned, in spite of herself.

As she looked up, she noticed a pair of humans looking at her and whispering to each other. The men were dressed in black jackets and tricorne hats and carried muskets slung over their shoulders. She scowled at them, which made them flinch and look away, pretending they hadn't just been talking about her. Blackcoats. They were about as much use as a rubber cutlass.

She scanned the crowd and spotted several more of the black-coated militiamen, moving among the crowds with muskets and crossbows, trying to look tough and make sure no one stepped out of line.

Newton had seen them too. He gave a hand signal, and the watchmen split up and fanned out through the crowd to board dinghies, just like they'd discussed. If they were seen together the blackcoats might get nervous, and according to Newton it was always best to work quietly. 'Incognito', as Hal put it. That was why Slik hadn't been allowed to come tonight. You just couldn't trust him to stay quiet for long enough.

Tabitha's boat was manned by a cheery-looking dwarf with a short blond beard and a red handkerchief knotted round his head. He gave her a wink as she climbed in.

'*Wraith's Revenge?*' she asked.

'Aye.'

Tabitha sat next to a pair of scrawny goblin sailors. The dwarf sang a sea shanty in a deep, warbling voice as they pulled out into the harbour, while the goblins swigged from a flagon, competing to tell the rudest jokes they could think of and snorting with laughter.

Clusters of lights glimmered all around them – flotillas of ships and barges, lashed together for the occasion and loaded with revellers. The dinghy was heading for the largest, made up of three vast warships – the *Behemoth*, the *Fighting Fury* and the

Wraith's Revenge. Music drifted over the water, louder and louder, the closer they came.

On board, the party was even more raucous than it had been on the quayside. Musicians played on the fo'c'sle, sawing away at fiddles and pumping squeeze-boxes. Below them, the decks bounced under the weight of breathless revellers, bobbing up and down to the jigs and reels.

Tabitha stepped over the gunwale, glancing back across the water. Newton's boat hadn't arrived yet. That meant she had a bit of time to investigate before she got stuck being the lookout. With luck, she might even find Phineus Clagg before the other watchmen got on board.

She set off, edging around the makeshift dance floor towards a set of tables laden with food. There were saffron cakes with cream filling, sugared nuts and glazed fruits, sweet biscuits from the town's confectioners and rich shokel buns, imported from the New World and decorated with golden sugar paper bearing the Cockatrice Company's purple emblem – a little reminder of who was paying for the party. Tabitha grabbed a slice of cake and bit into it. Soft red icing oozed out, and crumbs scattered onto the deck. It was delicious.

Munching on her cake, she climbed the stairs to the poop deck and joined a small crowd gathered around a local fisherman, One-hand Wallis, who was looking after the ship's supply of fireworks.

'This here, ladies and gents, is the firework to end all fireworks!' he crowed, pointing to an enormous multi-coloured rocket. 'Wait till you see this one: it's the shark's teeth. It'll blow your breeches off, and no mistake!'

'What's it look like then?' someone called out.

Wallis tapped his nose theatrically. 'Ah now, well, that'd be telling, wouldn't it? You'll know it when you see it though, that's for sure. The Flaming Nancy, I call it. Saving this one for later – for the grand finale. Just you wait.'

Tabitha felt a heavy hand fall on her shoulder, and looked up to see Frank's big, green, grinning face.

'Hello there, young missy. Don't you have a job to do?'

She rolled her eyes and ducked away from him, stuffing the rest of the cake into her mouth. Well, if she wasn't allowed to hunt for Clagg herself, at least she'd be the best lookout the Demon's Watch had ever had. She headed for the railings at the front of the poop deck, where she had a good view over the whole ship.

There was a lot to see, besides the dancers. Clowns, grog vendors, games . . . Someone had even set up a target for a knife-throwing contest. Muscled sailors pushed to have a go, and their tattooed arms sent blade after blade thudding into the painted target. Tabitha wished she could join in and show them how it was done. There was no way she'd lose.

She pushed the thought from her mind and scanned over the heads of the partygoers, picking out the few blackcoats who were on board. They seemed to be busy enjoying themselves, which meant they wouldn't be causing the Demon's Watch any trouble. Good.

Next, she looked for the other watchmen. Old Jon was on the fo'c'sle, smoking as usual, nodding along as another old elf spoke rapidly into his ear. There was Paddy nearby, chatting with an off-duty fiddle player. He caught her eye and gave her a wink. Last, she spotted Hal's floppy brown hair and Newton's shaven head, bobbing up and down as they threaded through the crowd, towards the door that led below decks.

Everything was going perfectly according to plan. Tabitha sighed and slumped over the railing. Looked like it was going to be another boring . . .

Wait.

There was another figure down there, a few steps

behind Hal. A human-sized figure, cloaked in grey and hooded. A figure moving slowly, but with purpose. Following.

Tabitha leaned forward, gripping the rail hard. Whoever it was hadn't bothered to dress up, but had gone to the trouble of hiding their face. That was very, very suspicious. Phineus Clagg? Or whoever Phineus Clagg was due to meet.

She watched, her heart pounding, as the grey, hooded person opened the door that Newton and Hal had just gone through and disappeared into the darkness beyond.

This was it! This was her chance. She was the lookout, wasn't she? So she was supposed to be looking out for things. Newt hadn't told her what to do if she saw something, so that meant it was up to her. Probably. Or if not, it was his own fault for not being clear enough.

She shoved her way back through the crowds and down the stairs, heading for the doorway, checking she still had her knives. Then she pushed open the door and stepped inside.

The noises of the party grew faint as Tabitha climbed down wooden steps into the belly of the *Wraith's Revenge*. Gradually, the chatter and music were replaced by the long, eerie groans of the ship itself, rocking gently in the waves. Tabitha forced herself to breathe deeply, slow and regular. She moved silently, listening as hard as she could, but hearing no one.

She was two decks down, and the distant thud of dancing feet mingled with the sounds of creaking timbers and lapping waves. It was cold, and the air was damp and heavy with the scent of rotten wood. She climbed down the final flight of steps to the hold, reaching inside her jacket and pulling out a slender knife, peering into the shadows.

Tabitha began to have a nasty, creeping feeling that it might have been a mistake coming down here. Where was the grey figure? Where were Newton and Hal? And why in Thalin's name hadn't she thought to bring a lantern? She could barely see two feet in front of her. She was alone and vulnerable, and she didn't like it.

A light flared up ahead, and something hard and cold jabbed into her neck. She reeled back, choking, her knife falling and skittering away into the darkness. She was going to die, she was going to—

'Tabs? Is that you?!'

Tabitha blinked, her eyes adjusting to the light.

There were two figures in front of her. Newton and Hal, risen up from hiding places behind piles of timber. Hal's hand was lit up like a glow-worm, bathing the hold in a ghostly light. Newton was just a few paces away, his black wooden combat staff pointed straight at her neck. Both of them wore expressions of horror.

'I'm sorry,' snapped Tabitha. 'All right? That hurt. I didn't mean to—'

A pair of hands gripped her throat and she was dragged backwards, coughing and gagging.

Chapter Seven

Grubb stared at the cat, struggling for words.

'What . . . what are you—'

'None of your business,' said the cat. 'Why don't you hop it?'

There were only two explanations for a talking cat. Either Grubb was in need of sleep, or . . .

Oh Thalin. Yellow eyes. Ginger hair. And that voice, proud like a gentleman's, with a hint of an Old World accent.

Things were starting to make a horrible sort of sense.

'It was you,' he said. 'At the Legless Mermaid.

You're that man who came and asked about the package and—'

'Congratulations, you're a genius.'

'So . . . you're a—'

'Shapeshifter. Yes. Full marks.'

'And you've been—'

'Following you. Right again.'

Grubb could hardly believe it. A shapeshifter. A *shapeshifter*. They were about as common as flying whales. Grubb had never seen one before. At least, he didn't think he had. Of course, the whole point of shapeshifters was that they could transform into an animal whenever they chose, and the rest of the time they looked just like ordinary—

'Oh, do stop gawping,' said the cat. 'I've enjoyed our little game, but I'm afraid I can't stay.'

It picked up the package in its mouth again, and sauntered off down the alley.

'Hey,' said Grubb. 'You can't take that. It's not yours. I know it's not yours. It belongs to . . . Well, it belongs to someone else.'

'Watch me,' said the cat over its shoulder, its voice muffled by the velvet.

Grubb felt the first stirrings of panic. He had to do something. Without the black velvet package he had nothing. There was no way Phineus Clagg would let him join the crew if Grubb had lost his precious package. He would have to go back to the Legless Mermaid, and he couldn't do that. Not now.

'Bring that back here,' he said, in the sternest tone he could manage. His voice cracked slightly, making him sound ridiculous. He swallowed.

The cat paused for a moment, a shadow at the end of the alley, and put the package down again.

'Brave,' it purred, 'but a little stupid.'

Grubb felt his face burn.

'I told you, it's not yours. I won't let you take it.'

The cat sniggered. It was the first time Grubb had ever heard a cat laugh, and it wasn't a pretty sound.

Without warning, the cat sprang back down the alley, straight past Grubb, the package in its mouth. He lunged after it, tripped over the snoozing imp and fell heavily. Barely stopping to think, he clambered to his feet and followed.

The cat darted left into a small side street, then right, and within seconds it had raced out onto the quayside, flying over coils of rope and dodging past empty barrels. Grubb sprinted after it, pumping his scrawny legs as fast as they could go. A gang of sailors on their way to the Grand Party turned to laugh and yell at him to slow down. They ignored the shape-shifter, of course. All they saw was a cat with something in its mouth – probably a dead rat. Nothing out of the ordinary there.

Grubb was breathing hard now. The cat was increasing its lead, and he knew he had to catch it before it slipped back into the side streets. But it stuck to the quayside, racing between patches of moonlight and lantern light. It must have known how easy it would be to lose him, to disappear into the shadows.

It was mocking him.

At last, it veered left down an alleyway. Grubb followed. His feet hurt, his legs ached and his breathing was coming harder and harder.

By the time he'd turned the corner himself, the cat was gone. He stopped and bent over, gasping for air and cursing silently. Well, that was that. It was crazy to think he could have caught it anyway.

'Well, well,' said the shapeshifter's voice. There it was, perched above him on a low rooftop, one paw resting on the package. 'Still here, are we? What a strange little creature you are. Want to try something more challenging?' It picked up the package in its mouth and trotted a short way across the rooftop, daring Grubb to follow.

He knew he should give up. But the cat was getting to him with its swagger, its confidence and its taunting voice. He couldn't let it escape.

The rooftop wasn't too high, and there was a pile of wooden crates below. Grubb pushed them against the wall and climbed up, clumsily grabbing the gutter and hauling himself onto the roof, straining the stitching of his new jacket almost to ripping point. He stood and felt the breeze on his face, cool and fresh.

For a second he looked into the cat's twinkling eyes, and then it was away. Grubb scrambled up the slope of the roof and slid down the other side. He leaped to the next house, forcing himself not to think about what he was doing. *You're just serving drinks, back at the Mermaid*. He skidded on roof tiles, knocking several loose and sending them smashing into the alley below.

As he reached the top of the next roof he caught a glimpse of the town laid out around him. Here and there a turret, a flagpole, a wooden crane rising above the houses. Fireworks exploding high above, lighting up the skyline. Far to the right, a forest of masts bobbing in the harbour. In an instant, he saw more of Port Fayt than he'd seen in six years at the Legless Mermaid. And then he was leaping to the next roof, and scrambling up another set of tiles. Something was nagging at the back of his mind – fear, maybe – but whatever it was, it didn't seem important any more.

The cat was always just ahead, running and jumping so smoothly it seemed almost to be flowing over the rooftops. But somehow, Grubb kept up with it. They were onto their fourth house, and their fifth. His breathing was ragged, his muscles burned and his knees were bruised from banging against gutters. None of that mattered though. He could catch it. He *knew* he could. He found himself grinning.

The gap between the fifth and sixth houses was wider than the others, but if a cat could do it, so could a mongrel boy. Grubb launched himself over, taking a quick glance at the alley below.

And his heart jolted.

What had got into him? What in Thalin's name was he smiling for? There was no way he could jump that. No way . . .

He landed on the rooftop with a horrible crunching sound.

'*Aaaaaaaaargh!*'

Something was wrong. Hot pain rushed through his ankle.

He reached down, and overbalanced. With a sick feeling, he realized he was tipping backwards. He waved his arms in wild circles. He just had time to cry out in panic, and then he was falling.

For a moment, Grubb had a vision of himself as he

might look to a passer-by. A strange, mottled runt of a mongrel, dressed in finery far too good for him, plunging down, down, down . . .

He closed his eyes as the cobblestones came up to greet him.

Chapter Eight

Tabitha twisted and rammed her elbow back as hard as she could. But the hands closed tighter, and her body flooded with a strange exhaustion, weighing down her limbs until she was numb and paralysed.

Magic.

Out of the corner of her eye, she glimpsed her captor – the hooded figure. To her surprise she saw that it was an old human woman. But her face was grey like a goblin's and disfigured with deep lines, more than could possibly be natural. She was snarling, her eyes wide, burning, black as death.

Tabitha's stomach pitched with fear.

'The Demon's Watch,' said the woman, and her voice was a low, growling whisper. She sniffed the air, and her crooked mouth twitched. 'Yes, of course. Such brave creatures. Ready and waiting – for me, perhaps?'

Hal suddenly went white, his eyes bulging out behind his glasses, gulping for air like a fish stranded on a beach. The light from his hand began to fade, and he staggered sideways, his face a mask of fear. The old woman smiled.

Newt sprang forward, swinging his staff so hard and fast that Tabitha was sure it would crack the woman's skull. But instead she caught it in mid-air and, impossibly, pulled him towards her. She gave a strange, exultant shriek and her arms began to expand, squeezing Tabitha and Newton in closer, absorbing and trapping them.

The light from Hal's hand went out, and they were in darkness.

The old woman shot upwards like a rocket. There was a juddering crash as they hit the deck above and went straight through it. Then another crash, and another, and a table of drinks went flying as they shot up into the night sky. There were screams and angry shouts. Tabitha caught a glimpse of Old Jon and Paddy trying to calm people down, and blackcoats on the *Behemoth* rushing for the gangplank to the

Wraith's Revenge, hastily loading crossbows.

Their captor threw back her head and howled again. She dropped out of the sky and balanced on the mainmast's highest yard, still grasping the two of them with inhuman strength, like a hawk with its prey. Tabitha squirmed, gasping for air and trying to escape her grip. But the old woman just laughed and thrust out her arms, dangling her captives in front of her, one in each hand. Out of the corner of her eye, Tabitha could see the deck, far, far below.

Yes. Going down to the hold had definitely been a mistake.

Musket shots rang out, and crossbow bolts whirred past. One tore into the furled sail below them. Another slammed into the mast.

'Where is it?' screamed the woman. 'What have you done with it?'

The words came rushing out, buffeting them like an angry gale.

'Where is Captain Phineus Clagg? Tell me.'

Tabitha slipped down sharply, and was caught again by the wrist. She gasped, panting with fear, trying not to think about what was happening.

'Tell me, or I drop the girl.'

'Do that,' grunted Newton, 'and you'll be sorry.'

Tabitha would probably have wanted to punch him, if she hadn't been so utterly terrified.

The old woman's eyes grew wider and wider, two swirling black pits, deeper than the ocean. She leaned in, her cloak flapping about her like a demon's wings.

'It's you who'll be sorry, Captain Newton,' she hissed.

There was frantic movement down below on the poop deck. A blur of green – Frank, moving through the crowds around One-hand Wallis. Then Wallis was shouting and gesticulating, and Frank held him off with one arm as he tipped the gigantic firework to an angle, reached for a tinderbox . . .

'No!' yelped Tabitha. 'Wait, Frank, no!'

The Flaming Nancy launched in a cloud of sparks, with a screeching, shrieking roar, and party-goers threw themselves to the deck in panic.

On the yard, the old woman's eyes narrowed. She flung herself sideways at impossible speed, taking Tabitha and Newton with her, split seconds before the Flaming Nancy hit the mainmast.

There was a shatteringly loud *BANG*, and Tabitha was blinded by a rainbow of light. And then she was flung away like a rag doll, and at first she was almost floating in the air, and then she was falling, down and down, faster and faster, and Newton was turning in slow motion in the air beside her, and she opened her eyes half a second before she hit the water, and immediately wished she hadn't, and then there was nothing but a muffled roaring, and she flailed with her arms and legs, fighting her way upwards, reaching for air . . .

Tabitha surfaced, spluttering and choking. Newton appeared at her side, spitting out seawater and rubbing salt from his eyes. They bobbed in the freezing water, too cold to say anything for a minute or so. The top yard of the *Wraith's Revenge* was on fire, and the mainmast was studded with crossbow bolts and scorched black by the Flaming Nancy. But the old woman was gone.

A short swim later, and the pair of them were hauling themselves out of the water and scrambling up a rope ladder, back onto the ship. They stood, dripping and shivering, while Fayters crowded round them, all clamouring at once.

'You've ruined the party!' screeched One-hand Wallis.

'How in the name of the Ebony Ocean did you get up on that yard?!'

'Watchmen indeed,' huffed a troll woman. 'Wastes of space, more like.'

Tabitha was about to step forward and give them

a piece of her mind, when Newton laid a hand on her shoulder, holding her back. She looked up at him, and her heart sank. She knew that expression. Disappointment. Newt obviously thought this was *her* fault, somehow. They'd be having a chat later, she could just tell.

There was a commotion among the crowd as blackcoats shoved people aside and a tall, pale elf shouldered his way through. His uniform was pristine, and silver glinted on his shoulder and lapels. Tabitha knew him, but would have been much happier if she didn't.

The militiaman snapped open a heavy pocket watch and made a show of inspecting it.

'Evening, Mr Newton. It's a little late for a swim, don't you think?'

A voice called out from the crowd.

'What a party, eh, Cyrus? Night to remember or what?'

Tabitha spotted Paddy's head above the crowd, a big grin plastered on his face. The troll could never resist a chance to wind up militiamen.

Colonel Cyrus Derringer just smiled.

'A night to remember? Well, it certainly is now. And it's Colonel Derringer, if you please.' He turned his cold blue eyes on Newton. 'Care to explain yourself before my men blow you to pieces?'

Newton met his gaze, and said nothing. Cyrus's smile grew wider.

'Very well then, let's see. Aside from disturbing the peace, vandalizing three tables of food and ruining the firework display, you have somehow managed to smash a gaping hole right through one of the town's most valuable warships. And in case you hadn't noticed, the mast is on fire.'

'Really?' said Newton.

Derringer's eyes narrowed.

'You're in big trouble. You and your whole bilge-brained crew.' In one smooth motion, his sabre flashed from its scabbard and came to rest, the blade pressed against Newton's cheek.

It was a neat trick, but Newton didn't flinch. In spite of herself, Tabitha felt a flush of pride at his bravery.

'It's the blackcoats who are supposed to keep the peace in Port Fayt,' Derringer hissed. 'The Dockside Militia. Just remember that.' He stepped back, and smiled again. 'Tomorrow morning, the governor will be expecting you at Wyrmwood Manor, and I can't imagine he'll be very happy. The Cockatrice Company have spent a fortune on this party. If it was up to me, I'd throw the lot of you into a shark pit.

'Now get off this ship. Before I lose my temper.'

* * *

It was a little after midnight by the time the watchmen left the *Wraith's Revenge*.

Tabitha looked back from the longboat, towards the ship and its scarred mast. She'd had a taste of action at last, but she didn't seem to feel good about it. As a matter of fact she felt scared and sick, and she was glad to be going home.

Newton shifted seats to sit next to her.

'Tabs,' he said.

'I know, I know, but listen, I saw her go down below and I wanted to warn you. It almost worked as well – if I'd been a few seconds later I—'

'Enough.' There was real anger in his voice, and it shut her up at once. 'Tabs, you have to do what I say, understand? I know it's hard. You've lived with me for a long time. And maybe I've let you get away with too much in the past. But things are different now that you're a watchman.'

Well, at least he was admitting that.

'People could die, Tabs. Actually *die*. You saw that old woman. Do you understand what I'm saying?'

Tabitha opened her mouth to reply, but nothing came out. Instead she just bit her lip and nodded silently. The old woman's face loomed at the back of her mind, like a spider in a cupboard that she didn't dare look at. She had never seen magic like that before. Hal had learned some impressive tricks from the Azurmouth Magical Academy. On a good day he could even lift up a chair, using just his mind. But the old woman was something else. Something far more terrifying. Those strange black eyes . . . She shuddered.

'Who is she, Newt?'

Newton shook his head.

'I don't know. But we're going to find out.'

He was staring back at the ship, and Tabitha noticed that his knuckles were white, gripping onto his staff where it lay across his lap, safely retrieved from the *Wraith's Revenge*. Paddy had told her once that the staff was a gift from an old hobgoblin, a traveller from the lands beyond the New World. It was plain – three gleaming, black lengths of wood, slotted together – but for close combat, Newton never used any other weapon. 'The Banshee', he called it.

'I'm sorry, Newt,' she said, quietly. 'About going down below.'

'Aye.'

He wasn't listening, though. There was something in his eyes – some emotion that Tabitha had never seen before.

With a jolt, she realized what it was.

Fear.

PART TWO
Fayters

Chapter Nine

Wyrmwood Manor loomed ahead, all grey walls, battlements and turrets, perched on the edge of the cliff top like the shadow of a dragon preparing to swoop down on Port Fayt.

Newton wasn't looking forward to this. Not one bit.

A footman led the way down a gravel pathway, past palm trees, clipped lawns and hedges. It was strangely quiet, except for the crunch of their footsteps and the occasional cry of a gull. Here and there, Newton saw a tinkling fountain, or a fish pond. There were statues of ancient Old World heroes, posing with broadswords, bows and axes.

Whatever you thought of the Wyrmwood family, the gardens were beautiful. Even Slik seemed to be lost in wonder as he rode on his master's shoulder, hanging onto his collar. All the same, Newton felt uneasy. He was so used to the noisy, untidy bustle of the port he'd left behind. He glanced down at his grubby coat and nearly worn-out boots with a twinge of embarrassment. Ahead of him, the footman's golden jacket and white stockings were spotless.

At the end of the path, before the front doors, they came to a huge, antique bronze statue. It was of a human warrior from the Dark Age, wearing a serene expression and stabbing an ogre with his spear. Newton winced. It was probably a fine statue, if you were an art lover. Not so fine if you were an ogre, of course. But then, the Wyrmwoods had never been famous for their tact.

Newton realized he was rubbing at the red marks on his wrists again, and shoved his hands deep into his pockets.

Two blackcoats snapped to attention as the footman climbed a short flight of steps to the entrance. Newton glanced up at the manor before following. It towered against an overcast sky. It brooded. Could buildings brood? He didn't know. Either way, it made him nervous, that much was sure.

'Yuck,' said Slik. 'Ugliest heap of stone I've ever seen.'

For the first time that morning, Newton smiled.

The hallway was dim, and so cavernous that he could barely make out the vaulted ceiling. It was like something out of a ballad from the Dark Age. Softly glowing crystal chandeliers hung way above their heads. Murky oil paintings of long-dead Wyrmwoods covered every inch of wall. Their footsteps clicked on a black marble floor, echoing loudly.

'Wait here please,' said the footman, and disappeared up a wide carpeted staircase.

Slik jabbed Newton in the neck.

'Just curious, but how are you planning to talk your way out of this one?'

'I'm sure it'll be fine.'

He wasn't at *all* sure that it would be fine.

'If you say so,' said Slik cheerily. 'I'm sure the governor will understand. I mean, I suppose it's a shame you didn't actually catch that old witch. And the damage to the ship was a *bit* unfortunate. And the firework, and wrecking the party. I'm sure you'll think of something though.'

Newton bit his lip. The fairy wasn't making things any easier, but he still felt better for having someone with him. Even someone like Slik.

He considered the man he was about to meet. Eugene Wyrmwood, director of the Cockatrice Company and, as of yesterday morning, governor of Port Fayt. The three trading companies had shared power in Fayt for longer than anyone could remember – Cockatrice, Redoubtable and Morning Star. They took it in turns to rule, swapping every year at the start of the Festival of the Sea.

It was an old tradition that the new governor's company paid for the celebrations, in order to show off their generosity and enormous wealth. That meant that causing a scene at the Grand Party was a bad idea. And the fact that Eugene Wyrmwood also happened to be the single wealthiest and most well-connected man in all three companies didn't help matters.

Newton wasn't *scared*, of course. But perhaps he was a little bit *concerned*.

The footman reappeared at the top of the stairs.

'The governor will see you now.'

Newton took a deep breath.

'Do me a favour and keep quiet for this?' he muttered.

Slik snorted and blew a raspberry.

Governor Eugene Wyrmwood stood with his back to them, his oily-blue dressing gown shimmering like the skin of some strange sea creature, gazing through a vast viewing window at the back of his office. Beyond, far below, lay the sparkling expanse of the Ebony Ocean.

Thin strands of purple smoke coiled lazily upwards from a pipe in the governor's hand. Scrubbs' Purpurea tobacco, Newton reckoned. The finest that money could buy.

The governor turned to his visitors with a weak smile, and Newton saw that he was pale and anxious-looking. In the official portraits, Eugene Wyrmwood was a young man, bold and arrogant, with a fierce stare and shining black hair. In real life, he was a good deal older, with gentle eyes and grey hair, combed carefully to conceal a bald patch. He looked like a man who was longing to put his feet up.

'Good morning, Mr Newton. Come in, come in. Your first visit here, I believe?'

'Yes, your honour.'

'Very good, very good. Architecture has always been one of my greatest interests,' said the governor thoughtfully, as if Newton had asked him. 'The exterior of the manor house is chiefly based on the Old World castle of Vorlak the Strong, from the Northern Wastes, you know. Late Dark Age. But of course, our architects have made certain adjustments, mainly to the interior. For reasons of comfort, you see . . .'

Newton felt Slik shifting restlessly on his shoulder. Frankly, he sympathized – he'd never been that interested in buildings either. His attention wandered to the large bookcases of leather tomes that lined the room from floor to ceiling, to the globe sitting on Wyrmwood's desk, to . . . was that a child's doll, propped up beside it?

'. . . And of course, the East Wing has been altered substantially since Mother died,' Wyrmwood was saying, 'although there's much work still to be done.' His eyes glazed over. 'Mother was quite tireless in her dedication to the manor, of course. A splendid woman.'

He sighed.

'But forgive me. To business.' He pushed aside mountains of books and paper on his desk, and set his pipe down, before noticing the doll and hastily shoving it into a desk drawer. 'Ah, ahem, you, er . . . know Colonel Derringer, I believe?' He waved vaguely at a corner of the office.

Derringer stepped from the shadows, holding out his hand and smiling. Somehow, the elf had managed to brush up his black uniform to look even more perfect than usual.

'Mr Newton and I are very well acquainted, your honour.'

Newton nodded, but ignored the outstretched hand. He wasn't going to pretend they were friends. Not even for the governor's benefit.

Wyrmwood had settled into a large armchair behind his desk, and begun fiddling with a large gold signet ring.

'Very good. Well, gentlemen, I gather there has been a . . . *misunderstanding*.' He sounded almost apologetic. 'Colonel Derringer informs me that the Watch were a little disruptive, shall we say, at the Grand Party last night?'

'Dangerous and destructive,' put in Derringer.

Newton cleared his throat.

'We were following a smuggling lead. Turned out to be more serious than we'd—'

'Hardly the point, though, is it, Mr Newton?' interrupted Derringer. 'You're talking as if you were some sort of appointed official.'

Still, that smile.

Slik piped up. 'Better that than being some sort of—'

Newton coughed hastily to cover the last word. Slik had lasted almost two minutes without saying anything, and that was probably the best he could have hoped for. At least the fairy was trying to be supportive. Not that he needed an excuse to throw insults around.

Cyrus Derringer's smile turned icy.

Governor Wyrmwood frowned.

'Mr Newton, I'm sure you're aware that it is the duty of the Dockside Militia to police the town? That is the way it has always been. And whilst the, ahem, "Demon's Watch" has, admittedly, been highly successful at dealing with the, er, less *salubrious* elements in Port Fayt, its activities have never been properly sanctioned.'

Newton nodded, not quite trusting himself to reply. He might end up telling the governor exactly what he thought of that arrangement.

'Well, it's all most disagreeable. I can hardly approve of this sort of behaviour. Especially during the festival, and with the Pageant of the Sea a mere two days hence. We simply can't afford to have any distractions, and I daresay—'

'There's a witch, your honour. Here, loose in Port Fayt. A powerful one.'

'I beg your pardon?'

Derringer laughed unpleasantly.

'A witch?' he sneered. 'Surely you can't be serious? Everyone in Port Fayt knows that magic is prohibited without an official warrant.'

'A witch,' Newton went on, ignoring the elf. 'She used a draining gaze on Hal, and she can levitate, for Thalin's sake, and who knows what else.'

'How dare you tell such outrageous lies in front of the governor?'

'You were there, Derringer. If there was no witch, how do you think we got up onto the top yard?'

'I dread to think, but I imagine your own ridiculous excuse for a magician had something to do with—'

'Gentlemen, gentlemen, please.'

Governor Wyrmwood pulled a silk handkerchief from his dressing gown and mopped his brow.

'Now then, a witch, you say. That sounds most unlikely. We haven't seen the kind of magic you describe for decades. If this was the Old World, perhaps, or if we were still stuck in the Dark Age . . .' He chuckled. 'But we are a trading port. Not here, Mr Newton, not here.'

Newton opened his mouth, and was silenced by a raised hand.

'In any case, it seems to me that there is no real threat. A scuffle at a party. Undignified, yes. But nothing to be concerned about at such an important time of year. An investigation by the Watch would be both troublesome and unnecessary. Therefore, for the duration of the Festival of the Sea you are to cease all operations.'

'Your honour . . .' said Newton and Derringer at the same time.

The governor raised his hand again.

'Enough, please. I've made up my mind. My mother would never have stood for such nonsense if she were still with us. The Watch is not to operate during the festival.'

'But—'

'Now, if you gentlemen will excuse me, I have several other appointments this morning, and I fear I can already feel a headache coming on. You may show yourselves out.'

Stunned, Newton bowed and left the room. The governor had spoken, and he had no answer.

In the corridor he stood motionless, breathing heavily.

'That went well,' said Slik.

Newton grunted and rubbed at his ribs, still sore from the witch's grasp.

'You've been very lucky, Mr Newton.'

Derringer. The elf had followed him out of the room.

'Destroying a government vessel, vandalism, arson – I'd be perfectly content, if I were you. In any case, the town's safe with the Dockside Militia looking after it. Who knows, maybe this will teach you to leave the job to the professionals.'

Newton liked to think he was a patient man, but he'd already put up with a lot this morning.

'Remind me, are these the same professionals who let Captain Gore escape from the Brig?'

Derringer's smile froze. Slik sniggered.

'The ones who spectacularly failed to uncover the Mer Way unicorn rustlers? And then there's the Mandeville Plot . . .'

For once, Derringer stopped smiling and snarled.

'Even your marvellous watchmen couldn't save Governor Mandeville.'

'At least we were there. Where were you, laundering your uniform?'

The elf stepped in closer, his blue eyes narrowed with fury.

'Understand this, Mr Newton. If you step out of line just once, I'll have you in the Brig yourself, with all the scum you've locked up over the years. They'll be delighted to see you, I can assure you. So you'd better not let me catch your watchmen snooping around. Because if I do, it'll be the end of the Demon's Watch. For good.'

Chapter Ten

Tabitha couldn't believe what she was hearing.

'He can't do that! No one can do that!' She shot up from her stool in fury, then sat down again just as angrily. 'I mean, just because a silly, wet mummy's boy of a governor wants to show off with his stupid Pageant of the Sea . . . He can't shut us down like that! Can he?'

The watchmen were sat hunched around a table in the small, cosy serving room at Bootles' Pie Shop – their regular meeting place. There were no other customers in today, and as usual, Mrs Bootle had provided a vast platter of steaming hot pies and jugs of cold grog. Even so, the atmosphere was gloomy.

'Don't worry, Tabs,' said Frank. 'I'm sure Newt's got a plan here. Right, Newt?'

Newton shrugged, and bit into a wedge of seagull pie.

'He's the governor,' he said, juggling the hot meat around his mouth. 'He doesn't want the Demon's Watch to investigate; that's his decision.'

Tabitha banged the table in frustration, making the plates and mugs rattle.

'But, Newt . . . that's just not FAIR! Wyrmwood's nothing but a spiteful, twisted old fool, and all he cares about is money and his stupid Cockatrice Company and his silly, stupid pageant. And while him and his rich fat friends are sitting on their bums getting even richer and even fatter, that smuggler and that crazy witch are going to be on the loose and you're saying that we can't do anything about it?!'

She jumped up again and began to pace around the room, fists tightly clenched. They couldn't give up without a fight, just when things were getting interesting. She was scuppered if she was going back to playing triominoes again.

'Tabs has got a point, Newt,' said Paddy. 'I mean, about that witch. Whole of Port Fayt could be in danger.'

Newton nodded slowly. 'Yep. Whole of Fayt could

be in danger, right enough.' And he tore off another mouthful of pie.

'This ain't like you, Newt,' said Old Jon.

The room fell silent.

Old Jon was sitting with his pipe, a little apart from everyone, puffing and gazing into the middle distance. From what Tabitha had heard, the elf had been a watchman back when Newt was still in his cradle. So if he had something to say, you listened.

Finally, Newton put down his pie.

'Don't worry,' he said. 'We're not going to let this go. No witch is going to run around causing havoc in *this* town. Not during the Festival of the Sea. Not at any time.'

Tabitha collapsed back onto her stool with a sigh of relief. Frank and Paddy exchanged grins. Old Jon carried on smoking and staring, while Hal nodded as he polished his spectacles. He was looking especially pale after what had happened on the *Wraith's Revenge*.

'But listen,' Newton went on. 'No one can know what we're up to. If we're found snooping around, Governor Wyrmwood won't give us another chance. And if Cyrus Derringer even suspects something's going on, we're sunk. Understood?'

'Understood,' said the watchmen, as one. Tabitha

felt a cold thrill run through her. Disobeying the governor was dangerous, of course. Very dangerous. But then, being a watchman wasn't exactly supposed to be a stroll by the quayside.

'So, first things first. Does anyone have any idea who this witch is or what she's after?'

Silence. Tabitha racked her brain.

'Any clues at all?'

'Well,' said Hal, frowning and replacing his spectacles. 'I very much doubt that she's a Fayter.'

'Right,' said Paddy. 'Unless she's really been keeping her head down, we would have heard about her before. A witch that powerful . . . I reckon she's new in town, and from the Old World, most likely. Yow!'

Frank had jabbed him in the ribs.

'Nice work, genius.'

'All right,' said Newton. 'That's not a lot to go on. So here's my idea – we find that contraband. Once we know what it is, we'll have a better idea of what's going on. And if the witch still wants it, she can come and get it.'

Hal raised an eyebrow.

'Forgive me, but is it really sensible to antagonize her so? A witch like that will be capable of—'

'It's not sensible. But we don't have a choice. The blackcoats couldn't handle this. And who knows what she's up to? So we've got to find that cargo. Way I see it, there's only one person who can tell us where it is, and that's—'

'Clagg,' interrupted Tabitha, determined to show she could help. 'Captain Phineus Clagg.'

'Exactly.'

Hal was still looking doubtful.

'That's all very well, but do we have any idea how to track him down? I'm sure you'll recall that he was somewhat . . . absent from the Grand Party last night.'

'We'll track him down, all right. We just need a little help.'

The pie-shop door swung open, and all eyes turned to it.

'Afternoon, all,' said Jeb the Snitch.

He sauntered in, dressed in a particularly violent pink and blue waistcoat and grinning smugly. Tabitha groaned. Crafty, sneaky, treacherous . . . Jeb was a perfect example of everything that the League of the Light said was wrong with goblins.

'Well, if it isn't the Snitch,' said Paddy. 'Reckon that look says you know something we don't.'

'Know a lotta things you don't, mate.'

THUNK!

Tabitha found she had slammed a knife into the table.

'We don't need this clown, Newt. He's trouble, and anyone can see it.'

'Oh, clown, is it? That's rich, coming from the circus troupe who smashed up the *Wraith's Revenge* last night.'

Tabitha began reaching for another knife, but found her arm trapped firmly in Frank's big green fist.

'Where'd you pick up this one?' sneered Jeb. 'Down the shark pits?'

'All right, enough,' cut in Newton, before Tabitha could come up with a halfway decent retort. 'Jeb, have you found out where Captain Clagg has been hiding himself?'

'Course I have. What do you take me for, an amateur? First things first, though. Got my payment, have yer?'

'Aye. The usual. No more, no less.'

Jeb sighed.

'Then I got two words for yer – Captain Gore.'

It took a few moments to sink in.

'Captain Gore, the pirate?' said Frank. 'The sickest, bloodthirstiest pirate in the Ebony Ocean?'

'Know any other Captain Gores?' enquired Jeb. He hopped up onto a stool, grabbed a fresh pie from the mountain in the middle of the table and poured himself a helping of grog, all the while ignoring Tabitha's baleful glare.

'Gore and Clagg've got themselves a little score to settle. Few years back, out in the tropics, Clagg sold Gore thirty barrels of finest Azurmouth firewater. Got a pretty price for them too. Except after the deal was done, it turned out it weren't actually firewater in the barrels – it were seawater. Gore and his pirates've been after Clagg ever since, looking to get their own back. Seems yesterday, they finally caught up with him. Captain Gore's bosun, that ol' ogre Tuck, with all them swirly black tattoos, he found the smuggler in some dockside tavern and dragged him kicking and screaming back to their galleon. The *Weeping Wound*, it's called. It's anchored out in the bay, so you best hurry. Gore won't be stopping in Port Fayt for long. Man's got ships to plunder.'

Tabitha shrugged her way out of Frank's grip.

'How come you know so much about Captain Gore?'

Jeb smirked at her.

'Know all kinds of things, don't I?'

There was a long pause.

'Right,' said Paddy, at last. 'So you're saying, if we want to talk to Phineus Clagg, we'll have to ask Captain Gore for him?'

'Seems that way. And if I was you, I'd ask nicely. 'Specially if you want him in one piece.'

'So we'll ask,' said Tabitha fiercely. 'We're the Demon's Watch, aren't we? What's the problem?'

'The problem,' said Frank, 'is that Captain Gore is a maniac. The sort of maniac who gives other maniacs a bad name. I heard he fed his cabin boy to a shark once. Then ate the shark.'

Jeb cackled and stuffed more pie into his face.

'True enough,' said Newton thoughtfully. 'There's no way Gore will just let his victim go. But if a smuggler tricked him, then so can we. We'll just have to use a bit of cunning, that's all.'

Chapter Eleven

'Joseph Grubb, look at the state of you!'

A moist cloth dabbed at his face, and he squirmed.

'Sit still, it's only a handkerchief. There, that's better.'

He giggled and blew a bubble.

Elijah Grubb put on the sternest face he could manage. 'Now, time to eat up all them greens, young'un. Can't have you wasting away.'

'No chance of that, Eli. If he carries on like this, we'll be needing a wheelbarrow to cart him around in.'

Joseph giggled again. His mother wagged her finger at him, pretending to be cross.

'And all that giggling. He's a right little terror.'

'Terror,' gurgled Joseph.

They both laughed. Mr Grubb took Mrs Grubb in his arms and kissed her, his tough grey goblin skin pressed against hers, delicate, white, human.

They were at home, sitting around the little dining table in their house with the green front door. Mother and Father, both there, both safe. He had thought they were dead, but here they were, alive. Everything was so wonderful, Joseph felt like he might burst.

There was a knock on the door, and Mrs Grubb went to answer it. Standing there, in the rain, was a blackcoat.

He couldn't hear what the man was saying, and he could see only his mother's back. But somehow, suddenly, with a searing pain, he knew.

Father was dead.

They had come for him. Humans. Men he'd worked with on the docks. Men who had seen him with his pretty human wife. Men who were supposed to have been his friends.

Joseph looked across the dining table at the man he'd thought was his father, and saw that there was something wrong with his eyes. They weren't supposed to be yellow, were they? And his face wasn't supposed to be furry and ginger, was it?

'Eat up those greens, mongrel,' said Mr Lightly, 'or I'll . . .'

He flinched.

'Hold still,' said his father.

'It hurts.'

'That's because you fell off a roof.'

Where was he?

'Hold still, I said.'

'Mother?'

The room was darker. Much darker. Somewhere, he could hear her crying, and he reached out for her.

'Do you want me to tie you up? Or are you going to stay still?'

'Mother!'

Everything was going back to how it was before. Father gone, Mother crying. And soon she would be gone too. He sobbed.

'Father?'

'I'm not your father, boy.'

The room was darker than ever, and he was alone. Darker, and darker, and darker . . .

A figure crouching over him in the gloom, yellow eyes glinting, holding something small and black.

Where was he? Was he dead?

He tried to get up, but was pushed down again.

Half asleep, he settled for rolling over instead. Everything was going to be fine. He was sure of it.

'Tough as a shark,' the figure murmured. 'If you only knew what it was you took . . .'

And Grubb slept, again.

'Joseph, did I ever tell you the story of how the world began?'

'Tell me again.'

They were sitting on a pier, just Joseph and his father, swinging their bare feet to and fro above the waves – Joseph's grey-pink, his father's just grey – watching for the flashes of merfolk tails, out in the bay. In the distance, the sun was setting, staining the Ebony Ocean crimson.

'Long, long ago, before humans or goblins or elves, the land was crafted by demons and seraphs. They made everything – the Old World, the New World and the Middle Islands, the mountains and seas and the creatures that walked the earth. The world is soaked in their magic, Joseph, and it's that same magic that magicians use in their spells, even today.'

Joseph nodded, his eyes wide.

'Now, many years later, war broke out between the creatures of the Old World. That was the Dark Age. And in those days, the humans used to say that the seraphs had made them in their own image, and that it was only the other creatures – the imps, trolls, ogres and so on – that were shaped by the demons.'

'What do you think, Father?'

Elijah Grubb smiled and put an arm around his son's shoulders.

'I think they worked together. There's a little bit of demon and a little bit of seraph in everyone, Joseph. Don't let anyone tell you different.'

He pointed over the water.

'Look, there's one – a merman. See it?'

Joseph looked, but the merman had gone. And when he turned back to his father he found that he was alone on the pier, and the ocean was swirling and churning and slipping, slipping away from him . . .

Where was he?

Where was he?

Chapter Twelve

The Marlinspike Quarter was its usual grubby self. Youths loitered on corners, and crooked salesmen flogged stolen goods at makeshift stalls. Above them, washing billowed on lines strung between houses, most of it looking so grimy it was hard to believe it had actually been washed. A wrinkled old troll sat cross-legged against a wall, cranking out a tune on a hurdy-gurdy, while a half-starved monkey slept peacefully beside him. There was a soft clink as Newton tossed a coin to join the few that lay on a scrap of cloth in front of him. The troll nodded, almost imperceptibly, and carried on playing.

'Where are we going?' asked Tabitha.

'You'll see.'

Tabitha sighed loudly. She hated it when Newton was mysterious. Which, unfortunately, was most of the time.

'Fairies,' called a salesman. 'Best messenger fairies, cheap as brine! Fairies from the Old World and the New!'

They clamoured in their cages as Newton and Tabitha passed, reaching out tiny arms, begging to be bought. Tabitha tried not to look. Newton didn't want her to have a fairy – said she was too young to need one – which was completely ridiculous, of course, and totally unfair.

'When are we going after the smuggler?' she asked, to take her mind off the fairies.

'Soon enough. We need a few things first.'

'Well then, I'm going to Thalin Square to see the decorations.'

Newton looked at her for the first time since they'd left Bootles'.

'No, young lady. You're coming with me.'

'Why should I? You won't even tell me where we're going.'

A pained, anxious look passed over Newton's face, as he realized that she had a point. Tabitha hated that look, almost as much as him not telling her what was going on. It meant he thought he wasn't looking after her properly, and for some reason it never failed to make her feel bad.

'I'm sorry,' he said. 'I should have explained. We're going to . . .' He trailed off, looking over her shoulder.

'Where? We're going to where?'

But Newton was already striding past, his attention fixed somewhere else entirely. Exasperated, Tabitha followed.

They were heading for a dwarf standing on a street corner. The stranger had long black hair, a black moustache and a black beard, all matted, greasy and wildly out of control. He was holding his coat open, displaying a hodgepodge of pans, spoons and knives that dangled from the lining. Tabitha reckoned the coat must have been made for a troll, because it was far too big for its current owner.

The dwarf caught sight of Newton, grinned, then turned tail and fled. Unfortunately his legs were too short and his merchandise was too heavy for him to get very far. He clanked a short distance down the road and then stopped, bent over, puffing and wheezing to catch his breath.

'Well, if it isn't the Ghost,' said Newton, strolling up and patting him on the back. 'Good to see you.'

'It's plain Jack Cobley now,' said the dwarf, peering

up at Newton with bulging, bloodshot eyes. 'And I ain't done nothing wrong.'

Tabitha tried not to breathe in through her nose. The dwarf stank of something, and it definitely wasn't shokel buns.

'I doubt that, Jack,' said Newton. 'But relax. I'm not going to throw you in the Brig. Not this time.'

'Oh thank you, thank you, thank you!' gibbered the dwarf, pathetically grateful. 'Me smuggling days are over, you know that. I learned me lesson, sure as the sea. Never want to see the inside of the Brig again, long as I live.' He shuddered.

'Good. I need to ask a favour.'

Instantly, the dwarf became suspicious again.

'Favour? What favour?'

'That old sloop you had. You used to run dragons' teeth in false barrel bottoms, back in the day. Remember?'

'Aye,' said the dwarf, his brow creased as he desperately tried to work out where this was going.

'What happened to her?'

'She's anchored out in the bay. But I ain't used her for a long time, Newt, I swear. She's a wreck. It'd cost me more to repair her than buy a new boat, and I can't afford that. Not on the money I make selling this junk.'

He waved a saucepan, forlorn.

'Perfect,' said Newton. 'We'll take her off your hands.' He opened his money pouch and counted out ten ducats. 'This do?'

The dwarf's eyes lit up and he snatched the money. 'Yes, sir, that'll do nicely.'

His eyes fell on Tabitha, and he stared. She looked down at her feet, and clamped her teeth together. Here it came.

'Hey,' he said, grinning. 'Hey, I know you.'

'All right,' said Newton. 'It's time to go now.'

'No, wait, you're that girl, ain't you? The Mandeville kid. I'm right, ain't I? That fancy blue hair dye don't fool me.'

'What if I am?' growled Tabitha, taking a step forward and glaring at him. 'It's no business of yours, you washed-up bilgebag.'

'Enough,' said Newton, putting himself between them. He took Tabitha by the arm, and effortlessly moved her away.

'Ain't you gonna ask me where I berthed it?' the dwarf called after them.

'I already checked,' replied Newton. 'North side of the bay. Berth three hundred and forty-three.'

It was only when they'd turned the corner that he let go of her.

'I wasn't going to do anything,' she snapped, rubbing her arm. It had been a gentle grip by Newton's standards, but it still hurt. 'Why do you always have to treat me like a baby?'

'You need to watch that temper,' said Newton, ignoring her question entirely. 'It'll get you into trouble.'

'You don't understand what it's like, being recognized all the time like that. How could you? It's not as if your parents were . . .' She choked back a sob, and was immediately angry with herself for getting so upset. All those stupid feelings about her mother and father were bubbling up inside her again. The hurt and the loss. How could she be so pathetic, still? She'd been a baby when they died, for Thalin's sake . . .

Newton stopped and turned to face her, placing his heavy hands on her shoulders.

'You don't know much about my parents, Tabs,' he said softly. 'And listen, ignore people like Jack Cobley. He's an idiot, and idiots are a ducat a dozen in this town. Being a good watchman means being in control. That means staying calm. If you lose your temper, you could put all of us in danger. Do you understand?'

When Newton spoke like that, it was hard not to listen. She nodded, dabbed at her eyes and took a deep, quavering breath.

He reached out to ruffle her hair, then pulled his hand back fast, clearly remembering how much she hated hair-ruffling.

'Come on then,' he said. 'Let's go and find the Ghost's boat.'

They set off again.

As they walked, Tabitha glanced sideways at Newton. He didn't look much like her real father. Or at least, how she imagined her real father had looked. Her eyes wandered to his wrists, and the red blistered marks that ran around them. She had tried to ask him about those marks once, but he'd just muttered something and changed the subject. *You don't know much about my parents, Tabs*. Well, it was true. There was a lot she didn't know about him. Her real father would have told her everything about himself. Her real father wouldn't have kept secrets from her . . .

Suddenly, Tabitha felt very alone.

'Why was he called the Ghost?' she asked, trying to sound like she was feeling fine now. 'Was it because he was hard to catch?'

'Hardly. He's an idiot, remember? We called him the Ghost because every time we caught him he went white as a sail.'

That made her chuckle.

Newton stopped and looked at her. He was wearing his anxious expression again.

'Look,' he said slowly. 'I, er . . . I know you hate being the lookout. So this time, with this smuggler, I thought, maybe . . . Maybe you should have a chance to do some real watchman work. What do you think?'

Tabitha felt her jaw drop.

'Really?' was all she could say.

He nodded and gave her a slightly clumsy pat on the shoulder.

'Just promise me you'll be careful. If everything goes to plan, you'll be totally safe.'

Safe? Tabitha pretended she hadn't heard that.

Chapter Thirteen

Governor Eugene Wyrmwood stood at the head of the table, eyeing it uneasily. The tablecloth was starched and spotless. The knives and forks were polished and shining like mirrors. There were crystal bowls laden with exotic fruit, and lit candles in golden candelabras, bathing the dining room in a soft, warm glow. It was perfect. And yet, he wasn't hungry. He wondered if he might be sick. But no. He was simply trying to find an excuse to leave.

A glance around the room didn't make him feel any better. A footman stood in every shadowy corner, still and silent, each one wearing the gold and purple velvet livery of the Cockatrice Company. Along both sides of the table stood the wealthiest Cockatrice merchants in Port Fayt, each one behind his allotted place, all waiting to sit. Only the place at the far end of the table, opposite the governor himself, was empty.

The diners were all dressed in their finest clothing, and all of them were getting fidgety, casting more and more glances at the empty place as time wore on.

The governor smoothed out his combed, pomaded hair and checked his coat for what felt like the hundredth time, making sure it was still as pristine as it had been thirty seconds ago. It was. He reached into his pocket, drew out a large golden pocket watch and checked the time. That didn't make him feel any better, either.

To his right, Mr Skelmerdale cleared his throat and leaned over.

'I don't like it, your honour,' he murmured.

Skelmerdale had a particular way of saying 'your honour' which made it sound more like 'your uselessness'. He was tall and bony, with close-cropped white hair and dark eyes which seemed constantly glaring, like a strict headmaster's. Governor Wyrmwood found himself wishing, yet again, that his mother was here. She wouldn't have put up with Mr Skelmerdale for one minute.

'He should be here by now, for Thalin's sake,' muttered Skelmerdale. 'He should have been here an hour ago.'

'Yes,' said Governor Wyrmwood. 'Indeed. Oh dear.' There didn't seem much else to say, so he fiddled with his cuffs instead. He'd always known that being governor of Port Fayt wasn't going to be easy, but tonight was shaping up to be even more fraught than he'd expected. The Cockatrice merchants had only elected him director because he was the last of the Wyrmwoods – the wealthiest family in Port Fayt. That didn't mean they liked him, though. Far from it.

He could already feel the first pulsing of a headache coming on.

Skelmerdale turned his glare on the empty chair and muttered something about manners, appropriate behaviour and lack of respect.

'Mr Skelmerdale,' hissed an elderly imp, Mr Rotheringham, at Eugene's left. 'You simply must guard your tongue when the ambassador arrives. We can't allow relations with the League of the Light to become any worse than they already are.'

'Worse?' snorted Skelmerdale, glowering down at the imp. 'How could they possibly get any worse?'

'Need I remind you,' huffed the imp, 'that the League controls nearly every major port in the Old

World? That trade is a meagre trickle as it is, and that unless they are prepared to lift these dratted sanctions—'

'Curse the League,' snapped an elf further down the table. 'How dare they presume to—'

'But it would be foolishness to—'

'I'll say what I like! You can't tell me to—'

The governor pulled his handkerchief from a sleeve and dabbed at his brow. It was an all too familiar argument, and the timing was exceptionally bad.

Thankfully, at that moment the doors to the dining room swung open, and an unusually portly elf in Cockatrice Company livery entered. It was Governor Wyrmwood's butler. The voices died down almost at once.

'Your honour,' announced the butler. 'His grace, the Duke of Garran, ambassador of the League of the Light, has arrived.'

There was a shift in the room. All trace of the bickering disappeared instantly. Instead, there was a tense, expectant silence.

'Very good,' said the governor, his voice wavering only a fraction. 'Show him in, will you?'

And before the butler had a chance to reply, the Duke of Garran glided into the room.

The Cockatrice merchants couldn't help themselves – they stared. The Duke was a small man, with pink skin so perfect and flawless that it looked like it belonged to a child. He was dressed in white, from the white satin tricorne that he handed to the butler, to his white silk stockings and white leather shoes. Even his eyes seemed to have no trace of colour. They swept around the room, quietly judging everyone and everything within sight.

Nothing but those eyes seemed to fit with the dreadful rumours surrounding the Duke of Garran. *He collects the severed heads of trolls*, the governor told himself. *He hangs goblins upside down for days, just for fun. He has baby imps thrown on bonfires*.

'Good evening, your grace,' he said.

The Duke of Garran moved his lips into the exact shape of a smile, without actually smiling.

'Thank you, Mr Wyrmwood.' His voice was soft, gentle and cold. 'I hope you have not been waiting long?'

'Not at all,' the governor said quickly, before Skelmerdale could interrupt. 'Please, let us sit.'

The Cockatrice merchants gratefully pulled back their chairs and collapsed into them. Not one of them was used to standing up for as long as the hour they'd had to wait. Normally, it was other, less important people who waited for them.

'Well, your grace,' said the governor, tucking his napkin into his collar and finally beginning to relax. 'I must say, it is a truly *splendid* honour to welcome you to Port Fayt, and to my dear home, Wyrmwood Manor. I do hope you find it to your taste. It was my great-great-grandfather who conceived of the original design, you know. The exterior is, of course, based on the castle of Vorlak the Strong, in the Northern Wastes, as I'm sure you'll have noticed, and . . .'

His words died as he looked up. Everyone had sat down – except the Duke of Garran. Several of the merchants were exchanging anxious glances.

Governor Wyrmwood forced himself to smile.

'Won't you, er, have a seat?'

'Unfortunately I cannot stay for dinner,' said the Duke. His colourless eyes flickered, momentarily but obviously, towards a pair of troll merchants seated near his end of the table, and for an instant he looked as if he had swallowed a morsel of rotten fish. 'I must return to the Old World on the next tide. Urgent business.'

'But the sanctions,' said Mr Rotheringham, his voice a little higher than usual. 'I mean to say, I understood that we were going to be discussing the

League of the Light's sanctions against Port Fayt.'

The Duke turned his glassy stare on the imp.

'There is nothing to be discussed. The trade sanctions will not be lifted. Not without considerable evidence that the Cockatrice Company, the Redoubtable Company and the Morning Star Company are all fully committed to the way of the Light.'

'The way of the Light,' said Skelmerdale, in a tone which was dangerously close to a growl. 'Are you referring to your purges? To the removal of so-called "demonspawn" wherever you find them? To the wholesale slaughter of goblins, trolls and ogres by the League's troops? Heads displayed on spikes? Barbarism not seen since the Dark Age?'

'I believe I will take my leave of you now, gentlemen,' said the Duke, ignoring what had just been said.

'Good riddance,' roared Skelmerdale. He stood, towering over the table, his face purple with anger. The other merchants stared at him in horror. 'Port Fayt will never submit to the way of the Light. We are not murderers here, *your grace.*'

'Sit down,' pleaded the governor desperately. 'Please, Mr Skelmerdale, sit down. I apologize, your grace, the Festival of the Sea is such a stressful period for all of us . . . I'm sure you can understand . . .'

'I understand.'

'Um, do you? I mean, excellent, well, perhaps we could put this all behind us, and—'

'I understand perfectly. And I will not forget this, Mr Skelmerdale.' The Duke of Garran tapped his head with a plump, pink finger. 'I have a very good memory. Very good indeed.'

He turned on his heel and glided out of the room, taking his white satin hat from the butler as he went.

There was a long, uncomfortable silence.

'Well?' said Skelmerdale at last. 'It's true, isn't it? The League will be at odds with us so long as Port Fayt allows all people to live here peacefully.'

'Perhaps,' said the governor, 'a little more delicacy might have been appropriate . . .'

'Delicacy?' scoffed the elf who had spoken up earlier. 'The League has never been delicate with us. What about the assassination of Governor Mandeville?'

Everyone seemed to stiffen a little at the words. Skelmerdale and Rotheringham cast anxious glances at the governor.

'We have never repaid the League for that,' the elf went on. 'You, of all people, your honour, should remember—'

'ENOUGH!' bawled the governor, making several merchants flinch. His head felt like it was exploding now, and he clutched at it, trying to control the pain. 'That's quite enough. The Mandeville Plot was a long time ago, Mr Bentham, and I had hoped that we had put it behind us. In future, I would prefer it if you did not mention the matter.'

The table had gone very quiet again. The elf opened his mouth to reply and then thought better of it. Some merchants fiddled with their cutlery. Others became very interested in the tapestries on the walls. A few stared intently at their empty plates.

The governor stood. He felt suddenly weary, and embarrassed.

'Thank you, gentlemen. I, er, I hope you will forgive my little, um, outburst. And please excuse me, I will not join you for dinner. I find I am not hungry.'

He dropped his unused napkin on the tablecloth and practically fled from the room, feeling the stares of the merchants every step of the way, and almost colliding with the servants bringing in the first course – a large silver tureen of soup.

Chapter Fourteen

Grubb's eyelids blinked open, then closed again. There were two people in the room with him now. They were talking to each other, and their voices came to him distantly, as if through a fog. He dozed, half listening.

'Do you understand how much it's worth?'

'Yeah, yeah, but the deal was—'

'Forget the deal: that was before I knew what I was stealing.'

'Two hundred, that was what we agreed, weren't it?'

'I took it to Mr Harrison, you see. The toymaker.'

'The what?'

'Let's just say, Mr Harrison sells other things as well as toys. The point is, the imp was able to identify it for me. This is a leash, my dear, deluded friend. Do you understand what a person could do with this?'

'What do I care? It's worth ducats is all I know.'

'Three hundred.'

'Maw's teeth! Stinking thieves, yer just don't know when to stop. Thieving out of yer own employer's pocket . . . Yer'll be stealing my flaming shoes, next.'

'Four hundred.'

'All right, all right, steady on. Three hundred. Done. But you're a crook. Can't trust nobody in this town.'

There was a jingle of coins. Grubb rolled onto his side. The voices seemed to be getting fainter and fainter, but he was fairly sure they were his mother and father.

'Where did you go?' he asked them. 'I'm so glad you're back. Why did you leave me alone again?'

'Wake up,' said his father.

'But it's still dark. I'm so sleepy . . .'

'I said wake up, mongrel.'

Ice-cold water crashed over him. He jerked upright. He was drenched, and very much awake.

'That get your attention then?'

It all came back to him.

The package.
The cat.
The rooftops.
The fall.

He was sitting on a makeshift bed of straw heaped on a stone floor, still wearing the imp's fancy shirt and jacket. A yellow glow spilled from a lantern onto a goblin crouching over him – one who looked extremely irritable. Now that Grubb was awake, it was no surprise to see that the goblin wasn't his father after all.

Out of the corner of his eye, he could make out huge oak barrels looming over them in the darkness at the edges of the room. A cellar, somewhere. How long had he been unconscious? Hours? Days?

'And this,' said the goblin, putting down the empty water bucket, 'really takes the cake. Bringing some grogshop runt here. Some mongrel. What in all the sea am I supposed to do with him?'

The other shrugged. He was standing in the shadows, but a sliver of light from the doorway fell on the side of his face – pale freckled skin, ginger hair, the glint of one eye, yellow, like a cat's . . .

'I could hardly leave him lying in the street. He saw me take it.'

'So why didn't you just deal with him? You're too soft, that's your problem.'

The shapeshifter ignored that and examined his fingernails.

Letting out a long sigh, the goblin stood.

'All right, you can buzz off now. Got yer payment, ain't yer? We're done.'

'Very well. A pleasure doing business with you, Jeb.'

The door opened and closed with a bang.

The goblin called Jeb scratched his head and inspected Grubb. His clothes looked expensive but thrown together, so that they were mismatched. He was wearing a canary yellow coat with a dark blue waistcoat, heavy gold earrings and a belt buckle that glittered with jewels. Grubb glimpsed black velvet sticking out of the goblin's belt. The package, stolen by the cat the night before. Or was it two nights ago?

'Had a nice rest, have we?' enquired Jeb.

'Yes, thank you,' said Grubb.

He carefully flexed his leg, and found that there was no pain at all.

'My leg . . .'

'You can thank that ginger weevil for that,' said the goblin sourly. 'Now get up. You're coming with me.'

'Where am I?'

'You'll find out. On yer feet.'

Grubb stood up slowly. His limbs were stiff. He wasn't sure he really wanted to go with Jeb, but it didn't seem like he had much choice.

'Are you a friend of Phineus Clagg?' he asked.

'What? No. Friends are for mugs. I'm a businessman.'

'So . . . what are you going to do with his package?'

The goblin grinned, running his tongue over his pointed teeth.

'Sell it, of course. It's bound to be worth something.'

'But it's—'

'Enough.' He shoved Grubb towards the door. 'Right little troublemaker you are, ain't yer? Chasing after a shapeshifter in the middle of the night, then lying around snoring and moaning all day yesterday, and now you're up asking all these stinking questions. What do you think you are, the Demon's Watch or something?'

Grubb couldn't help himself.

'It wasn't his to take, sir. Not yours either.'

That won him a cuff on the back of his head.

'Ow!'

'Keep your trap shut, mongrel. Clear?'

Grubb nodded. There didn't seem much point in arguing about it.

Jeb pushed him through the door and up a flight of stone stairs. Grubb could feel his heart pounding. The shapeshifter might have looked after him, but he was far from convinced that Jeb would do the same. Someone who paid hundreds of ducats to have things stolen for him could be capable of anything.

They turned into a corridor and climbed more stairs, wooden this time, dimly lit with lanterns that hung from hooks on the walls. Above the creak of their footsteps, Grubb heard the muffled sound of people chattering and laughing. Stamping their feet, shouting and singing. The sound grew louder.

At the top of the stairs they came to a thick red velvet curtain guarded by a man and a troll in spotless white shirts and red waistcoats, each carrying a stubby blunderbuss. Grubb swallowed hard and stopped, but Jeb shoved him forward again and nodded to the guards. They nodded in reply and pulled aside the curtain.

And then they were inside.

It was a theatre, of sorts. Or at least, Grubb thought it was a theatre. He'd never been inside one before, but knew what they were supposed to look like. A vast crystal chandelier lit the auditorium. There was dark red wallpaper and brass fittings, ornate moulding papered in gold leaf and a vast, domed ceiling. Everything looked old and worn.

Here, the noise was deafening. It came mainly from below, where Grubb could see spectators standing, crammed into the lower galleries and round the edges of the auditorium. They were jostling, waving at friends, shoving each other to get a good look at the performance area. But from this angle, Grubb couldn't see what they were watching.

They had come in at the highest gallery, where the spectators were well-dressed and silent. They sat in plush armchairs, fans fluttering, pipe smoke hanging heavy above them. Bully boys loitered in the background, and Grubb saw sabres, pistols thrust into belts and even the odd musket. He'd never seen so many weapons in his life.

'What is this place?'

Jeb opened his mouth to reply, but at that moment there was a wave of shouting and cheering, drowning out his words. It sounded like 'Harry's Market'.

That couldn't be right.

Grubb looked around, hoping to see some way to escape. There were doors further along the gallery, but he had a feeling that if he made a run for it, the dangerous-looking guards would be on Jeb's side.

There was no way he could get past them. He was stuck with his captor.

'Jebedee, my lovely!'

'Harry, you old scoundrel.'

The newcomer was an elf, tall and spindly, with curls of grey hair crawling out from beneath a tricorne hat. He wore a coat made out of some strange grey material that Grubb didn't think he had seen before. On his shoulder sat a messenger fairy, wearing an identical coat and hat.

Harry and Jeb began speaking fast in hushed voices, too low for Grubb to hear what they were saying. So instead, he edged forward to the front of the gallery to see what everyone was watching.

He caught his breath. In an instant, he knew why there were so many armed men around. He knew what Jeb had said when he'd asked where they were. He even knew what Harry's jacket was made of.

Where the stalls and thc stage should have been, there was a gigantic pool of water, foaming and churning.

Of course it wasn't Harry's *Market*. It was Harry's *Shark Pit*.

Chapter Fifteen

Grubb had heard all about shark pits.

The blackcoats had been trying to shut them down for years, but they were still going strong in secret, hidden in warehouses and theatres like this one, all over Port Fayt. He tried to pick out a shark fighter in the bloody water, but the dark shapes were moving too fast. They were merfolk, according to Mr Lightly. A land dweller wouldn't stand a chance in the pit. Sometimes they did it out of choice, for the glory of it. But more often, the shark pit owner would send his boys out to sea with nets, hunting for recruits. They were locked away like lobsters in underwater cages, only allowed out to train, and to fight in the pits. If Thalin could see this town now . . .

A figure breached in a fountain of spray, leaping up several feet above the surface. Grubb glimpsed taut, muscled arms, a slender trident and the silver tail flicking off drops of water. The merman's body flashed as it turned in the air and slipped underwater once again.

The spectators were roaring and cheering as loudly as they could. Most of them probably had bets on the bout. It wouldn't be pretty if the shark fighter lost, but that didn't seem to matter to them. There were tales of punters making their fortune at the pits. Then there were other tales, about those who lost but couldn't afford to pay. The owners of the shark pits weren't often all that understanding. And of course, the sharks needed feeding.

Grubb spotted something grey, sleek and fast below the surface, and shuddered. He had seen mermen before, of course, swimming out in the bay, sometimes even coming up to the dockside piers to barter and trade sunken treasures with Fayt merchants. But a shark – that was something else entirely.

'Admiring my beautiful sharkies, my dear?'

Grubb had been so busy watching the pit below that he hadn't noticed Harry coming up behind him.

He felt the elf's slender fingers resting on his shoulder, and fought down the urge to push them away. Jeb sidled up next to him. The package was still stuck into his belt, so close that Grubb could have reached out and taken it.

'Yes, sir.'

'Well, no wonder, duck. Look at that splendid coat o' yours . . . I'd say you're a gent who appreciates the finer things in life.'

Jeb guffawed.

'Just like my clients here.' Harry gestured around the gallery. His voice was shrill, and would probably have been ridiculous if its owner wasn't such a strange, terrifying individual. Grubb could see his clothes up close now – the rough texture of the shark hide, spattered with dark patches. He didn't have to ask what had made those stains.

'This is the top brass up here, and no mistake, my dear. See that gent with the fan?' He pointed out a lanky troll in expensive-looking clothes, whose face was caked in white makeup. 'That's the Actor. No doubt you've heard of him, a man of the world such as yourself? No? The man runs nigh on every street gang and gambling den in the Marlinspike Quarter.' Harry lowered his voice. 'Came over from the Old World two years ago. His whole family had been killed, see? By the League of the Light. Bayonets, it was.' He poked Grubb in the stomach. 'Just like that. Dead as dead can be. They hung the bodies up outside the village and all, to show as how only humans were welcome there. Charming, eh? But that's the League for you.'

Grubb tried not to think too hard about what Harry was saying. Stories of the League's cruelty had been popular in the Legless Mermaid for months, and on the days when Mr Lightly hit him more than usual he had always reminded himself that at least he wasn't living in the Old World.

'Anyway, where were we? Ah, yes, that fine woman sitting next to him is Lady Harlequin. She might look pretty, but don't be fooled, dearie. She'd slice your nose off soon as look at you.'

Grubb glanced down at his feet, hoping that the woman hadn't seen him staring at her. The fairy on Harry's shoulder saw what he was doing, and cackled.

'Then we have Lord Wren.'

Harry pointed to a large man with an eye patch, dressed in black and smoking a pipe. 'Associate of the Boy King. Ain't really a lord of course, my duck, but try telling him that.' He shrieked with laughter, making Grubb wince. 'Honoured guests, one and all, merchant or mongrel – if you'll pardon the expression. But you're a busy fellow; you don't want to hear old Harry wittering on like this. Expect you came for the shark fighting, yes? I can tell you a thing or two about shark fighting.'

He rubbed his hands together, his eyes gleaming.

'Now the shark fighters, they're cheap as brine, see? Any time we like, we can take a boat out and go fishing for more of 'em, you see. But the sharkies, they cost a pretty penny. Ain't easy to replace the sharkies, not the ones we use at Harry's. So we have to weight it a little. That's why the fighters only get tridents, my dear. Expect you've been wondering about that.'

Grubb hadn't. He was feeling claustrophobic, desperate to get away from this place, and from Harry's horrible voice. There was something peculiar about the shark pit owner's eyes. Something not quite sane.

'Gives it a touch of authenticity. A touch of old-fashioned charm, if you like. It's quaint, isn't it, my lovely? Crowd loves it. But the point is, they're easy on my sharkies, them tridents. The sharkies, on the other hand, that's different. Doesn't matter what they do to the merfolk. Take Florence. She's in there now with two of my best fighters, but she can handle them, oh yes. Little darling's a bull shark. Ideal for my purposes. Not too big, but nippy. Got some teeth on her too, my lovely . . .'

There was a sudden, fast movement from below and a muffled scream, and blood foamed through the water. The shark pit erupted with howls and hoots and the stamping of feet.

Harry squealed in delight. 'There we are, my dear,' he said, clapping his hands together. 'See what I'm saying? Florence is our star performer.'

Grubb looked down at his feet again, feeling like he might be sick. Out of the corner of his eye, he could see shark pit flunkeys fishing bits of dead merman from the water with long-handled nets.

'She's got the taste for it now,' piped Harry. 'One's never enough, eh?' He gave another piercing laugh. 'Always room for dessert, ain't there?'

Something about the way he said it caused Grubb to glance up. Harry was looking at someone beside him. Jeb. Grubb saw the goblin draw a finger across his throat.

He knew what was about to happen. And there was only one thing he could do about it. He lunged forward, seized the package from Jeb's belt and held it out at arm's length over the edge of the balcony.

'Don't touch me!' His voice came tumbling out. 'Don't touch me, or I'll—'

Too late. Harry's bully boys moved in from behind, grabbed him and lifted him up and over the balcony.

'No, no, wait!' howled Jeb. 'I meant cut his throat, don't throw him into the . . .'

And then Grubb was falling towards the pool, still grasping the package tightly in his hand, with Harry's mad, shrieking laughter in his ears.

His brain froze as the world span around him. He saw the men with nets scurrying away, a few surprised faces turned upwards, gawping as he hurtled down, and then he smacked into the surface, and everything was dark, and all sound was muffled.

He was plunged deep into the pool, his body rigid with fear, but his mind jerking into action. He could taste blood. His eyes flicked open, and he saw scarlet tendrils snaking through the water like seaweed.

He had to get out. He had to get out.

And then he saw it.

Her.

Florence.

A shape in the water ahead. Dark and indistinct, but unmistakable. And with a lazy flick of her tail, she was coming towards him.

Don't move, he told himself. *Maybe she'll think I'm dead. Maybe she hasn't seen me after all. Can sharks see? Or do they just smell?* What was he thinking? He should be thinking about his parents, his home, his short, short life, whatever it was you were supposed to think of before—

The water quaked as a smaller shape darted in on the left, and then there was more blood, and Grubb felt strong hands gripping him, and he surfaced.

The roar of the shark pit came back to his ears. He coughed and spat out water, as a big man hauled him up and out of the pit. A young mermaid bobbed in the water where Florence had been, raising a blood-stained trident in triumph. She had white hair and green eyes, and when she saw Grubb looking at her she nodded. The cheering from the spectators was deafening.

'There you go, lad,' said the big man. 'Ain't right putting a land dweller in the pit.'

Saliva flooded Grubb's mouth, and he threw up violently on his rescuer's shoes.

'Whoa – watch it, mongrel,' said the man.

'Sorry,' said Grubb faintly. 'Thank you.' He flopped into the man's arms, taking heavy, gasping breaths. He was alive. Weak, sodden and still vaguely nauseous, but alive. He found, to his surprise, that his fingers were still clamped around the sodden velvet package.

Three more men jumped over the barriers and came staggering towards them. They were holding tankards, spilling the contents all over the place.

'Ha ha,' said one. 'A mongrel in a fancy coat.'

'I want one,' slurred another sadly.

'Nah, it's not a mongrel,' said the third. 'It fell from the sky, didn't it? It's a shooting star.'

They giggled, and one hiccupped, which set them all off again.

'Hey, mongrel,' said the first one, bending over to talk to Grubb. 'You come with us, eh? A drink for the little runt who went into the pit with Florence and survived.'

'We should keep him for luck. Make wishes on him and that. 'Cos he's a star, see?'

'What do you say, mongrel?'

Grubb tried to think it through. Whoever these men were, they were obviously too drunk to care why he fell from the top gallery. And one of them had been decent enough to rescue him. He would probably be safer with them than he would be with Jeb and Harry. *Probably*. He looked up to the balcony where his captors had been. They were gone. Most likely, they were on their way to get him right now . . .

'All right,' he said. 'I'll come with you. But can we please leave right now?'

The men cheered and slammed their tankards together.

As they drank, Grubb slipped the black velvet

package into his jacket pocket. The next chance he got, he was going to open it and find out what was inside. Maybe Captain Clagg wouldn't want him to, but after the encounter with Florence, that didn't seem to matter so much.

If he was going to be killed, he deserved to know why.

Chapter Sixteen

Slik was probably the smartest fairy in Port Fayt. Far too smart to be hanging around with a couple of stinking trolls, anyway.

He sat high up on a yardarm, shivering in the wind and waiting for the Bootles to finish changing on the deck below. The Ghost's old sloop was a right heap of junk, just like its ex-owner. It could barely hold the three of them safely. Thalin knew what would happen when Captain Gore's pirates came tramping on board.

His eyes streamed in the fresh sea breeze, and he rubbed at them with his fists. From their position, anchored out in the bay, he could see all of the ships in the harbour – even more than usual, thanks to the festival. Beyond, Port Fayt was laid out like a toy town, bathed in midday sunshine.

'Aren't you ready yet?' he shrieked down. But either the twins didn't hear him, or they chose to ignore him.

They looked ridiculous, Slik reckoned – overgrown green-skinned monsters wearing fancy merchant clothes, wigs and all. Most trolls were too stupid to make a living as traders, so Captain Gore was going to have to be a complete bilge-brain to fall for this. Thankfully, by all accounts he was.

Gore's galleon was anchored in the distance, sails furled, on the other side of the bay. The *Weeping Wound*. Slik could just make out its blood-red hull. Somewhere on that ship was their target – Phineus Clagg. Captain Gore himself had gone ashore, but when he returned, his prisoner would be getting it in the neck. And probably a fair few other bits of him, if a tenth of the stories about Gore were true.

That was, if the plan failed.

'Ready, Slik?' called one of the trolls, his big, ugly face looking upwards. Slik could hardly tell the pair apart, and frankly couldn't be bothered to try.

'I've been ready for half an hour.'

The other troll pointed out over the water to a

longboat that was making its way from Port Fayt towards the pirate ship.

'There you go, then. Hop to it.'

Slik rolled his eyes and dived off the bowsprit, head first, letting the momentum build before setting his wings buzzing and swooping out over the water. 'Hop to it . . .' he muttered. 'Stinking trolls . . .' They could take a hop into the ocean for all he cared.

The waves blurred below him, and within seconds he was touching down on the longboat's prow, swaying slightly as he steadied himself.

'What do you want?' growled a voice from overhead.

Slik looked up, wrinkling his nose in distaste.

It was the man himself.

The notorious Captain Gore.

The most brutal man in all the Ebony Ocean.

Or the most smelly, at least.

The pirate captain towered above, one foot on the gunwale, while ten gigantic men worked the oars beyond. He was short, bald and ugly, and looked as evil as a demon that had got out of bed on the wrong side. His left arm was made of wood and half-rusted prosthetic steel. He wore black breeches, black boots, a black waistcoat and a large black leather belt, its black iron buckle shaped into a black crab. From the belt there dangled a butcher's cleaver, a selection of knives and several more unusual metal implements, all clearly modified to screw into the wrist of the captain's replacement arm. Each one looked as if it was designed to cause a slightly different form of extremely intense pain.

Slik cleared his throat.

Here goes.

'My masters want to ask a favour,' he said, pointing back at the sloop. 'There are ducats in it, if you're interested.'

'That so,' said Gore. 'Ducats, eh?'

He turned back to his oarsmen.

'Hard a-port!'

'Aye-aye, Captain!'

Hmm. Apparently Captain Gore was even more stupid than they'd expected.

Back on the sloop, Frank and Paddy introduced themselves as merchants. They had to pay a brief visit to Port Fayt but, naturally, they didn't want to leave their cargo unattended. Perhaps the good captain could look after it for them?

Next, the twins led the way down to the hold, with Slik hovering beside them. One held up a lantern, and the light fell on row upon row of chests, stretching away into the darkness. The other threw open the nearest lid to reveal a mound of antique velvet gowns studded with jewels.

Captain Gore looked like a child who'd just been given his birthday cake. After all, he wasn't to know that the gowns had been bought at a cheap costume shop that very morning, and that all the other chests were empty.

'Don't you fret yourselves,' he chortled, completely failing to hide his glee. He pointed out one of his men – a huge ogre covered in swirling black tattoos. 'My colleague Bosun Tuck here will fetch the whole crew, to help carry the . . . er, I mean, to help guard your precious wares. You gents have got nothing to worry about.'

It was all Slik could do not to laugh out loud. A blind imp could see that Gore was planning to take the cargo back to his own ship and sail away with it. He was simply too greedy to figure out that it was him being tricked, and not the other way around.

'My dear Captain,' said one of the twins, putting on a ridiculous falsetto accent. 'If you don't mind my asking . . . your arm – what happened to it?'

'Oh, that,' stammered Gore, tapping the steel prosthetic with his one remaining hand. 'Erm, a shark ate it. Big bleeder had got hold of a young cabin boy, see, and I was trying to rescue him from it.'

Or feed him to it, more likely.

'We can't thank you enough,' squeaked the other twin.

'You can't imagine what this means to us.'

'Here's twenty ducats for your trouble.'

'In fact, take forty ducats.'

'Yes, forty ducats. Honest men are so hard to find nowadays.'

'Ain't that the truth.' Gore beamed.

Slik rolled his eyes and darted up out of the hold, flitting across the deck and away from the sloop, towards the cliffs where the *Weeping Wound* was anchored.

He almost felt sorry for the old bilgebag.

Almost.

It was creepy in the cave. Too creepy by half, if you asked Tabitha. The darkness, the drip-drip-dripping of water from the rocks up above . . . even the gentle lapping of the waves against their dinghy was making her nervous. The only light came from a small entrance tunnel at one end, just big enough for a boat to pass through, if its passengers ducked down. Tabitha knew that the *Weeping Wound* was anchored beyond, a short distance away. And if the pirates found them in here somehow, there'd be no escape.

She took another deep breath, wiped her sweaty palms on her coat, and gripped the oars. She had barely slept last night, knowing what was going to happen today. It was scary, of course, but she couldn't think about that. Newton was giving her the chance to do something real for once. Now all she had to do was make sure that everything went perfectly, and maybe, finally, he'd see that she was a proper watchman.

A twin gleam shone from Hal's spectacles, as he pushed them up his nose.

'We're agreed, then? No fighting, if we can possibly help it.'

Tabitha nodded, then remembered that Hal probably couldn't see her.

'Sure,' she said, and silently stuck her tongue out at him. Hal was so cautious it was a wonder he ever got anything done.

A tiny dark blot appeared in the light from the tunnel. It zipped into the cave, wings whining faintly.

'Slik,' said Tabitha, and her body flooded with relief and adrenaline. 'All going to plan?'

'Surprisingly, yes. That pirate's thicker than Mrs Bootle's custard. The trolls are on their way back to the port now, and Gore's bringing all his men over to the sloop. Just don't mess your bit up.'

'Very well,' said Hal. 'Tell Newton that we're on our way. We'll meet them back at the rendezvous.'

Slik grumbled something, luckily too quiet to hear, as he disappeared out through the entranceway.

Tabitha rowed them carefully towards the tunnel, blades dipping silently in and out of the water. When they got there they shipped the oars, lay flat on the bottom of the boat and reached over the gunwales to push against the rocks, guiding themselves through with their hands until they were out, blinking, in the open air.

Gore's red ship loomed before them, lying at anchor less than two hundred feet from the cliff they had just left behind. Further away, Tabitha could see the last of the pirate longboats heading west, towards the Ghost's sloop. Towards the decoy. She grinned. It was working, just like Newton had planned.

The pair of them took up the oars again, and began rowing fast. Every second they were out on the open water was a risk. What if Gore had left guards on the ship? He'd have been mad not to. And if they were spotted . . .

Finally, they came up alongside the galleon. Tabitha

fished around in a canvas bag and brought out her boarding hatchets. It was going to be a steep climb, but she'd practised long and hard, and she knew she could do it.

'No need,' said Hal softly, and pointed further along the hull. The pirates had left a rope ladder dangling over the side.

Tabitha sighed and stowed the hatchets again. She wanted to get out of this alive, obviously. She just didn't want it to be too easy.

They tied the dinghy to the bottom of the ladder and then clambered up, Tabitha first, trying not to bang or scrape against the hull. When she got to the top, she drew a knife, holding the blade pinched between thumb and knuckle, and peered over the gunwale. The deck was empty, except for one man, tied to the mast with enough rope to hang a giant. The man was overweight and filthy, and his long, greasy hair fell in a tangle around his face. It could only be Phineus Clagg.

He looked up, just as she was scrambling over the side, and his face broke into a hopeful grin.

'Afternoon,' he said. 'I'm Clagg. Captain Clagg.'

Tabitha ignored him and crept across the deck, Hal following. She held her knife in a throwing position, keeping a lookout for Gore's pirates. But there weren't any. Apparently the captain had decided to bring his whole crew to help carry the chests of non-existent dresses back to his galleon.

Disappointing.

'I don't like this,' said Hal, peering down a hatchway. 'There must be someone on board. Gore wouldn't leave his prisoner free to escape.'

Tabitha shrugged, and began to inspect the ropes binding Clagg to the mast.

'While yer here,' said Clagg, his smile strained, 'I don't suppose you could possibly see your way to giving me a hand, could yer?'

'All right,' said Tabitha. 'Don't get your breeches in a twist. We're here to rescue you.'

'Er . . . really?'

'That's right. So just shut up and do what we say.' She spun her knife round and got to work prising open the knots. In less than ten seconds, Clagg was free. He grinned, rubbing at his arms where the ropes had pressed into his skin.

'Thank yer kindly, miss. Much obliged.'

'Wonderful,' said Hal. 'Now let's get off this ship. I, for one, would prefer not to be here when our kind host returns.'

'Right,' said Clagg. 'I'll be off then.'

'No,' said Tabitha. 'You're coming with us.'

'Ah, now there's a kind offer, but you're busy folk. I wouldn't want to impose.'

'I said, you're coming with us.'

Tabitha took hold of one arm, and Hal took the other. They turned back towards the dinghy, and stopped dead.

Standing between them and the rope ladder was a squat, muscle-bound troll, dressed in a filthy vest, breeches and a tiny tricorne hat, perched at a ludicrous angle on his head. One green-skinned arm was covered in a spectacular selection of tattoos – a severed head, a skeleton with horns and an axe dripping blood. The other was holding an actual, real axe with a blade the size of Tabitha's head. Fortunately it didn't seem to have any blood on it. Yet.

'Who are you?' asked the pirate stupidly.

There was only one thing for it.

Tabitha spun her knife and sent it flashing through the air. It was just like target practice. Except this time, the blade landed in the troll's hand instead of the bull's-eye.

'*UUUUNNNGGAAARGGH!*'

Hal was whispering fast, one hand pointing at the pirate, who had dropped his axe and was bent over clutching his hand and squawking like a seagull trapped in a barrel. Then the air seemed to wobble, and the troll stopped still, silent and limp, as if all the energy had drained out of him at once. His huge body swayed once, twice, and collapsed on deck with an almighty thud.

Tabitha tried to slow her breathing down to a normal rate. She felt pretty close to collapsing herself.

'The knife was a little unnecessary,' said Hal, wiping his brow with a handkerchief.

'Well, if you'd only cast the spell sooner, I wouldn't have had to use it, would I?'

The magician sniffed.

'It's a complicated spell, which requires a lot of concentration. You can't rush these things. Besides, you know I hate violence.'

'Um, 'scuse me?' said Clagg. 'Can we go now?'

'Shut it,' snapped Tabitha. 'But yes. Let's go.'

They climbed down into the dinghy, Tabitha still trembling a little from the encounter with the pirate. It was the first time she'd ever thrown a knife at someone, and she wasn't entirely sure she'd enjoyed it. She glanced out over the sea towards the distant sloop, hoping for something else to think about. It was hard to tell from so far away, but it looked like it was lying very low in the water. It had probably never had a whole pirate crew on board before.

They started to row.

As the shock wore off, Tabitha began to feel light-headed. She'd done it. She'd boarded Captain Gore's ship, she'd rescued Phineus Clagg and she'd even dealt with a pirate. With a bit of help from Hal, obviously.

Maybe things would be different from now on.

Maybe Newt would realize she was better than just a lookout.

Maybe she'd be given all the important jobs.

Maybe she'd . . .

Her grin froze. There was a figure sitting on a rock beside the cave mouth, one leg dangling above the water, watching their dinghy come in and smiling at her. The figure of a large, shaven-headed human in a blue coat, with a tattoo on his cheek.

Newton.

He'd been there all along. She just knew it. Checking up on her. Making sure everything went to plan. Making sure it was safe.

Tabitha's excitement evaporated in an instant.

He still thought she was just a silly child.

Still.

The festival is always the busiest time of year in Harrison's Toy Emporium. Within the last hour alone, Mr Harrison has sold a fairy doll to a Redoubtable Company merchant, a rattle to a fisherman, a skipping rope to a trio of stout dwarf children . . . Now they are playing with it on the cobblestones outside his shop – too excited to take it home first.

Mr Harrison watches them through the window, humming to himself. He loves to see children enjoying his toys.

Out of nowhere, he remembers the peculiar man who visited yesterday, with the ginger hair and the yellow eyes, and the black velvet package. He shudders. For years, Mr Harrison has been providing certain other services at his shop, as well as toys. Services he wouldn't want the blackcoats to find out about. But recently, he has felt more and more exhausted by it all. It's about time he got on the straight and narrow. An elderly imp like him shouldn't have to spend his days worrying about getting arrested by the Demon's Watch.

The children finish their game and run home for dinner. It's getting late. Nearly time to close up for the evening. Mr Harrison ambles back to the counter – specially built, half-scaled so that he can reach over it without a footstool. He passes wooden dragons hanging from the ceiling, shelves loaded with puzzle boxes, cloth hand puppets of the Maw ('Warning: guaranteed to scare the little ones!'), models of legendary Old World warriors with moving sword arms and a hundred other brightly painted objects.

He begins tallying up the ducats he's made today. It's not a bad haul. Certainly not so bad that he needs to be risking his neck with his other business. Yes. Tomorrow, he'll throw out his wares and be done with it. It isn't worth the trouble. From now on, he'll be a toy seller, pure and simple.

He feels wonderfully calm, now that he's made his decision. After tomorrow, he'll never have to worry, ever again.

The door opens behind him.

'Ah, good afternoon,' says Mr Harrison, hastily tipping the ducats back into his money box. He reaches across the counter and picks up a small, painted wooden disc, with a length of string wrapped around it.

'Might I be able to interest you in this astonishing new device, just last month imported from the . . .'

He turns, and sees who has come in.

An old woman, wrapped in a grey cloak and hooded, so that her face can't be seen. His heart sinks. He can tell at once that she is the other *kind of customer. The kind who aren't interested in toys.*

He carries on with his pitch, knowing it is pointless.

'Now, this is just the thing for a grandson. Allow me to demonstrate, hm?'

He loops the string over a finger and lets the disc fall, then return, spinning up the string, into his hand. But instead of reaching his hand, as he expects, the disc jerks sideways and up, looping once, twice, three times around his neck. The string draws taut against his skin.

'I haven't come here for toys,' says the old woman.

Mr Harrison swallows. It's not easy, with the string around his neck.

'No, of course,' he gasps. 'Follow me, please.'

The string is still tight as he lights a lantern, draws back the red velvet curtain behind the counter and leads the way down the narrow flight of steps beyond. At the bottom is a heavy oak door. Mr Harrison draws a key from his coat pocket and opens it.

This room is even smaller and darker than the toy shop, with rough stone walls and a low ceiling. The walls are lined with shelves, loaded with dusty jars, boxes and bottles in every size, shape and colour imaginable.

'What can I get you?' asks Mr Harrison.

The old woman hands him a scrap of paper.

He places the lantern on a shelf, fetches an imp-sized stepladder on wheels and gets to work, hunting down the items on the list, all the time painfully aware of the string that circles his neck. He picks out a tub of yellow sun-dust, a felt bag full of ground-up dragon bones, a tiny bottle of shark's blood, a jar of spiders' eggs . . .

Mr Harrison isn't a magician himself, but he knows a great deal about magic – and as he collects the ingredients, he mixes them together in his mind. A numb horror creeps through him. He understands. He understands just what the old woman is intending to do.

'Are you . . . Are you quite certain you need all of this?'

The old woman says nothing, but the string around his neck twitches sharply, making him gasp.

'Gaagh! Very well. Of course. Forgive me.'

Mr Harrison piles the last of the containers into a leather bag and passes it to her. And as her hand closes over the bag, the light of the lantern falls on her face. Mr Harrison can hardly believe his eyes.

'Maw's teeth,' he splutters. 'But I know you!'

He is too surprised to think clearly.

'I thought you were . . . How long has it been since you were last here, in my shop? Why, it must be at least eight, ten years?'

Then Mr Harrison makes a strangled sound. The string around his neck is drawing tighter . . .

And tighter . . .

And tighter . . .

PART THREE
Tormenta

Chapter Seventeen

The sky clouded over, and it began to rain. In the bay, there was a *splish-splash* as the first drops hit the sea, and a *pitter-patter* on furled sails. Within minutes it was bucketing down, sending Fayters scurrying for cover. Washing was hauled inside and awnings were rolled up. Cockatrice Company banners and bunting hung soggy in the empty streets, dripping garish dye onto cobbles slick with water.

There was a fire going in the cosy serving room at Bootles' Pie Shop. But all the same, Tabitha shivered as she watched the rain falling through the wet windowpane. In the excitement with the pirate ship earlier, she'd almost managed to forget about the old woman. That crooked grey face, hooked nose and cold, dark eyes. Now, as she looked out into the gloom, she remembered. The old woman was still out there somewhere. The spider in the cupboard. Maybe somewhere very close. Maybe hunting for them . . .

She gripped the smooth leather hilt of her favourite knife. Whatever that witch was after, Tabitha wasn't going to be frightened. This was supposed to be exciting. It was a chance to prove herself. A chance to turn Mandeville into a name that was respected, not pitied. If only Newton would stop mollycodd-ling her.

'Another pie, dear?'

'No thanks, Mrs Bootle, I'm full.'

Mrs Bootle tutted and shook her head. It was well known that the twins' mother didn't believe in people being full – especially not when there were pies to be eaten.

'Anyone else?'

Frank, Paddy and Hal were sat around a table, cheeks bulging with food. Even Old Jon was nibbling on a slice, although as usual, he was sitting on his own in the corner, gazing into the distance.

'Yes please, Ma.'

'Yum.'

'Excellent pies – my compliments to the cook.'

Mrs Bootle's face lit up again, and she bustled round with her tray.

Tabitha had no idea how the others could eat at a time like this. They were going to interrogate Phineus Clagg! They were going to find out what his mysterious cargo was and what the witch was planning to do with it. And the watchmen were just lounging around stuffing their faces.

The smuggler himself was in a chair by the fireplace, hands bound behind his back, while Slik darted around tying knots in his long, greasy hair. The fairy had disappeared for a while after the rescue – probably trying to steal sugar from someone – but, of course, he was back now. There was no way Slik would miss a chance to torment someone.

'Will someone call off this flaming fairy?' pleaded Clagg.

'Pipe down, will you?' said Frank, through a mouthful of pie.

'Yeah, shut it,' said Slik, with glee. He swooped in and jabbed Clagg hard in the forehead.

'Ow!'

''Fraid Slik only listens to Captain Newton,' said Paddy, putting on a serious face. 'But don't worry, he'll be here sooner or later.'

'You big, fat, drunken, useless lump,' Slik gloated,

poking Clagg's nose to emphasize each word. 'Just you wait till Newton gets here. You'll be for it then.'

He tugged on a fistful of hair.

'Ouch!'

'That's enough,' came a voice from the doorway.

Slik groaned, dropped down onto the table and stuck his tongue out at the smuggler.

Newton stepped into the room, his blue coat streaked with water, raindrops glistening on his shaven head. He looked down at Clagg, bathed in the light of the fire, and sized him up. Tabitha looked too. Stubbled cheeks, unkempt hair, unwashed clothes, a lazy eye, a single tarnished earring and a battered old coat. *Captain Phineus Clagg. A master criminal, who braved a tormenta*. Frankly, he didn't look up to much.

'Pie, Mr Newton?'

'No thanks, Mrs Bootle.'

'I wouldn't say no,' said Clagg.

'Tough,' said Slik.

Mrs Bootle bustled off to the kitchen, a single pie left on her tray. Clagg watched it go, sadly.

'Right,' said Newton. 'Clagg. Know why you're here?'

Clagg shook his head.

Newton sighed.

'All right, if that's how it's going to be . . .'

He pulled up a chair, sat down face to face with the hapless smuggler, took his pipe from a pocket and began stuffing it with tobacco.

'First I'm going to tell you what we know. Three nights ago, you docked in Port Fayt, carrying a cargo in the middle of the worst tormenta in a decade. Now, that's suspicious. Anyone trying to bring a wavecutter into Fayt during a magical storm is either insane, clueless or wanting to avoid the attentions of the revenue men. You don't look insane, Clagg, and from what I hear, you're not clueless either.

'So it turns out you're a smuggler. And more than that, you've got a cargo you'll risk your own life for – not to mention the lives of your crew. That's enough to get us interested. Then we run into your customer, who happens to be an extremely dangerous magician. A witch, in fact. So now we're very interested. Smuggling, that's one thing, see? But getting mixed up with illegal magic – that's a dangerous game indeed.'

Everyone was watching the smuggler now. He opened his mouth, and shut it again. A droplet of sweat crept down his forehead.

'I don't know where you come from, but here in Port Fayt the use of magic is banned without a warrant. Especially magic like we've seen that witch perform. So you're in big trouble, Clagg. But the good news is, I'm going to be generous. I'm going to let you go. As long as you help us.'

'And, er . . . What kind of help were you thinking of?'

'Fair's fair. I've told you what we know, so now you can tell us what you know. Three questions. One: who is the witch? Two: what is the cargo she's after? And three: where is it?'

Clagg squirmed.

'The thing is, matey . . .'

'Don't try to talk your way out of this. Answers. Now.'

The smuggler licked his lips, calculating fast.

'Well, what's in it for me, then?'

Tabitha scowled. Hal frowned a little and pushed his glasses up his nose. Paddy chuckled quietly, and Frank gave a low whistle.

Newton put down his unlit pipe. He sat still for a moment, then lunged forward, grabbed the front two legs of Phineus Clagg's chair and tipped it over the fire. The flames licked at the smuggler's back.

'*AAARGH!*' said Clagg. 'Mercy! Mercy!'

Slik spluttered with laughter.

'You're not getting this, are you?' said Newton, taking his time. 'We're not the Dockside Militia. This isn't an official investigation. Governor Wyrmwood shut us down, see? So right now, we're acting outside the law. And I'm sure a man of your experience will understand when I tell you . . . *we don't have any rules*.'

Paddy cracked his knuckles.

'They call us the Demon's Watch, you know. So don't think of us as the good folk. More like the dangerous folk. The folk who don't have time to play games with numbskull smugglers. Are we clear?'

The chair tipped back further, and further . . .

'Yes, *YES*, matey, clear as a cloudless sky.'

Newton let go and the smuggler jolted forward, the chair legs landing on the floor with a bang.

'So, are we feeling a bit more helpful now?'

Clagg gulped and nodded.

'All right, all right, you win. I'll answer yer questions. Untie us first though, will yer?'

'Aye. But no stupid escape attempts, please.'

Frank tugged the knots open, and the ropes fell to the floor. The smuggler wiped the sweat from his brow with a filthy coat sleeve.

'Yer not goin' to like the answers, by the way.'

'We'll hear them first, then decide if we like them.'

'Right y'are, matey. You're the boss.'

The watchmen laid down their pies and listened.

For a few moments there was no sound except the distant rain and the sputtering of the fire, while they waited for the smuggler to recover. Tabitha found that she was holding her breath, and let it out silently.

At last, Phineus Clagg began to talk.

Chapter Eighteen

'I met her three months ago, on a cold night in Scrimport. You've never heard of it, I'll wager, just a dead-end fishing town in the Duchy of Garran, back in the Old World. Miserable place, it is. Rains all day, every day. But we had to put in there for a few repairs to the *Sharkbane*. She's the fastest ship I ever owned, see, and I happened to know a shipwright in Scrimport who'd do the job, and no questions asked.

'Well, he takes it on, but it's three days' work. Three days in that sun-forsaken hole. So I goes to the tavern each night, and each night it's as empty and dead as ever. Only other living thing in there is the landlord's three-legged, one-eyed dog. Until the third night.

'On that night, no sooner am I sat down, than this woman's sitting at my side, as if she's been there all along. And I swear, for all that I've some company, the place seems emptier and deader and colder than ever before. Scared the life out o' me, truth be told. Something wrong about 'er. That hood she wears, and them eyes, wide as the ocean and black as night.

'And she never tells me 'er name, but she tells me she's setting sail to the Middle Islands soon, to Port Fayt. She has to be there in time for the . . . what do yer call it? The Festival of the Sea. Only there's something she needs. Something she wants me to bring for 'er, fast as I can. She hasn't the time to fetch it herself, and she's heard about me and ol' *Sharkbane* – swiftest ship in the Ebony Ocean. It's a simple job, but a long journey. The cargo's to be picked up from Port Hel, in the north, then brought to Fayt. And the price . . .'

Phineus Clagg's eyes had glazed over, in a daydream.

Tabitha poked him in the ribs.

'Yes? Come on, maggot breath, what price?'

'All right, all right, I'm just getting to that. The price . . . Ten thousand ducats.'

Out of the corner of her eye, Tabitha noticed Newton and Old Jon exchange a glance.

'And there, on the spot, she pulls a bag out of 'er

cloak and empties it on the table. Gold and silver coins just spilling out and onto the floor, like it means nothing to 'er. "Take the money," she says. "There's half for you now. I'll be in Port Fayt in exactly three months' time, at the Grand Party. Below decks on the *Wraith's Revenge*. Bring me the cargo. Then you'll get the rest of your payment." And I pick the coins up from the floor, and when I get up, she's gone.'

The smuggler sighed, leaning back in his chair.

'And that's all I know, lads. Honest. So are we done now?'

Newton shook his head.

'What did you bring for her?'

'The cargo, o' course. Weren't you listening?'

'We got that, genius,' said Tabitha, through gritted teeth. 'But you haven't told us what it is.'

'Oh,' said Clagg sheepishly. 'Funny you should ask . . . That's the thing, see – I don't actually know.'

'What do you mean, you don't know?'

'Sometimes makes things easier in my line o' work. She told me to pick up the cargo from an address in Port Hel. So I did as I was told. Dingy place, it were, down an alleyway near the docks. This old elf answers the door – funny-looking cove, all bent over, with eye-glasses – and he gives me a package, wrapped up in black velvet and tied with a silver cord. Small thing, it was, long and thin. This elf had the look o' magic about him, see, so I weren't going to take chances tampering with it. Not with ten thousand ducats at stake. I'll tell yer one thing though. From what I heard on the docks, I was right about the magic. That old elf was an enchanter.'

Paddy grinned.

'Now we're getting somewhere.'

'Can you be any more specific?' asked Hal briskly. 'What form of enchantments did he perform?'

'Search me, matey.'

'You know how you said we weren't going to like these answers?' said Tabitha, fingering her favourite knife. 'You weren't wrong.'

'Can you tell us where it is, at least?' tried Frank.

Clagg was looking uncomfortable again.

'Umm, not really.'

'"Not really?"'

'Well, the thing is, I, er, I lost it.'

There was a pause.

'You . . . *lost it*?'

'I was distracted! Cap'n Gore's men were after me, see? Bosun Tuck found me in a tavern, and then he were chasing after me with a giant cutlass, and somewhere along the way it must've slipped out and fallen.'

'Where?'

'Well, I'd had a few grogs, see, and o' course I didn't notice it falling out at the time, what with trying not to get my head chopped off and all, so . . . who knows?'

'Nobody kill him yet,' said Newton icily.

Tabitha sprang out of her chair and prodded Clagg in the chest.

'Fat lot of use you've been. You're saying you smuggled a mystery cargo for a nameless woman, and you don't know what it is, where it is, where she is or why she wants it?'

Clagg thought about it and nodded.

'Well, when yer put it like that it don't sound so good, but . . . Yup. I reckon that's what I'm saying. Now that I think about it, that cargo could be anywhere. Any ol' lubber could've picked it up and wandered off with it.'

There was a long, stunned silence.

Outside the window, thunder rumbled and lightning flashed. The sky grew darker as the storm swelled.

It was the second tormenta in a week.

The old woman hurls the pirate from the cliff top, and watches as his broken body spirals down to the rocks below, bouncing and jerking its way into the churning sea.

The wind bites at her and flings her cloak out behind her, but she pays it no heed.

Things are almost ready. Almost . . . And yet, still, the final element of the plan eludes her.

She found the pirate in a revolting tavern on the harbour front. A snivelling, scrawny elf, his eyes glazed, his hair clotted with sick. One glance had been enough to see that he was scum, and he proved no better when she took him from the tavern and began to ask questions. It hadn't taken long to get everything out of him, but she had enjoyed it, all the same.

The pirates took Phineus Clagg, that much she has learned. But somehow, he escaped. So she is back at the beginning. No Phineus Clagg, and no cargo.

She should have known better than to trust a drunken smuggler with such a vital task. But the captains in Azurmouth had told her there was no faster vessel than his. And there had been so much to prepare in so little time. A foolish, childish mistake. No matter. There is time enough yet. And whoever took it will pay. Dearly.

She will find it herself.

Or perhaps . . .

The old woman's eyes narrow.

There is one person in this wretched town who might help her. And after all, why should she do everything by herself?

The old woman twitches her cloak and flaps across to the next strip of headland, rainwater streaking away behind her. She raises her hands to the sky and inhales deeply. She can taste the magic in the air. She licks her dry, cracked lips, and lets out a roar.

The sky roars back, as if in approval.

Chapter Nineteen

The rain was relentless, but Tabitha trudged on at a steady pace, refusing to go any faster to escape it. She held her coat above to shield her, although it was already sodden and starting to drip onto her hair.

'Oi!' said Slik from her shoulder, as a droplet spattered him. 'Watch it, little girl.'

'Stinking fairy,' muttered Tabitha.

'I heard that.'

'You'd better stow it then, or you'll be hearing a whole lot more.'

The streets were almost empty, save for the odd figure dashing for shelter under a stone archway or a wooden balcony overhanging the cobbles. You'd never guess it was supposed to be the Festival of the Sea. This was so unfair. Why was it always her? She was just as good a watchman as the rest of them, so how come she always, *always* got the worst jobs? Still. Even after she rescued that rotten smuggler, practically single-handedly. And now, sent off into the rain to fetch grog for him, with no one but Newton's irritating fairy for company. *It'll help me think straight*, Clagg had said. Tabitha reckoned that a good, solid punch on the nose might do the job just as well – and save time, into the bargain.

She'd decided to have a mug of velvetbean before heading back. She was so wet and cold and miserable, she felt like she deserved a treat. And if she was late bringing Phineus stupid Clagg his stupid grog, well . . . he was only a stupid smuggler after all. Running errands for criminals . . . What next, offering directions to the nearest shark pit? Looking after their loot while they popped to the privy?

THE PICKLED DRAGON, said the sign outside the tavern. It swung, creaking in the wind, painted with a poor likeness of a tiny dragon stuck inside a bottle of firewater, its eyes crossed and its pink tongue hanging out. The lantern by the door glowed with a soft yellow light, glimmering off black puddles below.

For all Tabitha cared, it could have been called the Certain Death and stunk like an open sewer, so long as it was dry. She wrung out her coat in the doorway, squeezed the rain from her hair and strode inside, drawing out her money pouch, with Slik hovering in tow.

As it turned out, the Pickled Dragon was peaceful and cosy, and smelled perfectly fine – by Port Fayt's standards, at least. There was a fire in the hearth, and an elderly troll with milky, sightless eyes bent over on a stool beside it, picking gently on a cittern. The matronly dwarf landlady beamed at Tabitha from behind the bar as she polished the pewter tankards. Tabitha smiled back, and ordered her velvetbean and the flagon of grog for Phineus Clagg. Then she chose a small table in the corner and sat down to wait, while Slik sat on the table edge, swinging his legs.

She looked around. There were a few bedraggled sailors hunched over their drinks, and a pair of old soaks at the bar, knocking back firewater, dead to the world. Nothing out of the ordinary.

No, wait. Over by the window there were four men drinking, muttering to each other. From the glazed look in their eyes, Tabitha reckoned they'd been there for a while. She scanned their hard faces, broken noses and tatty clothes and decided that they were lowlife. At worst, cutpurses, or bully boys in a mob, maybe. Nothing to write home about.

But it was their companion who interested her. He was a small wiry boy, about her own age, with the pale grey-pink skin and slightly pointed ears that marked him out as a mongrel – half human, half goblin. He was wrapped up in a big blanket, his ears drooping, his mug untouched.

'I'm bored,' announced Slik. But she didn't care.

What was the story with that mongrel? Obviously he didn't fit with the others. It seemed like they'd taken him under their wing, but they were mostly ignoring him, chattering away to each other.

Her velvetbean arrived. She took a sip, savouring its smooth, silky sweetness. The guessing game could wait, for now.

The men stood. Three of them stumbled to the bar, and the other one to the door, leaving the mongrel to his own devices.

Then Tabitha saw something that made her sit bolt upright and spit her smooth, silky velvetbean right across the table.

'Rudge put fifty ducats on that red-haired merman,' the fat man jeered. 'Fifty! What's wrong with you, for the sky's sake?'

'He took out a tiddler in training, I heard. Just wasn't his day today.'

'Wasn't his day? You can say that again. He's in five pieces!'

The men cackled and crashed their tankards together, yet again.

Grubb felt like he'd been in the tavern for hours. He was exhausted, and fed up of hearing about shark fighting, and crooked bookmakers, and terrifying women he hoped he'd never meet. Now that he had decided to open the package, he couldn't wait to find out what was inside. But there was no way he could do it here, in front of his new friends. Twice he'd tried to go to the privy, to be on his own, but both times they had pushed him firmly back onto his stool.

'You hear about Jake's cousin?' said the big man who'd rescued him. 'The one who went to make his fortune in the Old World? He was shacked up in Azurmouth until last month. Got press-ganged onto a League warship.' He lowered his voice. 'Word is, the League of the Light control Azurmouth these days. And if the Duke of Garran and the rest of them have got the press gangs out, what does that tell you?'

'Who cares?' said the fat man. 'What's it to us? That's just Old World politics. The League can take a trip to the bottom of the ocean, for all I care.'

'"What's it to us?", you say? The League of the Light? Don't you know nothing?'

'I know we're humans. It's them poor ogres and goblins and that what need to worry. I heard they chuck 'em in big pits and bury 'em alive. Stick 'em on spikes by the highways and that. But we ain't demon-spawn, so those dregs wouldn't touch us.'

The big man shook his head.

'Don't be so sure, mate. We might be humans but we're Fayters. The League'd wipe this place off the map if they got a chance, humans and all. You think they'd let us go free? You've got another thing coming. And that's just it, see . . .' He leaned closer and lowered his voice. 'Over in Azurmouth, they're building up a fleet. An invasion fleet.'

There was a pause, then the fat man snorted.

'You get that from Jake?'

''S right.'

'Well, then. Man's a drunkard. And an idiot.'

The big man shrugged, disappointed at his friends' reaction.

'All I'm saying is, if the League of the Light is looking over the Ebony Ocean, us Fayters'll be the first against the wall. I just hope the governor's ready for it, that's all.'

'Bilge,' said the fat man. 'All that walrus dung has given me a terrible thirst. I need a drink.'

'I'll come too.'

'Good idea.'

'Fine,' said the big man, put out. 'If you don't believe me, it's your own lookout. I'm going to the privy.'

The four of them rose unsteadily, and left Grubb on his own.

Finally, the chance he'd been waiting for. Glancing up to check that his new friends' backs were turned, he took the package from under his jacket, pulled off the silver cord, and peeled away the dark, wet velvet.

He wasn't quite sure what he had expected, but it definitely wasn't this.

'Hey. You.'

Grubb glanced up, startled. It was a human girl, about his age, with long blue hair and a grumpy-faced fairy perched on her shoulder. She looked damp but determined.

'Er, hello,' he said.

'Where did you get that?' said the girl.

He felt himself blush.

'Oh, this?' He couldn't think what to say. 'This is . . . this is just a spoon.'

It was just a spoon. An ordinary, wooden spoon. The kind that Mr Lightly's cook used to stir pots of stew.

'I can see it's a spoon,' said the girl. 'I just saw you unwrap it. Where did you get it?'

Grubb had never been good at telling lies.

'Someone, er . . . Someone gave it to me, as a present,' he said. But it came out half mumbled and half garbled, and his ears twitched with embarrassment. It was a lame answer.

The fairy snorted, and the girl's eyes narrowed.

'I think you should come with me,' she said.

'Whoa, hold on,' said the fat man. 'Let's have a look at that.'

He and his friends were back from the bar, their hands full with slopping tankards.

'Yeah, hand it over.'

Grubb's cheeks were burning now. He had no idea what he should do.

'Don't want any trouble with you gentlemen,' said the girl in a cool voice. 'Seems like you've had one or two grogs too many tonight. Time you trotted home, and I'll take care of your friend.' She turned to Grubb. 'If you come with me now, I can promise you'll be safe.'

The fat man and his friends just laughed.

'You threatening us? A little girl?'

The big man who'd gone to the privy was back now, and the four of them stood in a semi-circle round the table. The fat man put the tankards down. Reaching into his jerkin, he pulled out a stubby, wicked-looking blade.

The background murmur of conversation died out almost at once. The blind troll's cittern tune came to an abrupt end. Everyone in the tavern was watching the man with the knife.

Grubb's stomach turned over. He could make out stains on the blade. *Probably just fish blood,* he told himself.

'Wouldn't do that if I were you,' said the girl. Her voice was tense now.

'Hands off, princess. The mongrel's ours.'

The fairy tugged at the girl's collar.

'Can we go now?' he said hopefully.

Ignoring him, the girl pulled up one sleeve to reveal a fresh blue tattoo of a shark on her forearm.

'I'm Demon's Watch, all right? So you'd better put that little toy away.'

Grubb thought he must have heard wrong. A watchman? He'd listened to plenty of tales about them in the Legless Mermaid. It was the smugglers and thieves of Fayt who had given the Watch its name.

They feared it even more than the blackcoats, as if they thought watchmen were the spawn of the Maw itself. But this girl was clearly no older than he was. There was no way they were going to be afraid of her.

Sure enough, the fat man just grinned wider, and his friends began to snigger.

'Demon's Watch, is it? Well I never. And what's your name, sweetheart?'

'None of your business.'

'Ooh, now now, manners . . . Well then, if you won't oblige, allow me to introduce my mates. These here are Privates Rudge, Sprunt and Waters. And I'm Sergeant Culpepper, of the Dockside Militia.'

'Ah,' said the fairy. 'Oh dear.'

'Colonel Derringer's going to hear about this, princess, never you fear. And most likely, the governor's going to hear about it too. So why don't you run off home, before things get any worse?'

The girl considered for a moment.

'Hey,' said Private Sprunt, screwing up his eyes and staring at the girl. 'Wait a minute. Don't I know you? Ain't you that Mandeville kid what—'

With incredible speed, the girl grabbed the nearest stool and slammed it into Private Sprunt's face. The fairy took off, yelping with indignation. Sprunt reeled backwards, bawling meaningless noises. The girl vaulted onto the table, leaped off the edge and planted her boots in the middle of Sergeant Culpepper's chest, knocking him off balance and sending him toppling onto the flagstones.

Grubb became aware that, somewhere in the middle of her acrobatics, she had drawn a long, slender knife and dropped it point first into the table in front of him. It stuck there, its black leather grip vibrating back and forth. Did she expect him to fight with her? But he didn't even know who she was . . .

Sergeant Culpepper was scrambling to his feet while Private Sprunt cast around for a weapon. Private Rudge was chasing the fairy with a bottle, swiping wildly as it shrieked obscenities at him and darted under tables, behind chairs and up among the rafters. The militiaman would have had no hope of hitting the fairy, even without ten mugs of grog under his belt. The bottle shattered against a chair leg and Rudge let out a surprised yelp, his hand cut by a stray shard of glass. The fairy cackled, and made a rude noise.

Private Waters, who had pulled Grubb out of the shark pit, was drawing a dagger from his breeches and fixing him with a look that was half murderous and half drunken.

Stay calm. Stay calm. Grubb shrugged off his blanket, put the wooden spoon down and pulled the knife from the table, his hands trembling. It was lighter than he'd expected. His body flooded with adrenaline. He stood, and his knees felt weak.

Private Waters brought his blade-hand back, and in the instant before he struck, Grubb saw that it was going high. He ducked. The man's swing was so hard it twisted him round, exposing his side. Grubb barged forward with his full weight, aiming to shove the militiaman off balance.

Unfortunately Private Waters was a lot more solid than he'd expected. Grubb bounced back and collapsed in a heap, his shoulder aching from the impact, his knife clattering onto the floor. The militiaman looked down at him blankly, as if he was a little confused about what had just happened. Then his eyes refocused, and he grinned and lifted the dagger again.

The girl with the blue hair appeared from nowhere and kicked at his feet, tripping him and sending him crashing onto the flagstones.

'Word of advice,' she said, grabbing Grubb's hand and hauling him to his feet. 'When you're in a fight, you're supposed to knock your opponent out. Get it? Not yourself.'

Grubb didn't even have time to be embarrassed before she was flinging him sideways. A broken-off table leg came slicing down in the space he'd just been standing in. As he reeled away, Grubb saw the girl hold the table leg down with her foot and punch its owner once, very hard, on the nose. Private Sprunt dropped the weapon and spun away, holding his face and wailing like a baby. The girl turned and snatched the wooden spoon from the table.

'Look out!' yelled Grubb.

Waters, Rudge and Culpepper were converging on her, brandishing a toasting fork, a broken bottle and a large, stale loaf of bread.

The girl froze for an instant, then, without warning, threw the spoon at him.

Somehow he managed to catch it.

'Hold that for a minute,' she said, as if she just needed to stop and tie her shoe laces. She picked up a chair, raised it over one shoulder and turned on the militiamen.

Grubb bolted through the door and out into the rain-lashed street, the wooden spoon clenched tightly in one fist.

He had no clue which direction he should run in, but he ran all the same, pounding through the downpour, his feet soaked within seconds as they splashed through the puddles. His lungs were burning. He turned a corner, then another. *Just keep running*. And then, to his horror, he heard boots hammering on the paving stones behind him. He lengthened his stride, pushing as hard and as fast as he could.

'Wait! Stop!'

But Grubb wasn't stopping for anyone.

The sound of the boots drew nearer, and nearer, and then it was gone. Grubb came tumbling down and his jaw smacked onto a paving stone.

'*OUCH!*'

'Now will you stop?' It was the girl with the blue hair. She was sprawled on top of him, pinning him to the ground. 'I said hold it for a minute, not rush off with it like a mad fairy.'

Grubb spat out dirt and rainwater.

'Who are you?'

He'd meant it to sound tough and defiant, but it came out as an exhausted whimper.

'I could ask you the same question. I'm Tabitha. Demon's Watch, remember?'

'Tabitha, right. That's great. I'm Grubb. Could you get off me now?'

'No. Oh, well, all right.'

She rolled off him, and he stood, straightening out his shirt and coat. They were soaked through all over again, and covered in filth from the road. He rubbed his jaw.

'We'll be safe now,' said Tabitha, glancing back down the road. 'Those idiots are in no state to come after us. It was a pretty good fight, wasn't it?'

'Er . . .' said Grubb.

'What kind of a name is Grubb, anyway?' said the fairy. He was back on Tabitha's shoulder, huddling under her ear to get out of the rain.

'Shut up, Slik,' said Tabitha.

'I'm just saying it's a funny name, that's all.'

'It's my second name,' said Grubb. 'My real name's Joseph.'

'Joseph, then,' said the girl, holding out a hand. 'Pleased to meet you.'

'Um, likewise,' said Grubb, not sure if he really meant it. He shook her hand.

'Can we go now?' said Slik.

'Fine. Go on ahead – you can tell Newton the good news.'

'Which good news? That you got into a fight with the militia, or that you've adopted a pet mongrel?'

'Hey,' said Grubb.

'Ignore him,' said Tabitha. 'Slik, you just tell Newton I've found the cargo we've been looking for. Unless that's too difficult for you?'

The fairy gave an exaggerated sigh, and darted off down the street, his wings shimmering in the rain.

Grubb watched the girl watching Slik.

'Are you really in the Demon's Watch?' he asked.

She nodded.

'Huh.'

He thought for a moment. He could give her the wooden spoon that all these crazy people were so desperate for. He could go back to the Legless Mermaid, and say he was sorry for running away, and take his punishment. Then maybe Mr Lightly would forgive him, and he could go back to waiting tables and cleaning up at the end of the day, and sleeping alone on the cold inn floor. He'd nearly died three times in the last two days. He was wet to the skin and every part of him ached. It was time to give up the adventure and go home. Give her the wooden spoon, walk away and forget all about it. That was the sensible thing to do. Wasn't it?

'Can I . . . Can I come with you?' he asked.

Tabitha smiled.

'Of course you can. In fact, I insist.'

Chapter Twenty

As he flew, Slik entertained himself by repeating everything Tabitha had said in a range of silly voices. *Unless that's too difficult for you* . . . A child, telling him what to do. He'd show her.

He turned down an alleyway, in the opposite direction from the pie shop. There was someone he needed to see. A secret someone. Someone who paid more sugar than Newton did.

A few streets later, he was knocking on a thick wooden door, and a red-coated bully boy opened it. Down a corridor, round a corner, and up to another door. A second bully boy ushered him in.

'Slik,' snapped Jeb the Snitch. 'Where in all the blue sea've you been?'

The goblin was pacing the carpet, in front of a large mahogany desk with a grey shark-hide surface. Harry was at the sideboard, his own fairy on his shoulder, pouring tumblers of a dark red liquid. Without the usual tricorne hat, his grey hair clung to his skull, matted and greasy, with the odd curl bouncing off at strange angles.

'Hello, sunshine,' he said.

Slik headed straight for the squashy leather armchair on the far side of the desk and settled down on one of the arms, keeping an eye on the creepy elf. He never felt completely comfortable here at Harry's Shark Pit, and it was mainly because of Harry himself. The pit pulled in a tidy haul of ducats, but weirdly, Harry wasn't interested in the money. All he cared about was his sharks. It was bad enough that he named them after a long succession of ex-wives. But, even stranger, there were rumours that he went down to the cages every night to chat to them, for hours on end. Port Fayt had its fair share of idiots. No one knew that better than Slik. But Harry was something else – plain mad.

'Come on then,' said Jeb. 'Let's hear it. What's the

news, Slik? What's Newton up to? Any sign of that stinking mongrel?'

'You need to relax, my lovely,' said Harry cheerily. 'Look at you, all tense.'

'Of course I'm tense,' said Jeb. 'I'm upset. I'm angry. Why shouldn't I be tense?'

'Won't do you no good, Jebedee.'

Harry handed a goblin-sized tumbler to Jeb and a fairy-sized one to Slik, and they knocked the drinks back. Slik coughed as the bitter liquid scorched his throat.

'What in all the stinking sea is this stuff?'

'Just a little cocktail I came up with.'

'It's disgusting. What's in it?'

Harry's brow creased as he tried to remember.

'Now, let me see. A measure of firewater, a dash of trout essence, a sprinkling of hot herbs from the New World and three fingers of griffin blood.'

Jeb and Slik both spat the liquid out, spattering the carpet and the shark-skin desk with red.

Harry and his fairy burst out giggling.

'Only joking, my ducks. No griffin blood.'

'That's not funny, Harry,' growled Jeb.

It wouldn't be so hard to believe that the elf would feed them griffin blood. The stuff was poisonous, but a crackpot like Harry was capable of anything.

'Like I say, my lovely, you need to relax. So you lost this time. Don't matter, you'll win another time. Let this mongrel boy go. He beat you, fair and square.'

Jeb's ears twitched with rage.

'Stow it, Harry. You really think I'm going to let this go? That package is likely worth thousands of ducats. Maybe tens of thousands. And when I get it back, I'm going to sell it and make a flaming fortune.'

'Here we go again, always ducats this, ducats that.'

'Better than skulking around here with a load of big bleeding fish.'

Slik held his breath. Harry's fairy squawked, took off from his master's shoulder and settled behind the decanter of cocktail, peering out from behind it.

Harry looked at Jeb, long and hard.

'Careful, my lovely,' he said finally. 'Careful what you say about my sharkies.'

'All I'm saying is, if you spent as much time on business as you do on mollycoddling those sea vermin, yer'd be a lot richer, I can tell yer that. I mean, look at this place.'

He threw an arm out, indicating the walls of the office. They were covered in elegantly framed oil paintings – portraits of sharks.

'It's not right, Harry, that's all.'

Harry crossed the room in two long strides and gripped Jeb by the collar, knocking his tumbler of cocktail to smash on the wooden floor. The goblin went limp, terror written on his face. The red liquid trickled around his polished leather shoe.

'*Gaaaaaagh!*' said Harry's fairy.

'Now see here, rat guts,' breathed Harry. 'You say another word against my sharkies, and so help me I'll . . .'

Slik cleared his throat.

''Scuse me, but do you want this stinking news or not?'

Harry released his grip. Jeb staggered upright, straightened his coat and coughed, trying to regain his usual smug demeanour.

'All right, all right. Come on then. What've you got to report?'

'What about the sugar you promised?'

'Let's hear it first.'

Slik gave an exaggerated sigh.

'Fine. About that package you're after. Bad news is, the Demon's Watch have got it now.'

'What's the good news?'

'Didn't say there was any, did I?'

Jeb thought for a moment, then sauntered over to Harry, who was busy uncorking another decanter of firewater. He reached up and patted the elf on the back.

'So, Harry, me old mate . . . You've got a whole crew of bully boys lying idle, and I was wondering if—'

'Forget it, dearie,' said Harry, brushing off the goblin and pouring firewater into a glass. 'I ain't sending my boys to fight the Demon's Watch, if that's your plan. If Newton's crew have got your package, the game's over. You lost. Time to move on.'

'That's what you think,' sniffed Jeb. He hoisted himself up onto the desk. 'And I don't need you, anyway, come to think of it. The Snitch has got another trick up his sleeve.'

'Meaning?'

The goblin grinned, baring his pointed teeth until he looked like one of Harry's sharks.

'Meaning, the Demon's Watch have got hold of a certain someone as well as that package – a certain someone that a certain very dangerous friend of mine is after. So I reckon a little partnership is in order. We can take the Watch together, see, easy as drowning an imp in a barrel. This friend of mine will get what he wants, and I'll get what I want.'

Slik nodded. It was his favourite sort of plan – devious and violent, and everybody won. Except the Demon's Watch, of course.

Harry sighed and shook his head.

'Your problem is you want too much, duck. It'll be the death of you, mark my words. Give it a rest, is my advice.'

'Give it a rest,' echoed Harry's fairy, from his master's shoulder.

'I'll give it a rest,' said Jeb, 'when I'm so rich I'm eating diamonds for breakfast.'

'Well, just be careful,' said Harry, and he knocked back his firewater. 'Them diamonds might give you terrible indigestion.'

Chapter Twenty-one

The Bootle brothers had been questioning Clagg for over an hour, and the man still couldn't remember which tavern he'd lost the mysterious package in. Newton reckoned it was hopeless, but the twins wouldn't give up.

'Can you remember anything special about this place?' tried Paddy.

Clagg frowned, gazing off into the middle distance. He'd finally been given some food, and was treating his interrogation as an annoying distraction from dinner.

'It had grog,' he said at last, and went back to gnawing on a raw, lumpy brown patata.

'Perfect. So that narrows it down to – oh yes. Every single tavern in the whole of Port Fayt.'

'. . . And eels. Wonderful eels.'

'Well,' said Frank, rolling his eyes. 'It's a start.'

'Here, ain't you got any pies left?' said Clagg. 'This patata thing tastes like soil.'

'You can have a pie when you tell us something useful,' said Paddy. 'And watch what you say about those patatas. Ma just got them fresh off a boat from the New World.'

'Well now, matey, seems I'm not much use to you gents, and I'd hate to be wasting any more of yer precious time. So how about I head back to me ship?'

Hal shot him a dark look.

'No? All right then, fair enough.'

Newton had moved to the corner beside Old Jon, and was loading up his pipe with tobacco. The elf's silence kept him calm, and helped him think.

Ten thousand ducats, just for a smuggling run.

Newton had a strong feeling that whatever was in the witch's package was bad news. It wasn't just the massive sum of money she'd paid for it. It was the timing, too. According to Clagg, she'd insisted the cargo was brought in on the first day of the festival. Now there was just a day until the Pageant of the Sea, which would be held tomorrow evening. Why was this happening now, at the most important time of the year for Fayters? So far, he had no idea. But he was sure that he didn't like it.

The door flew open, and Tabitha swaggered in. She threw herself into an empty chair beside Frank and swung her feet up on the table, looking extremely pleased with herself.

'Evening, you lot,' she said.

'Look what the cat dragged in,' said Frank, reaching out to ruffle her hair. Tabitha tried to brush him off, and didn't quite manage it.

'Ha ha,' she said, not at all amused. 'So have you got anything out of this smuggler?'

'Nah. He's got the memory of a cuttlefish.'

'A cuttlefish who drinks too much.'

'And not even a particularly smart cuttlefish who drinks too much, neither.'

'All right, all right,' grumbled Clagg. 'I'm still here, yer know.'

The twins ignored him.

'Slik back?' asked Tabitha.

'Not yet. I thought he was with you. Where's the grog? Don't tell us you forgot it?'

'Of course I didn't forget it. I just brought back something a lot better.'

She nodded at the doorway.

A small boy had edged into the serving room, without anyone noticing. Newton sized him up. A mongrel – goblin-human, with pointed ears and mottled skin – scrawny and hollow-eyed, dressed in a filthy white shirt, filthy breeches and a filthy red satin coat. He looked very unsure of himself, and very damp.

'Er, hello,' said the boy.

'You!' said Phineus Clagg suddenly. 'Don't I know you from somewhere?' He was frowning at the mongrel, a half-eaten patata poised halfway between plate and mouth.

'Who is this, Tabs?' asked Newton.

'This,' said Tabitha proudly, 'is exactly what we've been looking for. Show them, Joseph.'

Hot gravy dribbled down Grubb's chin. He took another big bite and sighed happily.

'You could close your mouth when you chew,' said Tabitha, not quite managing to hide her disgust.

'Sorry,' said Grubb. He blushed and gulped down the mouthful. 'I don't normally eat with other people.'

'I can see why.'

Grubb chuckled, but Tabitha didn't join in.

'Just hurry up, all right? Newt and the others will

want to hear about how you found that wooden spoon.'

The pair sat together in the pie shop's kitchen, with the kindly old troll lady called Mrs Bootle bustling around them. Grubb was glad Tabitha was the only watchman here, even though she seemed to be sulking. The others had been friendly enough, but he wasn't ready to answer all their questions yet. And, to his relief, the big man called Newton had suggested that he have a rest and a bite to eat. Apparently Phineus Clagg's wooden spoon was important in some way, though he had absolutely no idea why.

Anyway, it felt good to forget about it for a while. The kitchen seemed like the warmest, cosiest place in the world. There was a cauldron bubbling over the fire, and the scent of pastry, onions and meat wafting through the air, and the steady *thunk* of Mrs Bootle's knife as she chopped up carrots. It felt good to be out of his old wet clothes, too. Mrs Bootle had given him a clean shirt and breeches, and an old faded blue watchman's coat that she said had belonged to the troll called Frank when he was younger. The clothes were much too big, but Grubb didn't mind. He almost felt like he was a watchman himself.

'There we go,' said Mrs Bootle, and she tipped the carrots into the big cauldron. 'Now, can I get you two anything else? Another pie? A mug of velvetbean?'

'No thank you, ma'am,' said Grubb.

'"Ma'am", is it? What a polite young man. Your parents must be very proud.'

Grubb felt himself blushing again.

'Oh, I don't . . . I mean . . . Well, my parents are, er . . .'

'How about a slice of shokel cake, then? Freshly baked this morning, iced and—'

'We're fine, Mrs Bootle,' interrupted Tabitha. 'And Joseph doesn't have time for a four-course meal anyway.'

'Very well, as long as you're sure. Give us a shout if you need anything – I'm off to help Mr Bootle mend the bed in the spare room. There's this big crack in it, you see, from when an ogre stayed last—'

'Yes, thanks,' said Tabitha impatiently. 'We'll see you later.'

Grubb watched the girl, as the elderly troll left the room. It seemed like a funny way to talk to a nice old lady like that. Maybe that was just how you behaved when you were in the Demon's Watch. Somehow he doubted it, though. He took another bite.

'Wassh it ike, beena wasshman?' he said.

Tabitha raised an eyebrow. He swallowed and tried again.

'What's it like, being a watchman?'

She rolled her eyes, as if it was the most boring question she'd ever been asked.

'Well, I didn't really do anything before, so it sort of seems . . . normal.'

'Oh.'

'I mean, it's exciting now, of course. Because of this witch. But most of the time, it's—'

'What witch?' interrupted Grubb. He had barely any idea what was going on, and he was starting to get tired of it.

'The one who's after the wooden spoon, of course,' snapped Tabitha.

'But, I mean, a witch? Who is she?'

'Well, that's what we're trying to find out,' said Tabitha slowly, as if she was explaining something for the hundredth time. 'All we know is that she got that smuggler friend of yours to bring her a wooden spoon all the way from the Old World, and she probably won't be using it to make a big cake for the Pageant of the Sea.'

She folded her legs up on the chair, and warmed her hands on the kitchen fire.

'So . . . the troll brothers – the watchmen – they're twins?'

'Uh-huh.'

'And Mrs Bootle's their mother?'

'You ask a lot of questions.'

'I . . . Do I? I'm sorry, it's just . . . I've only heard stories before. About the Demon's Watch.'

Tabitha pulled a face.

'All right. Here's the deal. The twins are Frank and Paddy. They've been in the Watch since they were children. Newt spotted them in Thalin Square one day, chasing after a pickpocket, and he was so impressed that he recruited them on the spot. Then there's Hal – he's the one with the pasty face and the glasses. His parents always wanted him to be a watchman. They're merchants, so they sent him to the Azurmouth Academy for five years, and now he's our magician. The elf, the one with the long white hair who doesn't say anything – that's Old Jon. Newt says he's been a watchman since practically the Dark Age. Then there's me.'

Grubb was trying to keep up.

'So Newton's your leader?'

She frowned.

'That's right.'

'He seems kind.'

'Yes, *obviously* he's kind, but he's also . . . I mean . . .'

'What?'

She turned her big grey eyes to look at him, trying to decide whether to go on. Grubb suddenly found himself worrying that he might have bits of pie stuck to his face.

'Well,' she said, at last. 'It's just that sometimes, it's like he thinks I'm still a baby. He only let me join the Watch properly a few months ago, even though I'm as good as any of the others. And now I have to babysit you when I just found that spoon that we've all been looking for. It's just not *fair*.'

'So why don't you say something?'

'I do – I mean, I have, but it's not that simple. I sort of owe him.'

'What do you mean?'

'Because he looks after me. He's always looked after me. Ever since I was little.'

'But he's not your father?'

'No, of course not. Don't be stupid.'

She looked back into the fire. There was a long pause, and Grubb began to wonder if he'd asked one question too many. Then she spoke in a small voice, all trace of anger gone.

'Have you ever heard of the Mandeville Plot?'

He nodded.

'My full name is Tabitha Mandeville.'

Grubb's eyes grew wide. *The Mandeville Plot*. He'd

only been a baby at the time, of course, but everyone knew the story. It had been a beautiful sunny day, and the governor and his young wife, Jessica, had gone out walking by the docks. Most governors never bothered to leave their big manor houses in the Flagstaff Quarter, but Mr Alfred Mandeville of the Morning Star Company was known for visiting every part of town and meeting every Fayter he could – merchant or mongrel.

Only this time, somebody had been waiting for him.

Whoever it was had thrown two small bottles from an upper window, one for the governor and one for his pretty wife. Bottles of griffin blood. The Mandevilles had died within minutes, and no one had ever found out who the murderer was.

'You're their daughter,' said Grubb, in wonder.

She looked at him with such ferocity that he flinched.

'Don't you dare feel sorry for me, understand? I was just a baby when it happened. It's not like I really remember anything.'

'Fine,' said Grubb, desperately trying to work out what would be safe to say. 'So . . . your hair is . . .'

'Dyed. It's blonde, really.' She sighed. 'The watchmen found out about the plot, and they tried to warn my father, but he wouldn't listen. He said he didn't want to live in fear. Then on the day of the murder, the Watch tried to protect him, but they were too late. I think afterwards, Newt felt so bad about what happened that he decided to, sort of, be my father himself.'

'You were lucky.'

She looked at him in total bewilderment.

'Lucky?'

'That's right. Don't you think? You were lucky that there was someone who really wanted to look after you.'

'I . . . No one's ever—' She broke off, lost in thought.

Grubb hurriedly changed the subject, unsure if he had upset her or not.

'So did you ever find out who killed— I mean, who was responsible?'

Tabitha spat into the fire.

'The League of the Light,' she said slowly, as if each word physically hurt her. 'It was one of their agents, sure as the sea. They hated my father. Before he became governor, he visited the Old World, and saw what they were doing. He saw their troops rounding up trolls and goblins and putting them to death. "Bringing light into the darkness", they call it.'

At the thought of it, Grubb felt a prickling at the back of his neck.

'So when my father had a chance to change things in Port Fayt, he banned all League merchants from the Middle Islands. It was the least he could do. But from then on, the League wanted his head. They persuaded someone to kill him. And not just any someone. Someone important.'

'How do you know that?'

'I don't know it, but . . . Well, afterwards, the Demon's Watch and the Dockside Militia tried to investigate, and they were told to forget all about it. All three trading companies – Cockatrice, Redoubtable and Morning Star – they all joined ranks and swept it under the carpet. They wouldn't have done that if it was just some bully boy or something. So the murderer was probably one of them. One of the fancy folk who live in the Flagstaff Quarter. They just didn't want whoever it was to get caught.'

'So you never found out?'

'No. Well, not exactly.'

'Not exactly?'

She paused and looked at him again, as if trying to work out whether to trust him. He smiled stupidly, which seemed to make the difference.

'I did find out one thing. Eugene Wyrmwood knows something, for sure.'

'The governor? Why do you think that?'

Tabitha bit her lip for a few moments, then leaned towards him.

'One day – it must have been two, three years ago – I saw him giving a speech in Thalin Square. He wasn't the governor then, of course; just a senior trading officer in the Cockatrice Company. I was near the front, and he spotted me. As soon as our eyes met, he went white as a sail and stopped talking, right in the middle of a sentence. It was as if he'd seen a demon. We stood staring at each other for a few seconds, while everyone else was wondering what was going on. Then he told the crowd he was sorry, but he felt ill, and one of his juniors took over the speech. You see?'

She sat back, waiting for a reaction.

Grubb wasn't quite sure what to say.

'Umm . . . But that doesn't really mean—'

'I know it doesn't "really mean" anything,' she snapped. She hunched her shoulders and swivelled round to face the fireplace, obviously disappointed in him. 'Not for sure, anyway. I just have a feeling, all right? I just know that if I could get hold of that bilgebag . . .'

She trailed off, staring into the dying embers of the fire.

'I'm sorry,' said Grubb. 'I didn't mean to—'

She interrupted him crossly.

'Do you have parents?'

Grubb shook his head.

'Orphan?'

He nodded.

'Do you remember them? I wish I could remember more about my parents.'

'I can remember a bit. My father was a goblin. He worked on the docks, unloading cargo for a few ducats here and there. And my mother was a human. He met her in the velvethouse she worked at.'

He put down the pie.

'I'm sorry, you don't want to hear this.'

'No, I do.'

'Really?'

'Yes, I want to hear. Go on. Tell me about your home.'

'All right. If you're sure. It was a little old house in the Marlinspike Quarter.'

'Describe it.'

'White plaster and black beams. A green front door. Two tiny windows that were never clean, that looked out onto the street. The three of us, we lived on the ground floor, in one big room. You had to go outside to use the privy. We shared it with half of the street.'

'What were their names? Your parents, I mean?'

'My father was Elijah. He came to Port Fayt on a wavecutter from the Old World, when he was a baby. My mother was Eleanor. Her family had lived here much longer, practically since the days of Thalin.'

The memories began to surge through his mind, each one fighting to be the first out of his mouth.

'I remember my mother singing old sea shanties to get me to sleep, and I remember playing games with my father. I used to dress up in a sack and imagine I was the Navigator, and we'd pretend to go exploring together. And when it was bedtime, he'd pretend to be the Maw coming to get me, and he'd chase me round the room until I promised to go to sleep. I think I thought I'd live there for ever, in that house. I think I thought . . .'

Suddenly, he was finding it hard to breathe. He hadn't spoken about this for years. Not since Mr Lightly had taken him on at the Legless Mermaid.

'Hey,' said Tabitha. 'Forget about it. I'm sorry I asked.' She pulled out a handkerchief and passed it to him.

'No, I'm sorry,' said Grubb. He couldn't stop

himself now. 'There was always this . . . *problem.* Because my father was a goblin, my mother was a human and I was a . . . a mongrel. My mother used to get so upset about it, and my father used to tell her not to worry. But she was right to worry because . . . because one day, they came for him. It was a gang of men he worked with. They couldn't stand to see him with my mother, and they . . . and they . . .'

He stopped and rubbed his eyes with the handkerchief.

Tabitha reached across and patted his arm.

'I'm sorry,' she said stiffly. 'I'm so sorry.'

Chapter Twenty-two

Books lay everywhere: scattered on the floor, piled haphazardly on the windowsill and leaning against the chair leg. Dust hung heavy in the air, mingling with the purple fumes from Eugene Wyrmwood's favourite pipe.

He was hunched at his desk, peering through his reading glasses and flipping the pages of a large volume entitled *Dr Leopold Collingsworth's Encyclopaedia of Sea Demons*, while the thunder rumbled outside. K, L, M . . .

There it was.

The Maw. The demon that killed Thalin the Navigator – or so the story went.

He tried to concentrate on the book, but he had a headache again. The Festival of the Sea was a trial in itself, of course, what with the Grand Party and the pageant to arrange, but the visit from the League's ambassador had made everything far worse. Try as he might, he couldn't stop thinking about that awful dinner and the Duke of Garran, with his soft, pink face, and his cold, colourless eyes. Mother would have known what to do. She would have dealt with it all far, far better than he had. He shook his head, and tried again to push it all from his mind.

Few have set eyes on the Maw and lived, he read. *Fewer still have left accounts of the beast's appearance, and all these accounts conflict dramatically. This leads one to suppose that either i) the beast is possessed of the transformative properties of a shapeshifter, or ii) most, if not all, of the accounts are at best fanciful, and at worst entirely fabricated. On balance, I incline to the latter interpretation.*

The Maw is perhaps best known as the beast that slew Thalin the Navigator, the founder of Port Fayt in the Middle Islands. Thalin is said to have founded the town in the year 1214, and to have governed it successfully for ten years. Restless, and eager for new adventures, he then set sail with his three vessels, the Cockatrice, *the* Redoubtable *and the* Morning Star. *(It is a point of interest that these names were subsequently adopted by the three trading companies which have shared power in Port Fayt since the late 1500s.) Thalin's bearing is known to have taken him two leagues south of the Lonely Isle, where the Farian Sea Trench, home of the Maw, is believed to be located. Not one of the vessels was ever seen again. There is a popular rhyme for children concerning the Maw:*

> *'In the Farian Trench, the great Maw sleeps,*
> *Where sailors fear the dreadful deep . . .'*

The governor took off his glasses and slammed the book shut. There was nothing there that any Fayter didn't already know backwards. He pushed it away. Then, after a moment's hesitation, he opened his desk drawer and picked up the doll that lay inside.

It was nothing more than a few scraps of cloth, crudely sewn together, stuffed with beans and falling apart. A black-coated militiaman, with a stitched smile and a pair of buttons for eyes. A strange mixture of emotions swelled up in him as he looked at it.

There was a rap on the door, and a secretary poked his head into the room. At once, Eugene Wyrmwood dropped the toy and shoved the drawer shut, feeling his cheeks go red.

'I . . .' He cleared his throat. 'I sincerely hope this is important.'

'Yes, Mr Wyrmwood, sir. It's Colonel Derringer to see you. He says it can't wait.'

'Very well, send him in.'

He refilled his pipe, and rubbed his aching brow. He didn't like Colonel Derringer. The man was difficult and demanding, and he had a strong suspicion that beneath all the bowing and scraping, Derringer thought he was an idiot. Then, there was that horrible, smug smile . . .

The colonel marched in, wearing exactly the smile he had just been imagining. There was a fat man with him, dressed in a militiaman's uniform with the stripes of a sergeant. He looked distinctly sheepish, and Wyrmwood noted with distaste that he had a black eye.

The pair of them came to attention and saluted.

'Governor Wyrmwood, sir,' said the colonel, and coughed. Wyrmwood noticed for the first time that the room was really very smoky indeed.

'What do you want?' he snapped, sounding a lot more cross than he'd intended.

'I'm afraid we have a problem with the Demon's Watch, Governor,' replied Derringer, still smiling. 'Sergeant Culpepper here has something to tell you.'

'Culpepper, is it?'

The militiaman nodded, embarrassed. 'Yes, your honour.'

'Well?'

'Sir, me and some mates, er, that is to say, colleagues, we were drinking in the Pickled Dragon earlier, down in the Marlinspike Quarter. Well, I say drinking. We weren't, er, drunk or nothing. Well, Sprunt had had a few, but—'

'Get on with it, Culpepper,' prompted Derringer.

'Yes, sir. Sorry, sir. Just keeping an eye out, we were, mixing with the townsfolk, as you might say.'

Governor Wyrmwood drew out his golden pocket watch and examined it meaningfully. Sergeant Culpepper wiped a trickle of sweat from his forehead.

'Well, to cut a long story short, we were chatting to this one lad, see, a goblin mongrel, and this girl came up to us, with blue hair, and she rolls up her sleeve and shows us one of them Demon's Watch tattoos, and says we have to do what she says. Then she just went completely mad and attacked us. I, er, I just thought you ought to know, sir, seeing as how you banned them watchmen.'

'Why, exactly, did she attack you?'

'Oh yes. Sorry, sir. This mongrel had a wooden

spoon, all wrapped up in a scrap o' velvet. And this crazy girl wanted it for some reason.'

'A wooden spoon?'

'I can take the Demon's Watch tonight, your honour,' said Derringer. 'You don't have to worry about a thing. We'll throw them all in the Brig. Just say the word, and—'

'Quiet,' said the governor irritably. 'I'm thinking.' His headache seemed to have got a lot worse since Derringer had arrived.

What would Mother do?

As it happened, he knew exactly what she would do.

'Very well,' he said at last. He waved his hand vaguely, shooing them away. 'It can't be helped.'

'Yes, sir.'

The two of them saluted again, Derringer's other hand resting on the hilt of his sword. Eugene Wyrmwood was struck by a thought.

'One thing though, Colonel. No one is to be hurt. Do you understand? Not now. Not in the middle of the festival. I don't want you making a scene.'

Derringer's smile grew even wider, irritating the governor so much that he almost winced.

'No, sir. I wouldn't dream of it.'

When they had left, the governor picked up his

pipe and reading glasses again and opened a new book, puffing absently. But his concentration was gone. He reached for the antique globe that stood on the corner of his desk, and began to spin it. His fingers brushed over the vast bumpy surface that showed the Old World, over the Ebony Ocean that Thalin the Navigator had crossed so many years ago, on to the Middle Islands and Port Fayt, and on again, over the ocean, towards the New World.

Governor Wyrmwood sighed, and pushed the globe aside. Sometimes he almost doubted that the fabled Navigator had ever really lived. So many of the stories about him were scarcely believable . . . Not least the tale of the Maw. Could such a creature have existed? Could it still exist? And was there any way to know for sure?

The study was warm and cosy, but Governor Wyrmwood shivered, all the same.

He took another puff on his pipe, and rang for a secretary.

Chapter Twenty-three

'. . . And that's when Tabitha came along,' finished Grubb. He wasn't much of a storyteller, but he'd muddled his way through as well as he could, from the night of the Grand Party to the Pickled Dragon inn. At first he'd been so nervous, standing in the pie shop serving room and speaking to the Demon's Watch, that his voice shook. But if his audience had noticed, they'd been kind enough not to show it. It felt strange, being the centre of attention and having everyone listen to him. He wasn't sure he liked it very much.

Newton was the first to speak.

'Should have known better than to trust the Snitch.'

'So he sold us out, tried to take the cargo for himself,' said Tabitha. 'Doesn't matter. We'll make that bilge rat pay.'

'Aye,' said Newton grimly. 'We'll make him pay. Hal, what can you tell us about that wooden spoon?'

The magician was sitting hunched over a table, cradling the witch's contraband in his handkerchief and peering at it through eyeglasses. He took off the glasses and frowned.

'My hypothesis is that this wooden spoon is in fact a wand, enchanted for a specific purpose. However, Mr Phineus Clagg's old elfish enchanter must be a consummate professional, because I can't detect a trace of his work.'

'Explain.'

'Well, a poorer enchantment would leave a magical stain, which could aid identification. But here the spell is firmly locked into the wood, so securely that I cannot detect any trace of magic. That being so, there's no way to establish how powerful it could be, or even what kind of enchantment has been used. Until someone attempts to use it as a wand, it is no different from an ordinary wooden spoon.'

'A wand?' said Frank doubtfully. 'Shouldn't it be more . . . magic-y looking?'

Hal sighed and rubbed his brow.

'That is exactly the sort of ridiculous preconception that magicians have to put up with every day. Anyone can perform magic, you know – it simply takes considerable time and patience to learn. You don't need a flowing white beard and a cape with stars on it. Likewise, the appearance of a wand is entirely immaterial. What matters is that it is a physical object which can be used to direct magical energy. A wooden spoon is a perfectly common choice. It's cheap and readily available, nicely balanced, and it saves you the trouble of carving your own.'

'Right,' said Newton. 'Understood.'

'Er, can I say something?' said Grubb.

'Of course.'

They all looked at him.

'It's just, when I was in the cellar of the shark pit, I heard the thief who stole it talking to Jeb. I think they thought I was still asleep. But he said something about a *leash*.'

Hal's eyebrows shot up.

'What does that mean?' asked Newton.

'A leash is a particularly powerful enchantment, banned in every known state in the Old World, and in the Middle Islands. It allows a magician to penetrate another mind and manipulate it at will. Which is to say that if you know how to use this wand correctly,' he held up the wooden spoon, 'you can make someone do whatever you want.'

There was a long pause.

'So,' said Frank. 'Whose mind does this witch want to control?'

'Could be anyone's,' said Tabitha.

Paddy shook his head.

'Not anyone's. Ten thousand ducats it cost, to get this wand into Port Fayt. So whoever she's after is going to be someone important.'

'How about Governor Wyrmwood?' suggested Frank. 'There's no one in Port Fayt more important than him.'

Newton nodded slowly.

'That's possible. If you control the governor, you control the town. You could do anything you wanted.'

'The timing fits, too,' said Paddy. 'Why come to Port Fayt now, on the eve of the Festival of the Sea? Maybe it's because the governor has a whole year in office before the next handover. Thalin knows what the witch could do in that time with the governor as her puppet.'

Frank ambled over to Grubb, gave him a wink and punched him on the arm. Grubb only just managed not to yelp out loud. It hurt, a lot. But he could tell it was supposed to be friendly.

'You're a brave lad, you know that?' said the troll.

'Umm . . . I didn't really do anything.'

'Nonsense. You've got guts, and you're a quick thinker, besides. You got lucky, of course, getting fished out of the shark pit by those lads, but all the same—'

'That reminds me,' interrupted Tabitha, rescuing Grubb from his embarrassment. 'I forgot to tell you, those bully boys from the shark pit turned out to be blackcoats. They started making trouble, and we got into a fight, and . . .'

She trailed off.

Everyone was looking at her.

'Tabitha,' said Newton. 'These blackcoats . . . They don't know you're a watchman, do they?'

There was a long pause. Tabitha went very red, and began to fiddle with her coat buttons.

'Oh, Tabs,' said Paddy.

'But I . . . I didn't know they were blackcoats, until . . .'

'Exactly,' said Old Jon. It was the first word Grubb had heard him speak. 'You didn't know.'

Tabitha glanced around the room, but no one met her eyes. No one defended her. Grubb wished there was something he could say to help her, but no words came.

'Why didn't you tell us earlier?' asked Hal.

'I didn't think . . . I mean, they'd had enough grog to sink a galleon. They won't even remember.'

'You don't know that, Tabs.'

Tabitha opened her mouth, but couldn't find a reply. Instead she just shrugged and began to stare fiercely at a random patch of wall.

'We're in trouble,' said Newton, at last. 'If I know Derringer, he'll have gone straight to Governor Wyrmwood. And after that, he'll be after us.'

'But—' said Tabitha.

'Quiet now.' Newton's voice had turned instantly hard. 'You've done enough. You did well to find Joseph and the wand, but you were reckless. I've told you before, this isn't a game. You've still got a lot to learn.'

Tabitha looked close to tears.

'I can help, I . . .'

Frank placed a hand on her shoulder.

'We all make mistakes, Tabs.'

She drooped, looking down at the floor so that no one could see her face.

'We don't have much time,' said Newton. 'Any minute now, Derringer and his men will be—'

There was a gunshot, and the window shattered.

Chapter Twenty-four

'Everybody get down!'

Grubb felt a firm hand on his back, and then he was half falling, half shoved down onto his knees. Someone had snuffed out the lanterns. There was a splash and a hiss, and the fire was out too.

He blinked, his eyes adjusting to the shadows and the moonlight. He could hear the watchmen moving cautiously to the edges of the room, metallic clicks and scrapes as pistols were loaded and cocked. Another hand gripped his collar, and he was pushed up against the wall, squeezed in between the hulking figures of Newton and Frank. Phineus Clagg brushed past, scuttling for the corner.

'Good evening,' said a calm voice. It seemed to come from everywhere and nowhere at once, amplified by magic.

'Cyrus Derringer,' whispered Frank. 'Doesn't that scurvy elf have anything better to do?'

'I know you're in there, Newton,' said the voice. 'And I'm not in the mood for messing around. You and your men have exactly three minutes to come out, unarmed, with your hands in the air.'

'Or what?' shouted Tabitha. It sounded like she'd recovered a little in the excitement. 'You leave us alone and mind your own business?'

'Not exactly,' said Derringer, without humour. 'We smash this place to smithereens, and take every one of you to the Brig. Every one of you that survives.'

'No surprise there,' muttered Newton. 'Hal, can you see anything?'

Grubb could just make out the thin silhouette of the magician on the opposite side of the room. He was peering out of the window, into the darkness.

'Nothing.'

'Right. Frank, is there any way out of here that Derringer doesn't know about?'

'An old smuggling passage,' said the troll. 'It's not been used for almost a century, but the entrance is in the cellar. Comes out in the alleyway round the back of the shop.'

'Good. We'll split into two groups. Hal, Jon and the twins, you're with me. We'll stay here and hold off the blackcoats. Tabs, you get everyone else out through that passage. And keep an eye on that smuggler, while you're at it. Hal, let's have the wooden spoon.'

The spoon came skittering across the floor. Newton caught it and placed it into Grubb's hands.

'Joseph, you've kept hold of this so far. Tuck it in your belt and don't take it out, no matter what.'

'Yes, sir,' said Grubb, and his stomach stirred with a mixture of fear, excitement and pride. Newton seemed to respect him, and he wasn't used to that. It made him feel brave, as if he could do anything. He wouldn't let the watchmen down. No matter what.

'We'll all meet at the lighthouse in two hours' time. The keeper's a friend of mine. Everyone understand?'

Grubb's eyes were used to the light now, and as the others nodded, he thought he saw Tabitha scowling. But she didn't say anything, and neither did he.

'Go now,' said Newton. 'And keep your heads down.'

Grubb felt Frank's hand on his arm as he started to move.

'Hey,' he said. 'Tell my mother, sorry about the window.'

'We'll be lucky,' murmured Hal, 'if it's just the window.'

Was it really such a good idea, sending Tabs on her own to take care of Mr and Mrs Bootle? Not to mention the tavern boy and the smuggler. Well, it was too late to worry about it now. The boy Joseph seemed to have sense, at least. And anyway, Newton was going to need the rest of the watchmen here, if he knew Derringer. He cleared his throat.

'Evening, Cyrus. You're making a big mistake, you know?'

Amplified laughter filled the room.

'Oh, well, if you say so. You can go free, then.'

A musket ball shattered another window, and knocked a chunk of plaster from a spot dangerously close to Old Jon's shoulder. The elf didn't even flinch.

'Scum,' he grunted.

'All right, point taken,' called Newton. He eased back the hammer on his pistol. 'So why don't you come in here and we'll talk about it like honest folk?'

'I've got a better idea,' said Derringer, with a hint of a snarl. 'How about you stop wasting my time and get out here, now. You have two minutes.'

Well, Newton hadn't expected that to work. Now there really was no choice.

'Frank, Paddy. We're going to need more fire-power.'

The twins grinned matching grins.

'No problem.'

They crawled behind the shop counter, and emerged a moment later, crouched and hauling a large chest. Frank lifted the lid, and Paddy passed round the contents – a pair of muskets for Old Jon and Hal (Hal waved away the offer, and Jon took both), a blunder-buss for Frank and a hefty four-barrelled volley gun for Newton. Paddy handed them each bags of gunpowder and shot and a few grenadoes, and drew out a squat weapon with a gaping, flared muzzle and a bronze model of a dragon bolted onto the barrel.

'Maw's teeth, what is that?' asked Newton, tugging open a bag of gunpowder.

'My grenadoe gun. Dwarf design. Been waiting a long time for a chance to try this out.'

'It's a good thing your parents aren't here,' said Hal, eyeing the weapon with distaste. 'I'm not sure your mother would approve.'

Newton finished loading the volley gun, cast a quick glance around the room to check that everyone was ready, and took a deep breath.

'Derringer! You know as well as I do, we aren't coming out without a fight. So if your men don't have the stomach for it, you'd better let them go.'

'Very funny,' said Derringer's voice. 'One minute.'

Had it really been such a good idea, coming to the watchmen? So far, it hadn't been quite what Grubb had expected. It should have been the end of his problems, but instead he was hurrying through a darkened corridor in a pie shop, fleeing from the Dockside Militia and trying to protect a wooden spoon. And for company, he had a dangerous smuggler and two elderly trolls wearing nightgowns. Not to mention his new friend Tabs, who was stomping on ahead with a lantern, in a black mood. Grubb thought he might have found this whole situation funny, if it wasn't so completely terrifying. He glanced back down the passageway, towards the room where they'd left the watchmen – the watchmen that he'd only just met, and might never see again.

'Everyone stick together,' barked Tabitha. 'Stop dawdling at the back.'

Grubb broke into a trot to catch up.

'Hey, matey,' said Clagg, putting an arm around his shoulders. 'I can look after that spoon for yer if you fancy. Take a load off yer mind.'

'I heard that, walrus brains,' said Tabitha, without giving Grubb a chance to reply. 'You, Joseph. If he tries any funny business, wallop him.'

'Girls, eh?' muttered Clagg, as they went down a flight of steps. Fortunately, Tabitha didn't hear.

The cellar was dank and freezing. It smelled of age, of neglect and of fish that had gone off months ago.

'So where's this secret passage?' asked Tabitha.

'Well now, let me see . . .' said Mr Bootle. 'It's been such a very long time since I saw it last . . .'

'Yes, yes. We don't have much time.'

'But I *think* the entrance is . . . erm . . . behind there.' He pointed to a blackened old barrel with a trembling green finger.

Tabitha crossed the floor and tugged viciously at the barrel, grunting as she took out her frustration on it. It fell apart in a tumble of dead wood, and she collapsed backwards onto the floor.

'Rotten,' observed Clagg.

'Well, thanks,' spat Tabitha, rounding on him with gritted teeth. 'I'm so glad we've got you to—'

A burst of gunfire cut her short.

Grubb flinched. Mrs Bootle let out a scared whimper. The sound was muffled underground, but there was no doubt about it. It came from the street outside the pie shop.

'What are yer waiting for?' said Clagg. He was already yanking open a trap door, set into the wall behind the ruined barrel. 'Sky's sake, let's get out of here.'

The tunnel was narrow, not much wider than the smuggler. It wasn't so bad for Grubb, who was skinny even for a goblin boy. But he didn't like the thought of the large elderly trolls coming behind him, squeezing through the muck in their freshly laundered nightgowns. He felt something warm and wet under his hand, and wiped it on his breeches, trying not to think too hard about what it could be. Something scuttled over his other hand, and he pulled it back in shock. Whatever it was had gone. He focused on following the light of Tabs's lantern moving ahead of him.

The tunnel curved slowly upwards, longer than he'd expected. When he finally emerged, hauling himself through a trap door above his head, he saw why. They had crossed under the alleyway and were now on the opposite side. Grubb pushed past a stack of old crates that hid the exit and joined the others clustering against the wall, casting suspicious glances each way like rats hiding from a tavern cat.

The rain had stopped at last, but the air was chilly. There was a constant dripping noise from the overloaded gutters, and the cobbles were a network of pools and puddles. The alleyway was dark and empty, except for the crates and a broken ladder leaning up against a wall. Gunfire sounded distantly, but now it was mingled with shouts and screams.

Grubb noticed the elderly trolls, holding onto each other and shivering in just their nightwear.

'Here, Mrs Bootle,' he said, 'take my coat.' As she took it from him, Grubb gave Tabitha a look.

'Oh, right,' she said gruffly, taking off her own jacket and handing it to Mr Bootle.

'Thank you very much, Tabs.'

Tabitha seemed a bit embarrassed.

'Come on then,' she said fiercely. 'Let's get out of here. Before we freeze to death.'

Without waiting for the others to follow, she strode off down the alleyway.

A figure stepped from a hiding place in the shadows, into her path. A hunched, twisted figure, wearing long grey robes.

An old woman.

Ice pounded through Grubb's veins. The moment stretched on and on.

Chapter Twenty-five

'Where is the wooden spoon?'

Her voice was thunderous and ragged, like the bellow of a wild beast.

'Give it to me. Give it to me now.'

Grubb tried to stir his body into action, but it was too late. She was right in front of him, without seeming to move at all. Savage fingers clawed at his throat, gripping and squeezing so hard that he let out a gurgling cry of pain. He could feel the spoon tucked into his belt, and braced himself for the clatter of wood on cobbles. But the spoon stayed put, where his oversized shirt hid it from view.

'Where is it?' she hissed. Her voice had

transformed into something low, deadly and insidious. 'I know you have it, mongrel. He told me you had it. Tell me where it is, or I'll kill you.'

Grubb had no idea what to do. Maybe it was the witch's magic, or maybe it was just blind terror. But either way, his body was paralysed, and his mind was as empty as a blue sky.

He could see every detail of her crooked face; every crease and wrinkle. Her nose was hooked like a seagull's beak, and most terrifying of all were the eyes, cold and black as obsidian. He felt light-headed, as if he was going to faint, or be sick, or both.

And then, out of the corner of his eye, he saw Tabitha. Her face was flushed, her eyes were shining and Grubb knew what she was going to do.

'No, no, no,' he burbled. 'No.'

Tabitha shoved him into the wall. He flew out of the witch's grasp, and the fog lifted from his mind.

The wooden spoon was gone. And yes, there it was, in Tabitha's hand.

'No,' he yelled again, uselessly.

But already she was sprinting down the alley, heading for the back streets.

'Save yourselves,' she called out, her voice shrill with excitement.

Newton's words came back to Grubb. *You were*

reckless. I've told you before, this isn't a game.

The old woman was smiling. He couldn't see it – her face was hidden in the shadow of her hood – but he knew it all the same.

'Stop,' he said pathetically. 'Please stop. Leave her alone.' But his voice was just a hoarse whisper, and before he could try again, there was a blur of grey and the witch was gone, flying after Tabitha so fast it was as if she didn't need to touch the ground.

At last, his stupid body leaped into action. He scrambled up and began to run. But instead of carrying him down the alley, his feet connected with something, and for the second time that day he found himself heading for the cobblestones, face first.

Not again.

Ouch.

His shirt was soaked through. He rolled over, and found a figure crouching above him.

'Come on, matey,' said Phineus Clagg. 'You can't do 'er no good now. Thought you had some sense in yer.'

Grubb struggled to get up, but the smuggler gripped his shirt and held him down.

'Let me go. I have to help her!'

'Don't be such a bilge-brain. What do yer think a little goblin boy can do against a witch like that, eh?'

'You don't understand, I . . . I need to . . .'

'You need to calm down is what you need to do.'

Grubb looked around for help, and saw the Bootles. They were clinging onto each other, staring down the alley towards where Tabitha and the witch had disappeared. Their eyes were as big as cannon-balls, their faces white as sails.

Immediately, Grubb knew that the smuggler was right.

'I'm sorry,' he said, trying to pull himself together. 'Of course. I'm sorry. I wasn't thinking straight. We've got to get to the lighthouse, like Newton said.'

'That's more like it.' Clagg rose, offering him a hand to haul himself up. 'Good luck then, matey.'

'What . . . What do you mean, good luck?'

Clagg turned up the collar of his coat and shoved his hands in his pockets.

'I ain't going to that lighthouse so your Captain Newton can throw me in gaol.'

Grubb felt himself being carried away on a wave of desperation.

'But you can't go. I thought you—'

'Look here. Yer a good lad and I ain't going to watch you run off to yer death. But I ain't going to do what yer tell me, neither. Far as I'm concerned, the contraband's been delivered now. Not the way I would've liked, but you can't have everything. So there's nothing to keep me in this port of yours any more.'

'You mean you're going to leave?'

Clagg hesitated.

'Why don't yer come with me, eh? Get out of this mess, matey, that's my advice.'

Grubb could hardly believe what he was hearing.

'But what about these old folk? What about Tabitha?'

Clagg shrugged.

'Suit yerself. Me, I'm going for another plate o' them eels. Ain't tasted eels that good in a long time. And after that, I'm getting out o' this scurvy town. Ain't been nothing but trouble since I got here.'

He winked, turned and disappeared into the darkness.

Grubb watched him go, in a daze. 'Fine,' he said to the receding figure. 'You do whatever you want. Don't bother worrying about anyone else.'

But there was nothing he could do.

Grubb began to realize that his neck was aching from the witch's grasp. He reached up and found it was wet – horribly wet, and sticky. He looked down and saw drops of blood soaking into his shirt. For a moment he felt like he might faint, but he managed to rally himself. There were still things to be done. People were relying on him, and not just the trolls – Captain Newton and the Demon's Watch. He wasn't going to let them down, whether they were alive or . . . not alive.

The Bootles had barely moved throughout everything that had happened, except to shudder with fear and cold.

'Everything's going to be all right,' he told them, trying to sound confident despite the gunfire still sounding in the distance. 'Let's get out of here.'

He strode off, dabbing at his throat with a sleeve, and got almost halfway down the alley before he had to stop.

'Umm . . .' he said. 'Which way are we supposed to be going?'

Chapter Twenty-six

Slik couldn't wait for the fun to begin.

The rain was easing up now, and from his position – crouched on a rooftop opposite the pie shop, sheltering in the lee of a chimney – he had an excellent view of the action.

He could see Cyrus Derringer in the alley below, kneeling behind a barrel, using a spyglass to try to see inside Bootles'. Behind the elf, a black-coated, grey-haired militia magician waited for orders. Slik reckoned he'd spotted all of Derringer's men now. There were five hidden in the shadows to the left of the pie shop, bayonets fixed. Another five on the right. Muffled voices came from the chimney beside him, enough to suggest that Derringer had a detachment in the upper floor of the house, too.

A triple-pronged attack: textbook stuff. Just what you'd expect from an old stick-in-the-mud like Derringer.

Slik licked his lips. It had been a surprise to find the blackcoats here, of course. He probably should have gone straight back to Jeb the Snitch and warned him to hold off. But this was too good a chance to miss. What was going to happen when Jeb showed up with his 'dangerous friend'? Slik didn't know, but he'd bet his left wing it would be entertaining.

Derringer checked his pocket watch and slid his sword from its scabbard.

Then, gunfire.

It came from down the street. Scattered pistol shots and a tinkle of broken glass, followed by whooping and the strains of drunken, loud sea shanties, sung horribly out of tune. Derringer lowered his sword, turned to his magician and spoke in a fast whisper.

Slik grinned. *Here we go.*

A crowd of figures rounded the corner, carrying burning firebrands which lit up the street, and each other. They were a rabble of humans, dwarves, elves, imps, goblins, trolls and ogres, at least thirty strong, armed with cutlasses, blunderbusses, knives, clubs and axes. Most of them had daubed on crude black war paint, or knotted handkerchiefs around their faces. They came to a shambling halt in front of Bootles' Pie Shop, tossing their empty grog bottles to smash on the walls, sniggering and joking with each other and generally looking extremely unpleasant. One of them held a long pole with a black flag attached. It flicked out in the wind, revealing a large white skull with a white cleaver stitched underneath.

Jeb's dangerous friend stepped out of the crowd, squat and bald as ever. He was dressed in his usual black waistcoat with no shirt underneath, so that Slik could see his prosthetic arm – a network of carved wood and rusted metal.

Captain Gore.

This time, there was a large serrated blade attached where his left hand should be, and in his right hand he held a rusty, outsized butcher's cleaver. Jeb the Snitch stood at his side, dressed in a ludicrous pink coat. He looked very, very pleased with himself. Gore just looked very, very angry.

'This it, Jeb?' asked Gore.

'That's right.'

'Good. Nobody tricks Captain Gore and gets away with it. Nobody.'

He threw his head back and roared, sound ripping

from his throat. It should have been bloodcurdling, but Slik wasn't scared that easily.

'PHINEUS CLAGG,' the pirate bellowed at the pie shop. 'GIVE ME PHINEUS CLAGG!'

'And the wooden spoon,' said Jeb, rubbing his hands together.

'AND THE WOODEN SPOON!'

Slik heard Newton's voice from inside.

'Why don't you come and get it, you bilge rat?'

There were whistles of disbelief, and one or two angry shouts.

'You'll regret saying that, Newt,' sneered Jeb.

'Only thing I regret is trusting you, you two-faced lowlife.'

'Yeah, well, you've no one to blame but yourself. I always told you, Newt. You can't trust nobody in this town. Not even yer own fairy. It was him who put us onto you, in case you were wondering.'

There was no reply.

Captain Gore turned to his men and grunted.

'Slaughter them, boys. All of them. Take no prisoners.'

Pistols clicked as they were cocked and blades slithered and scraped from their sheaths.

Slik giggled with delight. The best bit was, the pirates were all too drunk or stupid to have noticed the militiamen. Derringer's blackcoats were still in hiding, waiting for orders, while their leader tried to decide what in all the wide blue sea he should do.

There was a musket crack from the room below, followed by an ill-concealed curse. Slik dodged back out of sight behind the chimney, as several pirates turned to look upwards.

'What was that?' he heard one say, stupidly.

Idiots, thought Slik. *Idiots all round*.

As if to prove his point, there was a sudden battle cry from the right-hand side of the pie shop. He leaned round the chimney, and spotted one of the militia detachments come pounding out from their hiding place, levelling bayonets at the startled pirates.

'*Yaargh*,' yelled the blackcoats. '*Yaaaaaaaaaaargh!*'

Idiots.

'Attack!' barked Derringer, leaping from behind his barrel. '*Attaaaaack!*'

Musket fire erupted from the room below, answered by more gunfire from the pie shop. The militia magician stood up, flinging out his arms and sending a shimmering shock wave smack into the nearest pirate. A crossbow bolt smashed a window. Another zinged over the rooftop beside Slik, wildly off target. A grenadoe arced its way out of Bootles' and landed among the pirate crew, with a flash and a deafening bang.

The pirates were caught in the crossfire. They panicked, charging blindly in all directions, hacking and slashing with their weapons.

'Militia!' roared Captain Gore. 'Take them down!'

'Barricades!' shouted Newton, bringing his volley gun down with a hefty thump onto the head of a pirate who was trying to clamber through the window. The man went limp and dropped the knife he'd been holding with his teeth. He hung, half in and half out of the shop.

If Newton ever got hold of Slik, that fairy was going to be in big trouble.

The door shook as pirates slammed into the other side.

'Frank, Paddy, prop up that door.'

The troll twins slung their weapons on their shoulders and started dragging over tables and chairs.

Old Jon let fly with one of his muskets, and was rewarded with a squeal of pain. Calmly, he began to reload.

'How's that spell coming, Hal?' called Newton, pulling a pistol from the unconscious pirate's belt.

'I'm trying to concentrate,' said Hal through

gritted teeth. 'These aren't exactly perfect conditions for magic, you know.'

Newton grunted and fired the pistol.

'Fine. Hate to rush you.'

On the far side of the room, a pirate was clambering through a broken window. Frank leaped at him, belted him round the head with a stool and shoved him back outside again.

Another came through the next window along, and Paddy stepped up, parrying a cutlass blow with his grenadoe gun, then gripping the pirate by his collar and heaving him into the room. The man's head connected with a table, knocking him out with a dull thud.

The door shook again. They didn't have much time before . . .

And there it was at last – the familiar shiver of a spell being cast. Newton turned to see Hal's hands filling with black smoke. Within seconds, it had spread out into every part of the room, blocking everything from view.

'There,' said Hal, from somewhere in the fog. 'Are we happy now?'

'Not until we're out of here. Everybody move!'

The watchmen scrambled out of the room, firing as they went.

Newton was the last to leave. He tugged out his tinderbox, lit the fuses of the last few grenadoes and tossed them through the window. There was no need to stay and hear the result. He flung himself out of the room, and slammed the door shut behind him.

The walls shuddered as the grenadoes went off.

Newton wiped sweat from his brow.

'Which way to the cellar?' he said. 'Reckon it's about time to get out of here.'

Slik couldn't stop grinning as he watched the Snitch flee headlong down the street, the goblin's polished shoes spraying muck onto his fancy pink coat. This was absolutely the best thing he'd seen in ages. Plenty of blood and guts, and here on the rooftop he had a great view with no danger whatsoever. The only thing that could possibly make it any better would be a nice big sugar lump to suck on.

He would have liked to see the Snitch get it in the neck too, to be honest, but the sight of him wetting his breeches and running away like a frightened mouse was good enough. And anyway, there were much more exciting things to see in front of the pie shop.

The pirates had got into a right tizzy when they

were attacked on both sides, and already, many of them were wounded or dead. Now they were fighting back though, and their natural savagery was overcoming the blackcoats' training. Slik sniggered as one militiaman fell onto the cobblestones, squashed under the weight of three freebooters. The blackcoat magician was still casting the odd spell, but he was sweating and panting from the effort, and Slik reckoned he wouldn't last much longer. On the left-hand side of the shop, Bosun Tuck was cutting a swathe through the blackcoats, his cutlass swinging in great, bloody arcs.

The tattooed ogre was impressive, but he was nothing compared to Cyrus Derringer. The elf moved steadily into the midst of the enemy, his sword arm dancing with deadly speed. Slik followed each deft blow, each parry and each lunge. Elves were usually pretty fast, of course, but this was something else. Derringer ducked a whistling axe blade, punched its owner in the guts, swivelled, deflected two cutlasses that were swinging towards him, shoved one of his attackers away and slapped the other with the flat of his blade. And then Captain Gore stepped in, blocking his path.

Slik squealed with pleasure. It was a delicious contrast. The slender elf, with his elegant swordsmanship, versus the mad butchery and unstoppable strength of Captain Gore. All around them the fighting died down, and a space cleared.

'Cut his bleeding head off!' roared the pirates.

The two leaders circled each other. Derringer's blade seemed to slide snake-like through the air, while Gore hefted his massive cleaver, his blade-hand held out in front like a pistol levelled at his opponent's head. He hawked, spat and leaped forward, his cleaver raised.

The pirates howled with excitement. Slik held his breath. Here it came. Death or glory. The greatest duel any of them would ever witness. A fight to the bitter end. Two champions, locked in mortal combat. It felt as if fate had brought the pair of them together for this one moment of intense—

There was a heavy thud as Captain Gore hit the ground.

Cyrus Derringer knelt and wiped his blade on the back of the pirate's waistcoat. He looked utterly calm, as if he'd done nothing more than gut a fish. Blood spread through the cracks between the cobblestones.

It was over. And Slik hadn't even seen the killing blow.

There were a full five seconds of silence before Bosun Tuck took the initiative. 'Run away,' he croaked.

And the pirates turned tail and fled like cockroaches from a flame.

Slik banged the rooftop with his fist. It wasn't fair! The fight had been getting better and better, and now the militia colonel had ruined it.

'The shop,' barked Derringer at his men. 'Don't just stand around – search the pie shop, you sea slugs.'

The militiamen began to advance warily, nervous of the black smoke that billowed from the pie shop's windows and chimney.

But Slik had lost interest. With a flick of his wings he was away, skimming over the rooftops. That stinking Derringer and his fancy swordplay . . . Still, at least Newton and the Snitch had got what was coming to them. On balance, he decided, it had been a good night.

He flew high above the town, grinning as the rooftops blurred below him and the air rushed past. Wheeling around a warehouse, he dropped down into the street below and whizzed round a corner, upsetting a horse that was tied up outside a grogshop. He laughed.

It felt good to be free, away from boring, serious Newton and cowardly, useless Jeb. Maybe he should leave Port Fayt for good. There was a thought . . . But on the other hand, there was still plenty of sugar to be earned here. Perhaps he could find someone who was worthy of his services. And even if they weren't, it would be fun betraying them later.

Yes, that was what he needed. A new employer.

Chapter Twenty-seven

Grubb's foot slipped on a bump in the road, and sank deep into a puddle. He groaned as the water seeped into his shoe. Just what he needed.

'Are you all right, dear?'

'I'm fine thanks,' said Grubb, trying to sound like he wasn't bothered. The truth was, he was dejected, not to mention embarrassed that the elderly troll couple seemed to be coping with this unplanned night-time ramble a lot better than he was.

It was freezing up on the hillside. The wind rustled the grass and ripped through Grubb's damp clothes, painfully cold. He hugged himself to keep warm, and looked up again at the distant silhouette of the lighthouse tower. It didn't seem to be getting any closer.

It didn't help that his brain was endlessly churning over what had happened in the alleyway. The witch's face, twisted like a mask to scare little ones. The last glimpse of Tabitha, looking back triumphantly, grasping the wooden spoon . . .

No, it was no good thinking about that. He focused on what the witch had said, running the words through his head, over and over. *He told me you had it.* 'He'. Who was 'he'? Grubb tried to think like a watchman. Who could have told the witch where to find him? Jeb? The shapeshifter? But that made no sense. It was someone who knew that he had the wooden spoon; that was for sure. Could it have been one of the Demon's Watch? No, that was ridiculous . . .

His brain was starting to spin, and to distract himself he stopped and looked back at the lights of Fayt, glowing like stars.

But at once he thought of Tabitha, who must have been captured somewhere among those dark buildings. What would Newton say? He had no idea where she was. No idea where the wooden spoon was. The Demon's Watch had saved his life and taken care of him, and he'd messed everything up. He'd even begun to hope that he could join the Watch himself, but of course that was impossible now. Even if they'd survived the fight at the pie shop, there was no way they would accept him after this.

His ears drooped and his eyes started to fill, making him feel even worse. He dabbed at them angrily with his sleeve, turning away from the Bootles so they wouldn't see. He was as useless as a sea slug, just like Mr Lightly had always said. And worst of all, because of him, Tabitha was alone with that witch . . .

'Master Grubb,' said Mr Bootle. 'I hope you're not feeling sorry for yourself?' He laid a gentle hand on Grubb's shoulder.

'There's nothing you could have done, dear,' said Mrs Bootle. 'Nothing anyone could have done. Even Newt.'

It was just the sort of thing Grubb imagined his own parents would have told him. Mr Bootle even looked a bit like his father – just two or three times bigger.

That made him smile, so he gave up pretending and sniffed loudly.

'I suppose. I just wish I'd done something.'

'Nonsense,' said Mrs Bootle. 'You've looked after us, haven't you? Your parents would be so proud of you.'

'Best thing we can do now,' said Mr Bootle, 'is to

get to the lighthouse and wait for Newt. Can you manage that?'

Grubb nodded.

'Yes, Mr Bootle. I just—' He yelped. The old troll's fingers were digging hard into his shoulder.

'What's that?' asked Mr Bootle, in a shrill voice.

Then they all heard it. A pounding of hooves, and a clatter of wheels.

'Oh, Thalin,' whispered Grubb. 'The bushes. Let's hide in the bushes.'

The Bootles moved as fast they could, but the carriage came into view before they'd even reached the side of the road. They'd been seen. They must have been seen.

His pulse racing, Grubb looked around desperately for something he could use as a weapon. He hadn't managed to protect Tabitha, but he would protect the Bootles, if it was the last thing he did.

'Keep going,' he hissed. 'And stay down.'

There was a fallen tree by the roadside, and he snapped off a wet branch. It would have to do. It was too late to hide himself, so he crouched down where he was, in a patch of nettles, and waited, fingers numb on the damp bark of the branch.

There were whinnies and a jangle of reins, and the carriage came to rest a few feet away. He could smell the horses and see their breath puffing in the night air. He saw the figure of the driver in a tricorne hat, staring down at him. A troll. He tightened his grip on the broken bit of wood, and tensed, ready to charge.

'Joseph?' said the driver. 'What are you doing down there?'

Mr Bootle stood up from behind a bush.

'Paddy?' he said. 'What are you doing up there?'

Paddy Bootle took off his hat and grinned.

'Well, we were going to meet you lot at the lighthouse. But I don't want to interrupt your game of hide and seek. Who's winning?'

'"*He told me you had it*",' Newton repeated, when Grubb's story was finished. 'So the witch isn't working alone. Someone's helping her.'

It was dark in the carriage, and Grubb could only just make out the shapes of the watchmen sitting opposite.

'Well,' said Frank. 'Whoever it is has to be a total bilge-brain. Anyone can see she's as crazy as a crate of crabs.'

There was a glint of eyeglasses – Hal shaking his head.

'I disagree. Whoever is helping her certainly hasn't got bilge for brains. They might be a little reckless. Someone with a lot of ambition, perhaps . . .'

'What are you saying?'

'Do you think it was a coincidence that the witch was waiting in the alleyway at the *exact time* that Derringer's blackcoats attacked the pie shop?'

There was a pause, while the magician's words sank in.

'Cyrus Derringer,' said Newton.

'You think he's helping the witch?' said Frank doubtfully.

'It's possible. Maybe he arranged to attack the front of the shop, while she hid around the back.'

'But what would he get out of it?'

'Power, I reckon. Derringer doesn't care about money, but if the witch promised him some position – special advisor to the governor, or something – that would get him interested.'

Frank whistled.

'So he spends his whole time acting like he's better than us, and then he goes and sells out the whole stinking town.'

'Maybe,' said Newton. 'But let's forget about him for now. The witch has the wooden spoon. That means we have to warn Governor Wyrmwood. And we have to do it fast.'

'Yes,' said Hal. 'But Wyrmwood Manor will be

crawling with blackcoats. And in any case, we don't even know for sure that it's the governor that the witch is after.'

'True enough. But right now, it's the best guess we can make. So unless anyone has a better idea . . . ?'

'What about Tabs?' said Grubb. Even in the darkness, he felt them looking at him. 'We have to save her first, don't we?'

For a few moments, no one answered. Then Grubb felt Frank's big hand on his shoulder.

'Joseph, the witch isn't interested in Tabitha. Most likely she's on her way to Wyrmwood Manor right now. Either Tabs is with her, or . . .' He trailed off, leaving an uncomfortable silence.

Old Jon leaned forward and handed something to Grubb. It was heavy, made of wood and metal. A pistol.

'You'll need this,' said the elf, 'if you're coming with us.'

Grubb nodded dumbly. He was coming. Of course he was coming.

'And what about us, if you please?' snorted Mrs Bootle. 'What are we to do while you're off gallivanting in the governor's manor?'

'Don't worry, Mrs Bootle,' said Newton. 'We'll drop you at the lighthouse first.' He reached up and rapped on the top of the carriage, and they moved off with a jolt. A shaft of moonlight glanced in at the window, revealing the watchmen squeezed onto the bench opposite. All of them were frowning.

The carriage rolled on in silence. Grubb gripped his pistol tightly, his knuckles white.

'Do you think she'll be all right?' he said after a while.

Newton looked out of the window. Old Jon drew a knife and tested its edge with a finger. No one answered him.

Chapter Twenty-eight

The cool wet cloth soothed Eugene Wyrmwood's forehead, blotting out the pain and the dark thoughts. *Just try to forget*. He closed his eyes, sank back into the armchair and squeezed his hand tighter around the doll.

A picture of the watchman, Newton, flashed into his head. *A witch, your honour. Loose in Port Fayt*. He had demanded to investigate, and Eugene Wyrmwood had said no. What other answer could he have given?

By now, it was quite possible that Newton was dead.

He gritted his teeth. *Don't think about it. Think about the doll*. That always kept him calm.

He could remember, vividly, the day he got it. Every detail, every smell and every sound . . . Funny things, memories.

He had only been a boy, of course. Eight years old. Back then, his mother made him study all day, every day. But once a week she took him through the town – to the fairy market, to the velvetbean exchange and to Mr Harrison's Toy Emporium. Arabella Wyrmwood was the only child of Isaiah Wyrmwood, director of the Cockatrice Company, and it was her duty to represent the company's interests in Port Fayt. So once a week, young Eugene was allowed a few moments in the Toy Emporium, while Arabella spoke with the imp who owned it.

Even now, he could picture the shop as if he were still standing in it. The rows of dangling marionettes, the heaps of bright red balls, the hoops, skipping ropes, whistles . . . And best of all, the militiamen dolls, lined up in perfect rows, with smart identical uniforms and smooth smiling faces. So unlike the reality – the blackcoats he saw on the streets, who started fights and got drunk and beat up thieves. So much better than the reality.

He spoke up once, as they left the shop, his hand clenched tightly in his mother's. He told her how much he liked the militiamen, and how he wished he could have one of his own.

Only foolish children play with toys, she told him.

Beneath the damp cloth, Governor Wyrmwood frowned.

He had become obsessed. After that day, every time they went to the shop, he only had eyes for the militiamen dolls. He stood, staring at them, longing for them, until they had to leave.

One day, a young elf girl saw the militiamen dolls, and rushed up and took one, and her father bought it for her with a smile. And Eugene's heart sank, and he hated the little girl, and then felt terrible for a week afterwards because it hadn't been her fault, not really.

But after that, he wanted one more than ever.

Then came the day itself – the day he could never forget. Eugene's mother had told him to wait and not touch anything while she and Mr Harrison went into the back room to talk. They left him there, alone in the shop, with no one watching.

A minute passed. His heart was racing.

Two minutes. His palms slick with sweat.

Three minutes. Could he do this? He had never taken anything before. Never spoken back to his mother. Never disobeyed her for one moment.

The door to the back room opened, and without thinking, Eugene reached out, took the nearest doll and stuffed it into his satchel. As he did so, his hand brushed against the next doll along, pushing it slightly out of position.

His mother entered the room, followed by Mr Harrison.

'Come along,' she said. 'We've wasted enough time here. Back to your books.'

Eugene nodded. His face was hot. There was no way he could hide what he had done. His mother would find out. And then he saw Mr Harrison notice something. The doll, moved slightly out of rank. And his eyes flicked to Eugene's satchel, and up to the boy's face.

He knew.

And then, most vividly of all, Eugene remembered what happened next.

The old imp smiled. Smiled, and nodded.

It was fine. It was going to be fine.

And then they were walking away from the shop, the doll safe in Eugene's bag, his hand clenched tightly in his mother's.

Governor Wyrmwood took the damp cloth from his

face, and looked down at the doll. It had lost its knitted tricorne hat and its tiny wooden musket. Its black coat had all but worn through, and one eye was lopsided.

He held the doll tighter, tighter than ever, as a tear rolled down his cheek. Somehow, it always seemed to make things better.

Only foolish children play with toys.

It is a glorious summer's day, and a couple are walking along the quayside, arm in arm. Sailors and dockers nod to them as they pass, tipping their hats and smiling.

Tabitha knows she is dreaming, because the couple are her parents.

Her father makes a joke, and her mother laughs. They are just like she always pictured them. Him – tall, broad-shouldered, dark-haired, handsome. Her – young, beautiful, her long blonde hair shining in the sun. Tabitha drifts after them like a ghost. She longs to catch up, but she can't move fast enough. She can't even see their faces, can't even hear what they're talking about . . .

And already, she can feel everything changing. The sunshine is too bright, the sky too blue, the rooftops jagged like dragons' teeth. She knows what is coming, and she opens her mouth and howls, but no sound comes out, and her parents keep walking, and there is nothing – nothing – she can do about it. Finally they reach the house with the open window, and Tabitha screams until she has no voice left to scream with. Her father glances once, briefly, over his shoulder, and for an instant she sees his face, and her heart burns with love and the pain of loss.

A pair of blood-red bottles streak from the open window, and shattering glass rings in her ears, and the world comes apart in fragments. There is her mother, falling, clutching at her face. There are blackcoats, racing towards them. There are shouts, and sobs, and calls of 'Poison!' And there is the open window. She strains, reaching up as high as she can, desperate to see inside.

There is a figure there, wrapped in shadows. Just out of reach.

If only she can see who it is, everything will be different. Everything will . . .

She is awake.

It is dark here, wherever 'here' is. The only light comes from a candle, somewhere beyond the tiny barred window in the door. There is no way of knowing whether it is night or day outside. She lies motionless on a cold, hard floor, as the minutes drag by.

At last, she sits up. Her head feels like the whole Pageant of the Sea is marching through it. Gingerly, she tries to make herself remember. There was running, turning and – yes – the witch, bearing down on her like a nightmare, eyes pulsing black. Hands gripping her like talons, and then . . . nothing.

She had the dream about her parents. Strange. It's been years since she last had that dream.

Tabitha rises, using the rough stone wall as a support. The room is tiny – big enough to lie down in, but she has to hunch to stand. She peers through the window and sees just a narrow corridor, a stool with the candle on it and no one there. She checks her belt and pockets. The wooden spoon is gone. So are her knives.

This doesn't suit her at all.

'Hello?' she shouts. She bangs on the door and tries to open it, but of course, it's locked. Angry, upset and scared, she sits back down again. She is exhausted.

Questions pile up in her head, fighting for her attention. Where is she? Where is the Demon's Watch? Are they safe? What happened to Joseph, the grogshop boy? She scowls. What does she care? He got her into trouble with Newton, after all. She knows that isn't fair, but she decides that she deserves a little self-pity.

There is only one thing she can say for sure. She isn't dead. The witch hasn't killed her. Funny. That means something, probably. She just isn't sure what yet.

She lets her head loll back against the wall, and closes her eyes.

When the girl is snoring steadily, the old woman steps out of the shadows in the corner of the room. She bends down and lifts a strand of blue hair away from the face. Yes. She did not recognize her at first, in the hold of the ship. But now, up close, the resemblance is astonishing. Such a proud, stubborn face. The old woman smiles to herself, as memories swirl in her mind.

PART FOUR
The Pageant of the Sea

Chapter Twenty-nine

Grubb darted out from behind an ornamental hedge, keeping as low as he could, and threw himself down behind the stone plinth of a statue. Peering round it, he could see the ground-floor windows of Wyrmwood Manor glimmering in the night, no more than fifty feet away. One last sprint across the lawn and they would be there.

He hefted his pistol. *Don't cock it until you're inside,* Frank had told him. *If it goes off before then, chances are you'll either shoot your leg off or alert the blackcoats. Or both.*

'Ready?' whispered a voice, from behind his shoulder. He turned and was face to face with

Newton, who was crouched with a long black staff resting on one knee. Grubb couldn't believe how silently the big man could move.

'Ready,' he said.

Newton signalled towards a fountain a few feet away, where Hal and Old Jon were lying in wait, then tapped him on the shoulder.

'Go!'

Grubb launched himself forward, past the statue, his feet slipping every other step on the wet grass. He tried not to think about what would happen if a militiaman spotted them. *Just run.*

There was a stretch of gravel at the end of the lawn, below the windows of the manor. As they reached it, each watchman dropped down into a crouch and crept up to the wall, as quietly as they could.

The four of them paused, panting, listening. Muffled voices carried from inside.

'How come we always get these stupid jobs?' said someone.

'What do you mean, stupid jobs?' came the reply. 'This is important, this is. The governor's life is in our hands.'

'Oh come on. Nothing's going to happen. As if anyone would be crazy enough to break into

Wyrmwood Manor the night before the Pageant of the Sea.'

Wordlessly, Newton pointed Grubb to the nearest window. Grubb nodded and edged along, his heart thumping, until he was right underneath. He stood and peered inside.

It was the largest room he had ever seen, with a long table running down the centre, draped in a white tablecloth – a dining room. Moonlight spilled through the vast windows, illuminating ancient tapestries on the walls, delicate carvings on wooden dining chairs and elaborate silver candelabras. Grubb saw that his pointed goblin ears were casting long shadows on the table, and he pulled his head back at once, trying to make himself as invisible as possible.

There were two black-coated militiamen in the room – one fat, with a sergeant's silver stripes, leaning back in a chair with his feet up; the other short and stout, sitting on the table and swinging his legs. Both men had crossbows slung on their backs.

It took Grubb a few moments to recognize them, now that they were in uniform. It was Sergeant Culpepper and Private Sprunt.

'The trouble is,' Sprunt was saying, 'Derringer don't like you. Think about it. Why else would we get stuck with babysitting the governor, when we were the ones what reported that stupid girl and her stupid spoon in the first place? You'd think it'd be us what get to help him deal with the Demon's Watch, but oh, no . . . It's Farringdon and Smythe, same as usual. He don't like you.'

'That's not true,' said Culpepper uncertainly.

'It stinking well is true. Corporal Finch told me.'

'Told you what?'

'Said he overheard Colonel Derringer talking to Sergeant Smythe. He said you were as useless as a grogshop what's run out of grog.'

'Walrus dung.'

'It is not walrus dung.'

Grubb turned back to the watchmen, held up two fingers and pointed out where the militiamen were in the room. Then he made the hand signal Frank had taught him for 'crossbows'. Newton nodded. He and Old Jon were both armed – Newton with his smooth, polished black staff, Old Jon with an ancient, gnarled oak cudgel. Two days ago, Grubb would have been shocked to see an elderly elf with a weapon like that. But after being thrown in a shark pit and attacked by a witch, not much seemed to surprise him any more.

'Well, all right,' came Sprunt's voice again. 'Maybe it is walrus dung. But facts are facts. We're sitting around here twiddling our thumbs, while the rest of the militia is off winning all the glory. Where's the justice in that? At least we get a night off, that's all I can—'

Cracks of musket fire rang out, and somewhere in the building, glass shattered.

'What in all the stinking sea is that?'

'Now!' roared Newton.

At the exact same instant, he and Old Jon smashed a window each and hurled themselves through. They leaped across the carpet like avenging seraphs – even Old Jon, who was probably about a hundred years old. Sergeant Culpepper and Private Sprunt had barely got the crossbows off their backs before their attackers were on them, staff and cudgel swinging in unison. Grubb shut his eyes.

Thunk! Crack!

And then he and Hal were scrambling through the broken windows, while Newton and Old Jon picked up the blackcoats' fallen crossbows and hurled them outside.

Grubb couldn't believe he was actually inside the governor's manor. He touched an exquisite wooden dining chair to make sure that it was real, and gazed up at the tapestries in awe. They showed hunting scenes from the Dark Age, with human horsemen, almost life-size, pursuing a deer through a forest.

'Bootles are doing us proud,' said Newton, nodding towards the East Wing, as he relieved the unconscious militiamen of their pistols and passed one to Old Jon. It sounded like a full-scale battle was going on.

'Just as well they're supposed to be the diversion,' muttered Hal.

Newton sighted down his pistol at an imaginary target.

'All right, let's go. Keep your eyes peeled, and your voices down. Remember, the witch might be here already.'

Grubb carefully cocked his own pistol, like Frank had shown him. His heart was pounding even faster now, and his palms were sweaty. He tucked the gun under his arm and rubbed his hands on his shirt. He was ready for anything, he told himself. But the thought of seeing the witch lurching out of the shadows again made his stomach knot tightly. He took hold of the pistol, gripping it hard, but keeping his finger well away from the trigger.

Leaving the noise behind, they made their way out of the dining room, over the vast marble floor of the hall and onto the carpeted stairway.

Grubb almost forgot his fear as he looked around him. The hall was so vast, it seemed as if it could have fitted the whole of the Legless Mermaid inside it –

although it was hard to believe that the Legless Mermaid even existed in the same world as Wyrmwood Manor.

They crept up the stairs, onto the first floor, down a dark corridor and round a corner. Newton motioned for them to stop, and paused, thinking. He headed on a short distance, then stopped again.

'Are you sure you remember the way?' asked Hal nervously.

Newton shook his head.

'No. This place is a maze.'

It was true. The moonlit corridors snaked in every direction – gloomy, wallpapered, lined with polished oak doors and gilt-framed paintings – and all looking exactly the same. The pictures inside the frames were the only things that varied. Some were portraits of long-dead Wyrmwoods. Others showed ships out on the sea. Most were scenes of ancient battles, with heroes armoured in silver and gold, slaughtering whole armies of trolls and goblins. The victims were rendered grotesquc, with lumpy black skin, giant fangs and red eyes.

They passed a large window, the moonlight shining through onto a painting that was almost twice the size of the others. Grubb gazed up at it. It was a portrait of Governor Wyrmwood seated in a chair, wearing an expensive-looking velvet coat, his raven-black hair slicked back and his eyes brimming with confidence.

'I think this is it,' said Newton, a few doors further down the corridor.

Grubb was about to move on when he was distracted by a smaller, older painting next to Governor Wyrmwood, half hidden in shadow. This one was neglected, covered in dust but beautiful. It showed a young woman with high cheekbones, a sharp nose, blonde hair scraped tightly back and a piercing gaze. She looked stern, maybe even a little cruel. There was something strangely familiar about her. MS ARABELLA WYRMWOOD read a gold plate below. Grubb looked up again. Her eyes held his attention. So dark, almost . . . black.

Cold and black as obsidian.

His jaw dropped. He felt like he had been punched. Could it really be . . . He looked closer at the painting, and his head swam. Once again, the witch's words flashed through his mind.

He told me you had it.

It was like Newton had said. The witch wasn't acting alone. But it wasn't Colonel Cyrus Derringer who was helping her.

'Wait,' he whispered. 'Everyone, wait a minute—'

'Everybody ready?' asked Newton, spinning his staff in one hand.

The watchmen nodded.

Newton's boot crashed into the door, sending it flying open into the room. He paused, tensed and ready for combat, his eyes flicking rapidly, expertly around the room.

'What in all the sea?' said a voice from inside.

'Wrong choice,' said Newton. 'Run.'

Blackcoats piled out of the room behind him as he raced back up the corridor.

'Hold your fire!' shouted one of the militiamen. 'Take them alive.'

Hal and Old Jon were already running, and Grubb joined them. They skidded round a corner, as Old Jon let fly with his pistol.

Newton was ahead of them, pulling open a smaller door.

'In here,' he whispered. The four of them bundled inside, and Newton turned a key that was sitting in the lock. 'We'll barricade the door. That should hold them up until—'

'What are you doing here?'

They all turned. The room Newton had chosen was a large, dusty library, full of towering mahogany bookshelves. Just like the rest of the manor, it was lit by moonlight – a pale glow came through windows that reached from the floor to the ceiling, at the far end of the room. But what struck them most was the figure who had just stepped from the shadows by the windows, in front of a large desk covered in books and scrolls. The figure who'd just spoken.

Governor Eugene Wyrmwood.

Chapter Thirty

The governor's face was a poor match for the one in his portrait. It was far older, lined, pale and hollow-eyed, as though its owner needed a good night's sleep. And in place of the proud, commanding gaze was an expression of absolute terror.

'Get out,' he said. 'Get out at once.' His reading glasses trembled in his hand.

'Governor Wyrmwood,' said Newton. 'Thank Thalin we've found you. Your life is in danger.'

'Wait,' said Grubb. 'It's not like that—'

But Newton hadn't heard him.

'The witch I warned you about yesterday, your honour – she's coming for you. She's in possession of an extremely dangerous wand, and she—'

'What are you talking about?'

'Arabella,' burst out Grubb. 'He's talking about Arabella Wyrmwood.'

Newton stared at him. The governor's mouth twitched, and his eyes glazed over.

There was a long silence.

'Arabella,' said the governor softly. 'Yes, that was her name.'

Grubb stepped forward.

'I saw the witch's face,' he said. 'When I was in the alley behind the pie shop. And then I saw it again, just now, in the painting in the hall. She was much younger, but I'm sure it was the same person. The witch is Miss Arabella Wyrmwood, who is . . .'

'. . . Governor Wyrmwood's mother,' said Hal.

The governor had turned paler than ever.

Newton shook his head. 'That doesn't make sense. Arabella Wyrmwood died, ten years ago.'

'But she . . . she can't have. I saw her. What if . . . what if she was in hiding, or something. Or . . . or . . .'

He looked to the governor for a hint that he might be right, but Eugene Wyrmwood was staring straight ahead, saying nothing. A sick feeling began to build in his stomach. If he was wrong about this . . .

There was a muffled beating on the door, making everyone jump.

'I'm busy,' barked Wyrmwood, which made everyone jump again. 'Leave me alone.'

'Yes, your honour. Our apologies.'

'Mr Wyrmwood,' said Newton, as the militiamen's footsteps receded along the corridor. 'We don't have much time. We need to know the truth.'

The governor's eyes were fixed on the carpet.

'I didn't know she was still alive.' His voice was a hoarse croak, and he swallowed. 'Not until this afternoon. She came to visit me, and asked me to help her find something. A wooden spoon. I said . . . I . . . And then, later, Colonel Derringer arrived with one of his sergeants. The man had got into a tavern brawl over the spoon. He didn't know what it really was, of course. But I knew. I . . . told my mother where to find you.'

He took out a handkerchief and dabbed at his brow.

'You'd better tell us what's going on,' said Newton, quietly. 'And tell us fast.'

The governor hesitated for just a moment. Then he turned to a glass display case that stood near the desk, lifted the lid and drew out something. It was the most beautiful sword that Grubb had ever seen. It looked like an antique from the Dark Age. The slender blade was carved with swirling patterns and the silver hilt was encrusted with white star-stones. The governor held it delicately, the blade flat on both palms, as if it might break at any moment. It was obvious that he wasn't used to handling weapons.

'This was the blade of Corin the Bold,' he said in a hushed voice, as if he might offend the sword by speaking any louder. 'Are any of you, by any chance, familiar with the Wyrmwood family's genealogy?'

The watchmen shook their heads.

'Corin was our most illustrious ancestor. He was a warrior and a hero. He roamed the Old World more than five hundred years ago, in the early Dark Age, fighting for glory. He dedicated his life to the protection of humanity. With this very sword, he slew countless trolls, goblins and ogres.'

He held the blade up to catch the moonlight, and for a moment, Grubb saw something unexpected in the governor's eyes. Was it . . . sadness?

'As you know, the League of the Light has sworn to honour the memory of men like Corin. They believe we have become corrupted by peace, and that war is the only way to sweep away the demonspawn and bring light to the world. Their work is well advanced in the Old World. Now they turn to Port Fayt. After that, the New World. They intend to bring a new dawn.'

Throughout his speech, he hadn't looked any of the watchmen in the eye.

'You are the governor of Port Fayt,' growled Newton. 'It's your duty to protect its people, not betray them to the League of the Light.'

Governor Wyrmwood winced.

'"Betrayal" is such a strong word. Admittedly, I was forced to conceal my mother's allegiance to the League, but—'

'They're insane,' said Hal, unable to keep the disgust out of his voice. 'They'd plunge us back to the Dark Age if they could. Do you understand that?'

'And what does the wooden spoon have to do with this?' asked Newton. 'What does that witch want with it?'

A pained look came over Wyrmwood's face.

'Please, don't call her that. I won't have her called that.' His voice shook with emotion.

'He's lost his mind,' said Hal angrily. 'We're not going to get anything useful from him.'

A tear rolled down the governor's cheek. He staggered and collapsed into a chair, clutching the sword tightly.

'Mother,' he whispered.

'I don't believe it,' said Grubb suddenly. 'I mean, I don't think you believe it. What you said about the League.'

The watchmen looked at him.

'Joseph . . .' said Newton.

But Grubb shook his head.

'No, it's all right. I think I understand.'

He crossed the floor and knelt in front of the governor. A little voice in his head was squealing at him, telling him that he was being stupid, that he couldn't do a thing to help. But he pushed it deep down inside, and tried to imagine he was someone strong and important, like Captain Newton, or Thalin the Navigator. He took a deep breath, and let it out slowly.

There's a little bit of demon and a little bit of seraph in everyone, Joseph. Don't let anyone tell you different.

'Mr Wyrmwood. You don't hate goblins and trolls and imps. You don't want them dead. I know you want to help your mother, but you're not like her. Please, you have to tell us what she's planning.'

The governor was staring at the sword in his lap, tracing a pattern on the blade with a finger.

'It doesn't matter now, anyway,' he said. 'It doesn't matter what I think.'

'What do you mean?'

'It will all be over soon. Mother will make sure of that.'

'Why? What is she going to do?'

The governor turned angry eyes on Grubb.

'She is my mother!' he said wildly. 'No matter what, she is my mother.'

'No, she isn't.'

Grubb regretted saying it as soon as the words left his lips. It was too much. The governor would be furious.

But no.

Instead he just sat, deathly still, his mouth half open. Grubb ignored the little voice screaming in his head, and stumbled blindly on.

'I mean, she was once, of course, but now . . . ?'

Still, the governor said nothing.

'My father was a goblin,' said Grubb, fighting to keep his voice steady. 'He loved my mother very much. I know he did. But that wasn't enough.'

'I don't want to hear this,' snapped the governor.

'They killed him, Mr Wyrmwood. They caught him one night on the docks, came at him with sticks and knives and . . . Because he was a goblin. *Just because he was a goblin.*'

The governor's expression was flickering between

anger, hurt and confusion. He was like a trapped animal, with nowhere to run.

'I don't want to hear this,' he said again, in a small voice.

'My mother died afterwards, Mr Wyrmwood. I was five years old. Arabella might be part of your family, but . . . but some things are even more important than that. You have to tell us. What is she planning?'

Governor Wyrmwood was staring past him, at something on the desk. Grubb turned. Among the litter of scrolls was a ragged old doll, dressed as a militiaman, propped up against a pile of books. And when Grubb looked back, there was some powerful emotion in the governor's eyes that he couldn't identify.

'She killed him, you know,' said the governor.

'She . . . er . . . who?'

'Mr Harrison. The imp. The toy shop owner. Killed him. That's what she told me.'

Grubb struggled to make sense of what Eugene Wyrmwood was saying.

'Did . . . Did your mother give you that doll? And she bought it from this Mr Harrison?'

Wyrmwood shook his head, and for the first time since they'd entered the library, he smiled. A strange smile, private and sad. But definitely a smile.

'No, no,' he said. 'Of course not. Only foolish children play with toys.'

There was a heavy silence, then the sword clattered to the floor and Governor Wyrmwood gulped in air.

'Oh, Thalin,' he gasped. 'Very well. The end of Port Fayt. That's what she's planning. The end of Port Fayt.'

Chapter Thirty-one

Grubb's hands were shaking, and his breathing was ragged. He sank down onto the floor, trying not to think about what he'd been saying, trying not to remember his parents. He shook his head fiercely. It wasn't the time or the place for this.

'Go on,' said Newton. 'Keep talking. Tell us everything.'

Colour was returning to the governor's cheeks.

'Yes, yes, of course. I will tell you what I can.'

He closed his eyes for a moment, as if preparing himself. When he spoke, his voice was low and calm.

'My mother . . . She began the study of magic when she was a child. By the time I was born, she was the most gifted magician in Port Fayt, although she kept it a secret, of course. She never married, and I never knew my father. He was a gentleman from the Old World, I believe. Mother and I were so happy until . . . until she began to meet with agents of the League of the Light, and to speak of continuing the work of our ancestor Corin. Then – it was ten years ago – something . . . something terrible happened, and she had to leave Port Fayt in secret.'

There was a knock at the door, but everyone ignored it.

'Afterwards, the Cockatrice Company gave it out that she had died. Only a few of us knew the truth – that she was forced into exile, and told never to return. She left because of a crime that she had committed, on behalf of the League of the Light. We couldn't . . . we couldn't let her go to the Brig.'

'What crime?' said Grubb. But even as he asked it, he realized what the answer was going to be. Tabitha's words were coming back to him. *That old fool Wyrmwood knows something* . . .

'The crime of murder,' said Governor Wyrmwood, in a hollow voice. 'The murder of the governor of Port Fayt, Alfred Mandeville, and his wife, Jessica. It was my mother who threw the bottles of griffin blood. My mother who killed them. *My mother*.'

Another knock at the door, louder this time.

'The Mandeville Plot,' breathed Hal. 'And now she has Tabitha Mandeville, too.'

'Oh, Thalin,' said Grubb.

The door crashed open and blackcoats barged their way in, muskets levelled at the intruders.

'Go away,' screeched Wyrmwood. 'Leave us alone.'

'Can't do that, your honour. Colonel Derringer's orders are to protect you and keep out intruders.'

'I'm the governor of Port Fayt, you idiot!'

The sergeant wrestled with the problem, and failed to find a solution.

'Just lay down your weapons,' he said at last. 'Then we can talk about—'

BANG!

The sergeant's head jerked backwards, and he went down like a log. Panicked, his men let fly with their muskets.

Old Jon's cudgel swung into the nearest blackcoat, knocking him into a bookcase and dislodging several massive tomes.

'Hold fire,' someone was shouting. 'For the sky's sake!' But the militiamen were already drawing sabres and pistols.

Grubb dived behind a bookcase as more shots were fired. He heard a strangled whimper of pain, and turned to look. It was Governor Wyrmwood, staggering back against his desk, his face screwed up in agony. One hand gripped a smoking pistol, still pointed at where the militia sergeant had been standing.

'How dare they?' he rasped. 'This is Wyrmwood Manor . . .'

Across the library floor, Newton fired a pistol from behind another stack of shelves, while Hal raced past and came crashing down behind the governor's desk. Grubb saw his lips moving, as he worked on a spell. He hoped it was a good one.

Peering round the edge of the bookcase, he saw Old Jon knock out another militiaman, and run back towards them. The other blackcoats seemed to have taken cover. Reloading, probably.

There were a good thirty feet of library floor between the watchmen and the blackcoats now.

'Mr Wyrmwood?'

The governor groaned. He was slumped against the front of the desk, blood seeping into the carpet from where the stray militia musket ball had hit him. He turned glazed eyes towards Grubb.

'Find her. You must find her.'

'Where?'

'Out at sea. Aboard the frigate *Incorruptible*. It's loaded with all the necessary equipment . . .' He coughed, and red drool bubbled down his chin.

'Go on,' said Grubb desperately. 'Where exactly?'

'Two leagues south of the Lonely Isle. But you must hurry. Tomorrow is when she'll do it. The day of the pageant.'

'And Tabs? Where's Tabitha?'

'Mother took her.' He spluttered, choking on blood. 'She wants her dead, of course.'

Grubb shot a nervous glance past the bookcase. There was a volley of musket fire, and several more books fell onto the floor. He spotted one of the black-coats scuttling closer, using the bookshelves as cover.

'Mr Wyrmwood,' he said quickly. 'What is the wooden spoon for? What is your mother planning to do?'

The governor said nothing.

'Mr Wyrmwood?'

And with a jolt, he knew that Eugene Wyrmwood was dead. The governor's lifeless body slouched, head lolling forward, just like the doll on the desk. Grubb bit his lip.

Hal stood up from behind the table, throwing his arms wide. The room seemed to tremble for a moment, and he collapsed against the wall, instantly drained of energy.

There was a creaking sound, and on every side the

vast bookcases began to fall, knocking into each other like giant triominoes and crashing to the floor in clouds of dust and books. By the time the noise had subsided, the library was unrecognizable. The Demon's Watch were surrounded by a barricade of bookcases, blocking them off from the militiamen. Books were scattered everywhere. For a few seconds there was silence.

Old Jon smashed the window with his cudgel. Behind him, there were scuffling sounds as the militiamen tried to find a way over or through the bookcases.

Newton swiped along the window pane with his staff, clearing the broken glass, while Old Jon pulled a coil of rope from his knapsack and tied it to the desk.

'Should hold the weight,' he said. 'As long as that desk's been made properly.' He tossed the rest of the coil through the gap where the window had been, and nodded at Grubb. 'Off you go, lad. Time to get out of here.'

The Bootle twins were waiting for them at the gates of Wyrmwood Manor. It was almost dawn, and the sun had begun to appear on the horizon.

'Hello, you lot,' said Paddy, slinging his blunderbuss over a shoulder. 'Did you find Tabs?'

Old Jon shook his head.

'Wait,' gasped Grubb. It had been a long sprint from the manor house, and he was only just getting his breath back. 'I know where she is. The Lonely Isle. That's where the witch is heading, and she's taking Tabs with her.'

Newton looked at him curiously.

'You've done well, Joseph,' he said. 'Better than the rest of us, that's for sure.'

At any other time Grubb would have been pleased, but he didn't feel like celebrating right now.

'So, we'll be needing a ship then,' said Paddy. 'And a fast one.'

'A vessel, on the eve of the Pageant of the Sea,' said Hal. He was pale and breathless, still recovering from the ordeal of his spell. 'That won't be easy to find.'

'True enough.'

'No, wait,' said Grubb again. This time they all turned to look at him. 'I think I know where we can find one. I think I know where we can find the fastest ship in the Ebony Ocean.'

Chapter Thirty-two

Slik was having a terrible night.

It had started well enough. The fight at the pie shop had been a riot, and after that, he'd just needed to find an idiot stupid enough to employ him. How hard could it be?

He'd tried the Marlinspike fairy market first, hoping to undercut the fairy dealers by selling himself cheap. But it was late, and the market was shut up by the time he got there.

So he'd flicked the rainwater from his wings and taken off again, still optimistic, this time heading for the grogshops. Drunkards were easy to swindle, in his experience, and during the Festival of the Sea they were always in good supply. The first customer he tried was a little too drunk – a stinking great troll who announced that he'd never tasted fairy before, and promptly tried to eat him. Everyone in the tavern seemed to think it was an excellent joke, apart from Slik.

At the next inn he'd found an elf who seemed interested. Slik had always believed that elves were honourable, trustworthy folk – perfect. But just as they were negotiating prices, the scrawny bilge rat slammed a mug down over him, trapping him on the table and drenching him with a stale slop of grog. Slik only managed to escape when a fight broke out and the elf got a dagger rammed between his ribs.

Wet, hungry and sticky from the grog, Slik was starting to wonder if leaving Newton had been the biggest mistake of his life. He could still go back to Jeb, he reckoned. Except that the Snitch would probably think he had something to do with the blackcoats turning up at the pie shop. That was what you got with goblins.

Finally, a few hours before dawn, he found a dry patch under an awning and began to arrange an old canvas sack on the cobblestones as a mattress. He could hardly believe that he, Slik, the fairy who double-crossed Captain Newton of the Demon's Watch, was going to have to spend a night sleeping out in the cold. He felt deeply sorry for himself.

'So,' said a voice from behind him. 'What have we here?'

Before he could move, his wings were pinched firmly together and he was lifted up to his attacker's face. What in all the blasted sea . . . ? It was a cat. A common cat had managed to sneak up on him and trap him. This was a new low.

For a few moments, Slik lost all self-control. He knew a wide range of colourful words that Newton hadn't liked him using, and this seemed like the perfect moment to try them out.

'How delightful,' said the cat, when Slik had finished.

At once the ginger fur drew back up to its forehead to become ginger hair, and the snub nose grew to become a human nose, and the paw that clamped Slik's wings together became a finger and a thumb. The ginger-furred cat was a ginger-haired man. Only his yellow eyes stayed the same.

A shapeshifter. Slik was impressed, and tried his best not to show it.

The man produced a sugar lump, large, silvery-white and glittering. Slik only just managed to hold himself back. He hadn't eaten since lunch time.

'You want some sugar, little friend?' said the shapeshifter. 'Because I'm in need of a fairy.'

* * *

Grubb pushed open the door and stepped inside the Legless Mermaid.

It was strange. Everything looked the same – the same smoky air and flickering lantern-light, the same driftwood tables and chairs, the same crowd of half-cut sailors – but it was all different, somehow. Smaller. After everything that had happened, to think that he had spent the last six years living here, day in, day out . . . It made him shudder.

The watchmen came through after him, and Frank closed the door. Grubb scanned the room. No sign of Mr Lightly, but there was Phineus Clagg, just as he'd hoped, sitting at the same table he'd sat at on the day of the Grand Party. This time he'd brought company. They were smugglers, by the looks of them – five or six, all leaning in to listen, and nodding earnestly as their captain held forth. The youngest, a boy not much older than Grubb, was frowning as he tried to keep up.

'So, Cap'n,' Grubb heard him say, above the chatter, 'when you escaped from this "Demon's Watch", was that before you killed all the pirates?'

'Aye, before,' said Phineus Clagg. 'No, after. But before the battle with the shark.'

His audience all nodded and chorused '*Hmm*'s and '*Aaaah*'s.

'And what about the beautiful governor's daughter, Cap'n?'

'Yeah, where is she?'

'Oh,' said Clagg, waving his hand as though it was unimportant. 'She, er . . . she went away. Now then, I reckon it's time for another round o' them bowel-busters, eh? And another plate o' them delicious eels!'

Grubb approached, with Newton and the twins behind him, ready to step in if they were needed. It made him feel ten times more confident.

'Excuse me, Mr Clagg,' he said.

Clagg peered up from his tankard and recognized him. A broad grin spread across his face.

'Well, blow me down if it ain't young master Grubb.'

Then he noticed the watchmen looming behind, casting a shadow over the table.

'Oh. You lot again.'

'That's right,' said Paddy, with a wink. 'Us lot. Did you miss us?'

'Grubb,' said Clagg. 'I trusted you, matey, and now this? It's low, that's what it is.'

'No, don't worry,' said Grubb quickly. 'They're not going to throw you in the Brig. I made them promise. We've just come to ask a favour.'

'A what?'

Grubb took a deep breath.

'We need to, er . . . borrow your ship and crew.'

The smugglers chuckled.

'Are you pulling me leg?' asked Clagg.

'We need to set sail at once, and we're headed for the Lonely Isle. It's less than a day's journey.'

The captain pulled a face and downed his tankard.

'Less than a day's journey . . . Well, matey, since you asked so nicely, I might consider helping you out. But if I do, I'll want something in return.'

'Name it,' said Frank.

Phineus Clagg jerked a thumb at the watchmen.

'This lot off me back for a year; let me do business in Port Fayt, in private. How does that sound?'

'A month,' said Newton sternly.

Clagg opened his mouth to argue, then shut it again. His eyes flicked upwards, as if he was trying to calculate how much cargo he could run in that time.

'All right, me beauties.' He grinned. 'Anything for old friends.' He turned to a fat dwarf sitting beside him. 'Bosun. Ready the *Sharkbane*. We leave in one hour.'

'That's more like it,' said Paddy.

There was a shout from the other side of the tavern.

'MONGREEEEEEEEEL!'

Grubb felt his ears twitch, and a jolt ran through his insides, as if his heart had fallen right through his body and onto the floor. He'd just been starting to think they might get out of here without hearing that voice again. No such luck.

There was a commotion among the other customers, as the large, purple-faced figure of Mr Lightly shoved his way towards Captain Clagg's table, wringing a dishcloth as if he was trying to throttle it. Grubb edged round the table, making sure there was some solid furniture between him and his uncle.

'MONGREL!' barked Mr Lightly again, and he slammed his fists down on the wood, making the tankards rattle. 'You stinking, sneaking cockroach! You troll snot! Where in all the blue sea have you been?'

'Mr Lightly, I—'

'How DARE you run out like that, you mongrel maggot? I've been up to my ears in work here, and without a soul to help me. Did you even think of me for one minute, you selfish little greyskin scum? You useless mottled bilge-brain? Well, let me tell you, mongrel, I'm going to have you mopping floors until you beg for mercy. I'm going to have you scrubbing dishes until—'

'Excuse me,' said Newton. 'Did you say *mongrel*?'

The tavern seemed suddenly very quiet. Oblivious, Mr Lightly shoved a plump finger at Newton's chest.

'Yes, that's what I said. And who in the name of

Thalin the stinking Navigator do you think you are, stealing my tavern boy away without so much as a—'

'Mongrel,' said Newton thoughtfully. 'That's a word for a dog. Not a person.' He stepped forward, his massive frame towering over the innkeeper, who was beginning to look a lot less sure of himself.

'My grandfather was an ogre,' said Newton. 'Do you want to call me a mongrel?' He took the dishcloth from the innkeeper's trembling fingers, and laid it on the table.

Mr Lightly shook his head, eyes wide as cannonballs. Grubb had never seen his uncle look so pale.

'You see these marks?' Newton held out his arms, showing the red blister scars that ran round his wrists. 'The League gave me these. The League of the Light. Long time ago, I worked in the zephyrum mines in Garran, back in the Old World, on account of my grandfather being an ogre. They took him, and I went too, along with all my family. We couldn't leave him in there alone. Ten years, I was in those mines. The things that happened . . .' He trailed off, leaving a long pause.

The tavern was in total silence now.

'I was a boy when I first went underground. I was lucky, though – I got out, and came to Port Fayt. Wish I could say the same for the rest of my family. So you see, I didn't come over the Ebony Ocean to hear talk like that. Understand?'

Mr Lightly nodded.

'Now, we'll be needing Joseph. And it's time we were off. You going to say goodbye?'

The whole tavern was watching. Mr Lightly opened his mouth, searching for something to say that might save face. And then he crumbled.

'Goodbye,' he murmured. 'Goodbye, mongr— er, Grubb.'

'Joseph,' corrected Newton.

'Er, yes, sorry. I mean, goodbye, Joseph.'

For the first time in his life, Joseph Grubb looked his uncle straight in his bloodshot, piggy eyes.

'Goodbye, Uncle,' he said. 'I . . .' He stumbled to a halt. He could say whatever he wanted now. The Demon's Watch would protect him. He could call Mr Lightly names, or try to explain how angry it made him when Mr Lightly had spoken about his parents – called his mother goblin-lover or traitor, or called his father greyskin or sneak, or thief, or worse. But after all those harsh words, all he felt was exhaustion, and relief that he would never have to listen to it ever again.

'I won't be coming back,' was all he said.

Chapter Thirty-three

The dawn was beautiful. Soft pink and orange light spread from the distant horizon, picking out the peaks of the rolling waves. Unfortunately, Tabitha was feeling far too ill to appreciate it. She groaned and retched violently over the gunwale.

'Never been out to sea before, eh?' said the helmsman.

'Go and boil your head.'

The man shrugged and went back to ignoring her, humming softly to himself.

She shook her head to clear it, and looked up at the sunrise, trying to work out which direction they were heading in. Sun rises in the east, sets in the west. So they were sailing north. Going fast, too.

Tabitha started to feel sorry for herself again, and didn't bother to fight it. She wished there was someone here with her. Even that grogshop boy Joseph would do. He was a bit wet, obviously, and not much good in a fight. But when you spent all day washing tankards, she supposed that was all you could expect. And he hadn't made a big fuss when she told him about her parents. Now that she had a minute to think about it, she supposed he was . . . nice, sort of. She missed him. Sort of. At least he—

Her stomach heaved without warning, and this time she really was sick, all down the side of the ship.

Dejected, she slumped down with her back against the gunwale, and pulled her thin blanket around her. She was exhausted. The night had been bitterly cold, and she hadn't felt like sleeping, anyway. All the same, might as well do something. In the morning light, she could see the ship properly for the first time, and began looking for clues – anything that would help her work out where they were going.

She was fairly sure it was a frigate, but that didn't help much. A blackcoat guarded the captain's cabin, his tricorne low, so that his face was hidden in shadow. Whatever was going on, apparently the militia were in on it too. *Scum*. Apart from that, there wasn't much to go on. Except . . .

The ship's dinghy was cluttered with a strange contraption of carpentry and metalwork, like nothing Tabitha had seen before. It reminded her of a crane, a miniature version of the ones that stevedores used to unload cargo ships. But instead of a block and tackle hanging from the end, there was a long metallic rod with a pointed tip. She recognized the blue sheen of zephyrum. The magic metal. Hal had told her about it once. Just like when you put an iron poker in the fire, the iron got hot, if you exposed zephyrum to magic, it got . . . magical. She screwed up her eyes, trying to work out what the machinery was for.

'Have you guessed yet?' said the old woman.

The voice came from nowhere, making her jump. She could have sworn that the witch wasn't anywhere near her a second ago. A vague anger stirred in her at the presence of her captor, but she was too tired and sick to do anything about it.

'Are you going to tell me?'

The old woman gazed out to sea. She looked different in the morning light. Behind the alley at Bootles' Pie Shop she'd seemed like some black demon from the Northern Wastes. But now her shabby grey cloak hung from her like the rags of a beggar, and what Tabitha could see of her face was pitiful – lined and twisted, ruined in some way. She didn't seem very magical. More like a sad, tired old woman.

'Do you know where we're going, child?'

'Why would I, for the sky's sake?'

'Of course, why would you?' The woman licked her lips. 'Have you ever heard stories of the Farian Trench?'

Tabitha's stomach lurched, but this time it wasn't because of the rolling of the ship. Yes, she had heard stories of the Farian Trench. Stories for children and old wives. She looked up into the witch's face, expecting to see some hint that she was being made fun of. But the witch just carried on staring out to sea, her face stony and still.

'We're really going there? To the trench?'

The old woman nodded.

'But . . . what . . .'

She tailed off. There could only be one reason to go to the Farian Trench.

And with a dizzying feeling, like standing on the edge of a cliff, Tabitha began to realize what the zephyrum rod was for. What the wooden spoon was for. What the old woman had been planning to do, all along.

'We will bring an end,' said the old woman, 'and a beginning.'

'You've lost your mind,' said Tabitha, fighting down her horror, along with the urge to be sick again. 'You must have. Why, in Thalin's name . . .?'

'I've been waiting so long for this,' said the old woman wistfully, as if she hadn't heard Tabitha. 'You cannot begin to imagine. I tried to cleanse this town once before, but I was repaid with exile. My friends cast me out and turned their backs on me. Even my son did nothing to save me.

'Ten long years I spent, away from my home in Port Fayt. Ten years gone, but not wasted. When I first set foot in the Old World, I understood so little. I longed for my fine dresses, and my mirrors, and my jewels. But I changed. I learned. I studied night and day in the libraries of Azurmouth, of Renneth and Ysiland. I knew that in the end I would return, and cross the Ebony Ocean back to Port Fayt.'

Her voice had grown soft, dreamy and contented.

'The times are changing, child. The League of the Light is conquering the Old World, their troops vanquishing all before them. Port Fayt will be next. It is a nest of demonspawn. A pit of darkness, ripe to be purged. And what more fitting end than this? What better time than now, at the Festival of the Sea, when

Fayters throng the streets for their foul pageant? Those who honour Thalin the Navigator will die for it.'

Tabitha bit her lip until she tasted blood. She could think of a lot of things to say about the old woman's plan, and not one of them seemed like a good idea. But she couldn't just stay silent.

'You can't really believe that filth about trolls and goblins being demonspawn. There was peace between the people of the Old World for centuries before the League came along. And even so . . .' She took a deep breath, and tried to stop her voice from shaking. 'This won't work. You're going to get us all killed.'

The old woman shook her head slowly, then drew something from her sleeve. The wooden spoon. She held it up, examining it like a duellist testing a rapier.

'But I have this, child. A wand enchanted by the elf, Caspar of Hel, the finest magician in all the north. Magical potency locked securely, hidden within the very grain of the wood. Untraceable. Undetectable. And yet more powerful than any trinket in all the Old World. It was a mistake to entrust such a thing to a reckless smuggler, but no matter. I have it now. And with this wand, there will be no danger.'

The deck creaked as a militiaman approached. Colonel Cyrus Derringer. Only this morning, he didn't seem like his usual, calm self. There were bags under his eyes, as if he'd had a sleepless night, and he looked uneasy.

What in Thalin's name was he doing here?

'Lady Wyrmwood. The navigator reports that the wind is fair, and we're making good time. We'll be at the trench within a few hours.'

'Very well. I will begin my preparations.'

Tabitha stared at the woman.

'Lady *Wyrmwood*?'

'Arabella Wyrmwood,' said the old woman. 'Yes, that was my name. As you can see, my coward son has been a help, at last. He provided me with this ship and crew, and of course, Colonel Derringer and his blackcoats.'

'But . . . So you're . . . Governor Wyrmwood's mother?'

'And you are Tabitha Mandeville. You do not have to tell me, child. I've seen those grey eyes before, ten years ago. You have your mother's looks, but your father's blindness to the truth.'

Derringer stepped forward and caught Tabitha firmly as she sprang up.

'You evil hag! You stinking witch! You monster!'

'I did not expect you to understand,' said the witch. There was a note of sadness in her voice. 'Your parents were corrupted. That is why I had to kill them. For the good of humanity.' She turned to look at Tabitha, at last. 'Do you understand why I've brought you here? So that you can see. See the destruction. See the twisted place that your parents tried to protect crushed into nothingness. See the triumph of the Light. You must see all this, child, before you die.'

'Can't we go any faster?'

'Now now. Patience, matey.'

Hal muttered something under his breath, but fortunately Clagg didn't hear.

It was strange, Grubb thought, seeing Clagg in command of a ship. He'd seemed a bit lost and helpless on land, but out here in the salt air he was in his element. He was bellowing out orders to his crew, one hand gripping the wheel and the other a large flask of something that Grubb reckoned probably wasn't water. Even the smuggler's lazy eye seemed to be behaving itself better now that they were out at sea.

Above them, the sails stretched out like billowing white clouds, carrying them forward. The wind was good, thank Thalin. Grubb had been nervous about his first journey in a real ship, but he was actually enjoying himself. He watched Clagg's men at work, tugging ropes and clambering on the rigging. At the prow he saw Newton, one foot on the bowsprit, staring grimly ahead and ignoring the bustle of the smuggler crew behind him.

Clagg noticed him looking, and chuckled.

'That's one crazy captain yer've got there, lad.'

Hal shook his head in disgust. He was sitting on a barrel nearby, his hands thrust deep in his pockets, looking acutely uncomfortable around the ragtag smuggler crew. 'He's trying to rescue our friend and arrest a dangerous witch. And all you can say is he's crazy?'

'Aye,' confirmed Clagg. 'It's crazy doing anything that don't earn you a nice tidy heap o' ducats, that's what I reckon.'

'So money is the only thing you care about?'

'He's not my captain anyway,' said Grubb quickly, hoping to stop the argument before it got going. 'I'm not Demon's Watch, remember? Just a tavern boy.'

'Well, matey, yer seem like a watchman to me.'

Coming from Phineus Clagg, Grubb couldn't be sure whether that was a compliment or not.

The smuggler's cabin boy arrived with a basket, and handed round breakfast: morsels of fried squid. Grubb took a piece. Hal made a face, shook his head and went below decks.

'We'll be there in a couple of hours,' said Clagg, tearing off a chunk of squid with his teeth and gulping it down. 'Two leagues south of the Lonely Isle. You can tell yer precious Newton if yer like. Beats me why anyone would want to go to the Farian Trench, anyway.'

Grubb stopped in mid-chew.

'What did you just say?' He swallowed.

'The Farian sea trench. That's where we're going, matey. Two leagues south of the Lonely Isle. You 'ave to know yer charts to be as good a smuggler as I am.'

'But the trench isn't real, is it? It's just a story.'

Clagg snorted.

'Course it's real.'

'This can't be,' said Grubb.

'This can't be what?' asked Newton. He was striding down the deck towards them.

'The wooden spoon. I think I know what it's for.'

'What? How?'

'We're going to the Farian Trench.'

Newton's face froze for just an instant.

'The Maw,' he said.

'Will someone please tell me what in all the blue sea you lot are talking about?'

Newton murmured under his breath:

'In the Farian Trench, the great Maw sleeps,
Where sailors fear the dreadful deep.'

'A sea demon,' said Grubb. He felt foolish saying it. Everyone knew that demons didn't exist any more. But Clagg had said it himself – why else would anyone go to the Farian Trench? 'The demon that killed Thalin the Navigator. In children's stories, it's said to live there, in the trench.'

'Not just in children's stories,' said Newton. 'In the Dark Age, no ships would go near the Lonely Isle. That's where it gets its name. Whole vessels disappeared, along with their crew.'

Clagg snorted again.

'Now come on, lads. A sea demon? You've been hanging round with airy-fairy magicians for too long, filling yer heads with daft old stories. Them demons died out centuries ago. The ones what weren't killed off by heroes on stupid quests, that is.'

'You don't know that,' said Newton. 'Miss Arabella Wyrmwood thinks this one's still alive, at least.'

'And that's why she wanted the wooden spoon,' said Grubb. 'It's a mind leash, but not for a person. For a demon.'

Chapter Thirty-four

The morning had turned grey and chilly, and at last the frigate was riding the waves above the Farian Trench.

A team of ten men had stripped to the waist and were shoving and straining as hard as they could to turn a capstan. The dinghy creaked downwards, taking its mysterious load down to the murky water.

The militia company were all on deck now. They were drawn up in two ranks of ten, all of them standing to attention, crossbows and muskets pointing skywards. It was an impressive sight, but Tabitha only had to look at their faces to see how nervous they were. None of them knew what was happening.

Arabella Wyrmwood had changed her clothes. The ragged grey cloak was gone, replaced by a thick white hooded gown with a golden sun embroidered on the back – the arms of the League of the Light. As ever, her hood was drawn up. She stood on the poop deck, a lone figure silhouetted against a vast, featureless sky.

Tabitha looked out over the sea ahead. Could the witch really raise the Maw from the deep? She tried to imagine the waters parting, and the sea demon raising its head above the waves. Did it even have a head? No one knew, of course. There was the statue in Thalin Square, and she'd seen pictures in books when she was little, but they were all just fantasies – imagined versions of the demon. Sometimes the Maw was an enormous green serpent with a coiling tail and gaping jaws. Sometimes a kraken, with thick, slimy tentacles. Sometimes a giant black creature with horns and red eyes . . .

Tabitha laid a hand on the gunwale to steady herself. She was feeling dizzy, her head swirling with vertigo. The beast that slew Thalin, rising again at his festival, to destroy the town he founded. She had to admit, it was just like the witch said. *What more fitting end than this?*

'Careful with that, you fools,' screeched Arabella at two sailors who were lowering a wooden casket into the dinghy. They nodded, wide-eyed with fear, and carried on as if the casket was made of glass.

There was a shout from the crow's nest.

'Ship ahoy! Due south.'

The captain drew out a spyglass and scanned the horizon. Tabitha could just make it out, a speck in the distance.

'She's coming from Fayt, my lady,' said the captain. 'Heading straight for us.'

'How fast?'

'Looks like a wavecutter. With this wind, she'll be with us in less than an hour.'

Arabella turned cold eyes on Tabitha.

'Your friends, no doubt. But they are too late. Captain, run out the cannons.'

'Yes, my lady.'

'Colonel Derringer.'

The militiaman saluted.

'Take charge of the ship, and deal with these maggots.'

'Er, very well, my lady. But perhaps . . . I mean . . . shouldn't we wait and see what they want, before—'

Arabella's face twisted with fury.

'Do not tell me what to do, elf,' she spat. 'You will deal with it. I have more important matters to attend to.'

'You do know what she's doing, don't you?' Tabitha cried out suddenly. 'She's going to raise a *demon* from the *sea*! Are you just going to stand around and let her do it?'

Arabella said nothing. Several of the sailors glanced at each other. Derringer looked searchingly at the witch.

'Look at her robes, for Thalin's sake!' yelled Tabitha. 'Are you blind? She's an agent of the League of the Light! She's going to kill us all.'

Derringer had gone very pale. He swallowed hard.

'My orders,' he said at last, 'are from the governor. I'm to protect Lady Wyrmwood at all costs.'

Tabitha almost screamed with frustration.

'You, girl,' said Arabella, her voice dripping with hatred. 'You come with me.'

She gripped Tabitha by the ear and pulled her towards the dinghy.

'It's them,' shouted Paddy, punching the air in triumph. 'She's flying the Cockatrice Company flag.'

He was right. The witch's frigate loomed up ahead, gold and purple fluttering above the mainmast. The *Sharkbane* was closing fast.

'Told yer I'd get yer there, didn't I?' Clagg grinned. 'This here is the fastest ship in the Ebony Ocean.'

'Is it, now?' said Paddy. It wasn't the first time Clagg had mentioned that particular fact.

Frank clapped a hand on the smuggler's back, almost knocking him off balance.

'Well done, Cap'n Cuttlefish. You've done something useful for once in your life.'

'We have to stop her from raising the Maw,' said Newton. 'Clagg, tell your men to get ready for a fight.'

The grin on Clagg's face froze.

'Er, now now, matey. Fair's fair. Yer didn't say anything about fighting, did yer? So how about we drop you lot off here, and be on our way?'

'Don't be such a baby,' said Paddy cheerfully.

'You big scaredy-fish,' added Frank.

'All right, all right, steady on. I ain't going to fight for nothing. What'll yer give me?'

'Self-respect,' replied Newton.

'A chance to redeem yourself,' said Hal. 'Prove that you're more than just a money-grubbing crook.'

'Hmm. That's very tempting o' course. How about all that, plus an extra month into our bargain, to do whatever I please. And whatever plunder there is on that there ship. Deal?'

The troll twins groaned, as one.

'Deal,' said Newton.

* * *

'That's far enough.'

Tabitha let go of the oars and slumped over them, her muscles aching. The weight of the witch's apparatus had made the short trip hard work. The dinghy bobbed gently in the waves, some distance from the ship. It was strangely quiet. The sea was calm, and the sky was empty. There was something spooky about this patch of water, Tabitha realized. It felt . . . wrong.

'Now, you won't be bothering me any more,' said the witch.

Before Tabitha could respond, she felt her hands being drawn together as if someone was pulling them. They met with a clap behind her back. She tried to stand, but her feet shot together in the same way. She tried to open her mouth to protest, but her lips felt like they were glued, and they wouldn't open. She was furious, but powerless. She could only sit and watch.

Arabella opened the wooden casket and took out several small bottles of powder and coloured liquid, a wooden pestle and mortar and a large book. She opened it and began to read out strange words that Tabitha didn't recognize.

At first it seemed as if nothing was happening. Then – was it her imagination? – the sky seemed darker than before, and a breeze began to blow.

* * *

There were no more than twenty smugglers, and not one of them looked like a fighter. They held battered old cutlasses, blunt axes and rusty firearms, and shifted round nervously, casting furtive glances at the enemy ship. Probably wondering how they'd let Clagg talk them into this.

At least the Demon's Watch seemed confident. Old Jon was sitting on a barrel, face as calm as ever, his cudgel across his knee. Frank and Paddy were stretching like athletes and practising sword strokes, both of them looking unusually serious. Hal sat cross-legged on the deck, his eyes closed, building up his concentration for spells. The smugglers' magician sat with him, a thin human wearing a dirty old coat. Newton twirled his staff in the air, effortlessly turning it into a buzzing blur, flicking it from hand to hand. Seeing the watchmen, Grubb felt a little less afraid. He lifted the short hand-axe that Paddy had given him, testing its weight and trying to imagine what it would feel like to use in battle.

'Listen, everybody,' said Newton, raising a hand.

Silence fell at once.

'Here's the plan. We don't have any cannon, but we don't have time to get into a fire-fight, anyway. So we'll head straight for them, let fly with a volley of small arms and then board.

'Now, we don't know how many men they've got on that ship. We don't know if they're just sailors, or militiamen armed to the teeth. But either way, I don't give a flea's spit. You might not all know Fayt like I do. But if we fail, a whole town could be destroyed – men, women, children and old folk alike. This is our chance to save their lives. Understand?'

There was a low murmur.

'Then Thalin protect you. Make ready!'

There was a cheer. Not a deafening one, but a cheer nonetheless.

'Battle stations!' shouted Captain Clagg.

'Going to need a lot more than blinking Thalin protecting us, if you ask me,' Grubb heard one smuggler mutter.

The wind was stronger now. It howled over the water, throwing up flecks of foam and tossing the dinghy to and fro. Tabitha felt a spot of rain on her face, then another, and moments later the sea was dimpled with the falling drops. The witch's voice rose with the wind, mingling with it, growing ever louder. She crushed powders in the mortar bowl, rubbed them into the wood of the machinery and cast liquids into the sea, reciting from the book as she did so.

To her astonishment, Tabitha noticed that the metal

rod was changing colour, shimmering faintly as if steam was passing over it. It began to glow with a dull, dark, throbbing light. Arabella Wyrmwood turned a winch and the arm jerked down, dipping into the water, deeper and deeper, until it was fully submerged.

The spots of rain turned to spatters.

Cannonballs thundered into the *Sharkbane*'s hull, sending up explosions of splinters. Grubb threw himself flat on the deck, paralysed with terror.

'My ship!' screeched Clagg. 'You filthy, wretched, stinking— *Gaaaargh!*'

'Stay down,' came Newton's voice, astonishingly calm.

There was a volley of shots from the Cockatrice vessel, but the smugglers and the watchmen were crouched down low, and the musket balls and bolts just ricocheted off the side of the ship and tore through the sails.

The wind was up now, and the *Sharkbane* was moving fast with it, closing on the *Incorruptible*. They were so close that Grubb could hear the voices of the enemy.

'Reload,' someone was saying. 'Quickly!'

'I've changed me mind,' howled Clagg. 'I want to go back to port!'

But it was too late for that. With a juddering, rending, ear-splitting crash, the smugglers' vessel ploughed into the frigate.

'Attack!' yelled Newton. '*Attaaaaaack!*'

Grappling hooks arced above, falling on the deck of the *Incorruptible*. Grubb roared as loudly as he could. He couldn't tell if it scared the enemy, but it made him feel better. He rose up, one foot on the prow, and leaped onto the witch's vessel.

There was a mass of blackcoats on board, most of them still reloading, but at the sight of the attackers they dropped their guns and drew sabres, letting out their own war cries. There were shots, screams, thuds and the clatter of steel on steel. Grubb could hardly tell what was happening. He flailed his axe around, desperate to keep the militiamen at bay, desperate to live.

He must have been moving forwards, because in a moment he was free, beyond the fighting. Glancing back, he saw the smugglers still attacking, breaking on the blackcoats like waves on a beach. Heart pounding, he crouched behind the foremast, out of view of the battle, and took in the witch's ship. Tabitha and Arabella were nowhere to be seen. But the ship's dinghy was missing. He looked out to sea, and there, not far away, he saw it. It was laden with strange machinery, and a white, hooded figure, and a girl with blue hair . . .

There was only one thing for it. He raced to the side of the ship, hopped up onto the gunwale and dived.

It was only when he was halfway to the water that it hit him how incredibly stupid he was being. Then the icy water hit him, twice as hard.

He surfaced, spluttering and rubbing salt water from his eyes. What in all the wide blue sea was he doing? Did he think he was some sort of hero, like Captain Newton? Of course he wasn't. He was just a tavern boy with a head full of bad ideas. *The Maw. Somewhere below him was the Maw.* He looked back at the sheer hull of the ship. There was no way back up. The water was so cold it burned.

So now there really was only one thing for it. He gulped in air, and began to swim towards the witch's dinghy.

Newton laid two men low with a couple of deft movements of the Banshee. One went out cold, the other howled and clutched his nose, blood spurting through his fingers. The captain of the Demon's Watch paused for a second, assessing the battle.

Most of the smugglers were easy prey for the trained militiamen and their deadly sabres. But others were putting tavern brawling skills to good use. Meanwhile, Paddy and Frank were carving a twin path through the enemy. Hal and the smugglers' magician fought back to back, hurling waves of magical force at their opponents and knocking them off their feet. Old Jon cracked two sailors' heads together and left them in a heap on the deck.

They were winning – except for one thing. Colonel Cyrus Derringer's slender blade danced around him faster than a fairy, dispatching the smugglers with contemptuous ease. He moved with a speed and agility only an elf could attain, fighting with one arm held behind his back, the way they taught in the fencing schools of the Old World. His blade was deadly, but it was his face that bore the mark of a true professional. It was expressionless, calm even in the heat of battle.

He had to be stopped.

'Cyrus Derringer! Want a real fight?'

The elf parried a goblin girl's cutlass and kicked her in the stomach, sending her spinning away with a shocked look on her face.

'Mr Newton. Is this rabble all you've got?' He flicked blood from his blade.

'You should be ashamed of yourself. You're betraying your home.'

'I'm obeying my governor,' snapped Derringer. But

Newton thought he saw doubt cloud his face for just a moment. 'And I'll send you all to the bottom of the ocean, if I have to.'

'Come on then,' snarled Newton. 'For Port Fayt.'

Grubb's arms and legs ached, his chest burned and his fingers and toes were frozen. However fast he swam, it seemed like he was getting no closer. He rose and fell with the waves, gulping in air whenever he could, catching a glimpse every now and then of Tabitha, her hands tied behind her back, her blue hair sodden and clinging to her face. And he saw the witch too, heard her terrible voice carrying out across the sea, strange, feral words tumbling out, calling on the Maw.

Arabella Wyrmwood's eyes were swelling and swirling, black as the night, and her voice was inhuman, the roar of a wild animal. Her body quivered as she channelled magical energy through herself, into the machinery and down into the depths.

And, with a sound so low, so deep that it was felt and not heard, the dinghy moved. It wasn't the wind or the waves or the rain. Tabitha was sure of it. Far below, beneath the ocean, something had shifted.

The rain became a torrent.

* * *

Cyrus Derringer tossed his sword from hand to hand, flicking it easily in circles, while Newton stood waiting, his staff motionless. The deck was slick with rainwater and blood. The fighting, the killing and the screams surged around them.

Newton sized up his opponent. The elf was fast, and his blade was faster still. But on the other hand, he was arrogant, too sure of his own success. Maybe, just maybe, it would be his undoing.

Derringer smoothed back his damp hair and skipped in at an angle, his blade curving round.

Newton sidestepped, the sword glancing off the Banshee. Almost without thinking, he brought the other end of the staff swinging round, just as Tori the hobgoblin had taught him, long ago. But it wasn't good enough. Derringer was already well out of range, his blade still spinning in his hand. The elf's speed made Newton feel clumsy, weighed down, as if he was moving through water.

The elf smiled, and his sword became a blur. In a moment he was up close, driving his opponent back, hacking and slicing in every direction at once. Newton parried desperately, evading blow after blow.

And then there was pain in his leg, and he fell heavily forward onto one knee. Triumphant, Derringer raised his sword . . .

Too cocky. The end of the Banshee jabbed hard into the elf's throat.

Derringer's eyes went comically wide with shock. The sword fell and he clutched at his throat, choking, staggering backwards, and slipped over on the wet deck. Newton was up in an instant, his weight on his one good leg. Derringer fumbled for the sword, and Newton kicked it away. Looking down, he felt a jolt of anger to see his thigh covered in blood. He shoved the elf down with the Banshee.

'Your governor,' he growled, 'told us to stop that witch, before he died.' He watched confusion and mistrust fight for control of Derringer's face. 'She might have been his mother, but she's with the League of the Light. Don't you get it? She's the enemy.'

'But the governor said—'

'Forget the governor. What do you think she's doing now? Calling a demon to destroy Port Fayt, that's what. And we have to stop her. Together.'

'Together?' Derringer repeated, in a daze.

The witch threw back her hood, and Tabitha winced at the sight. Her grey skin was stretched taut over her skull. A few strands of grey-white hair flew out in the wind, and her black eyes whirled and danced. She opened her mouth wide, and let out a howl that rolled across the ocean and shook the ships with its power.

'RISE! RISE! RISE!'

All at once the wind dropped, and the sea calmed.

There was a low rumble, and Grubb felt the water vibrate below him.

The rumble became a roar.

On board the *Incorruptible*, the fighting stopped. Everyone watched the ocean, dizzy with horror. Some knew what was going to happen, but could barely believe it. Others sensed something in the air, and were filled with a fear they couldn't explain.

Arabella Wyrmwood drew the wooden spoon from her sleeve and raised it high above her head in triumph.

It was coming. The Maw. *It was coming.*

The sea was torn in two.

Grubb might have screamed, but if so, he didn't notice. His body convulsed, and he was flung aside in a torrent of water, like a doll tossed away by a petulant child.

Newton saw it all.

A shadow fell across the ocean. While militiamen

and smugglers threw themselves flat down in terror, hid their faces from the world and grasped hold of anything they could find, he stood, transfixed, and watched.

The Maw made a sound – a warbling, bellowing scream that seemed to stop his heart mid-beat.

It was nothing like the statue in Thalin Square.

Grubb surfaced, gasping and spluttering out seawater. There was the boat, and beyond it . . . beyond it . . .

Don't look. Focus. Focus on the boat. Focus on getting to Tabitha before . . . before anything more could happen. He struck out desperately, fighting his way towards her.

Arabella Wyrmwood was chanting. Tabitha opened her eyes just a fraction, in case she caught sight of the nightmare that loomed above. The witch was standing, gripping the spoon, her eyes closed as she channelled all her energy, fighting to worm her way into the mind of the beast.

Tabitha wriggled, trying to free her hands and feet, but it was no good. They were stuck fast. And then a strange image came into her head. She remembered Joseph, in the Pickled Dragon, throwing himself at the big militiaman and falling on his backside. So brave, and so stupid.

Two could play at that game.

She wobbled to her feet and hopped backwards, just managing not to overbalance. Then she bent her knees and launched herself across the dinghy, as hard as she could.

Half a second too late, Arabella noticed what was happening. She lowered the wooden spoon, her eyes narrowed with rage . . . and then Tabitha crashed into her. They tumbled outwards, pressed together, Arabella spitting and snarling. Tabitha felt her hands and feet come unglued as the witch's concentration broke.

For a moment she caught a glimpse of something beyond Arabella's shoulder, among the waves – the mottled face of a mongrel boy, rising and falling with the sea – before the pair of them smacked into the water like twin sacks of ducats.

Grubb saw the dinghy rock, saw the splash, saw Tabitha emerge a moment later, no more than twenty feet away, blue hair plastered to her head. She cast about, spotted him, waved at him.

'Hold this for a minute,' she yelled, and something came curving through the air towards him, droplets falling away from it.

Grubb pushed himself up as high as he could go, and caught the wooden spoon.

'Go,' shouted Tabitha. 'Back to the ship.'

Grubb bobbed in the waves, panting, hesitating. He couldn't go back without her. Not this time.

Beyond, the demon let out another hideous scream. It rippled the water, turning his blood to ice. He didn't dare look at it, but out of the corner of his eye he saw that it was moving. *Oh, Thalin.* It was moving towards the ships.

'What are you waiting for?' shrieked Tabitha. 'We don't have much—'

And then something surged up out of the water behind her, seizing her collar and lifting her out of the sea, upwards and upwards.

Tabitha choked, clutching at her neck, trying to tear away the cold hands that gripped her from behind. Arabella Wyrmwood's hands.

She looked down and saw the dinghy ten feet below, saw Grubb looking up, eyes as big as cannon-balls, still holding the spoon. Her feet kicked uselessly in the air. She caught a glimpse of the witch's white robes.

White, like a seraph.

'That wand belongs to me,' roared the witch. 'Give it to me, mongrel. Give it to me, or she will die.'

Tabitha tried to tell him to go, swim, get away. But

all that came out was a strangled squawk. She watched him decide.

What would his father do? Or Captain Newton, or Thalin the Navigator? They would be strong enough to do the right thing, of course. To make the hard decision. To save a town, not just a single girl. But Grubb couldn't think about them, couldn't focus at all. There was only Tabitha, struggling, but too weak to get away. Tabitha, her face going red, then purple. Tabitha, who was kicking less and less now, as the witch gripped her tighter and tighter . . .

He pulled back his arm and threw the spoon.

And then the witch was swooping over the water like a great seagull, with Tabitha in one hand and the wooden spoon in the other. Towards the demon.

They had lost, Grubb realized, and it was all because of him.

He kept treading water, but he felt as if his insides were turning to stone. What else could he have expected? Arabella Wyrmwood was stronger, so much stronger than he was. *All that way for this.* There was nothing more he could have done, and no other way it could have ended.

He had never been strong enough, and now they were all going to die for it.

Finally, in despair, he looked up at the Maw.

The first thing he saw was the way the sky shimmered and distorted around it. The leak of demon magic, smudging reality wherever it moved.

The next thing was its size, how it rose above the ships as if they were toys floating in its bath. He would have laughed, if he could.

Next, how the Maw waded like a human – but as if the water was no obstacle at all, as though the demon and the ocean existed in two entirely separate senses. Its body was dark, the colour of seaweed, and every inch of it was writhing with violence. It was impossible to tell how deep below the surf that terrible body extended. Its back was curved and covered in spines, and its limbs were like spiders' legs, long, slender and pointed, sending great gouts of spray into the air wherever they struck the ocean.

The head was the worst thing of all. The Maw had no use for ears, nose or mouth. But its eyes were vast, like those of a fish ten thousand times magnified. They were the colour of a stormy sea, somehow at once emotionless yet smouldering with malevolence.

A demon. A monster. A nightmare.

It had almost reached the ships.

Grubb hauled himself into the abandoned dinghy, shivering. The Maw filled his mind, blocking out everything else so much that he almost felt calm. He gripped the oars and began to row, turning the boat towards the demon. Running couldn't save him. He would go down with his friends, with Newton and Tabitha. With Frank and Paddy, Hal and Old Jon. With Captain Clagg. He almost laughed to think of what he was doing. Maybe he'd gone mad. But it seemed as if there wasn't much point being sane any more.

In the distance, he could see the witch hovering, a white spot against the Maw's dark, shifting skin, still holding Tabitha. There was a scattering of musket shots from the frigate, trying to drive off the demon. But they might as well have been trying to stab a dragon with a feather.

The Maw reached out with a limb that curled around the mainmast of the *Incorruptible*, plucking it away, sails and all, and tossing it from the ship like a broken toothpick. There were screams.

The witch's plan was working. Of course it was working. She would kill them all, and then Port Fayt would be next. Grubb rowed harder, faster. *Might as well get this over with.*

The Maw snapped off the bowsprit, ripped away ratlines.

And then it turned.

Something was . . .

Something was wrong.

The witch's voice carried to Grubb, over the water; shrill, angry and, most of all, *desperate*.

The witch let go. Tabitha dropped, slid down a sail, bounced off a spar and crashed onto the deck. She lay there groaning, looking upwards, her body throbbing with pain.

Arabella hung in the space where the mainmast had been, grasping the wooden spoon two-handed as if it were a broadsword – but tightly, too tightly. Her eyes were bulging, and she was chanting faster and faster.

The demon had stopped its attack and turned towards Arabella. It was . . . Could it be . . . watching her?

And there, amid the screaming, the splintered wood and the people rushing in every direction, realization dawned on Tabitha. *She couldn't control it.* After all this, the witch had no power over the Maw. No power at all.

Arabella was gripped with rage. Tabitha could see it in her face. She took one hand from the wooden spoon and thrust it forwards, sending a black wave of magic surging towards the demon. Its flesh shook at the impact, and it let out a searing squall of noise.

She was trying to beat the Maw, as if it was just a stubborn horse, or a dog.

Somehow, Tabitha found the strength to let out a croak of laughter.

With liquid speed, the Maw swiped at its tormentor. The witch hurled herself backwards, white robes streaming in the wind. She darted behind the foremast, and the Maw's limb went crashing through a spar. It swung a second blow at her, and she climbed higher and struck the demon with another blast of black magic. Once again, the mouthless demon howled.

It reached for her and she soared upwards, higher and higher, as if she could escape the world itself.

But the Maw was faster.

Its limbs grew impossibly long, reaching up, overcoming her, grappling her, pulling her back downwards.

The witch managed to free one arm, and Tabitha saw her throw the wooden spoon at the demon. A final, desperate gesture. It bounced off, and disappeared into the surf below. The Maw gripped her arm and squeezed it to her side so that she was trapped, helpless.

The witch's eyes were wide open, and her face was

a picture of horror. She was nothing any more, nothing but a frightened old woman. And in spite of everything, pity stirred in Tabitha's heart.

Arabella began to scream, over and over, wordless sounds tearing their way from her throat, chilling Tabitha's blood, until she had to clap her hands over her ears. Eventually the screams gave way to sobs. But if the Maw had ears, it had no mercy. With a surging roar, it plunged back into the sea, taking Arabella Wyrmwood with it.

Giant, rolling waves spread out from where the demon had dived. Grubb tensed and fought to keep the boat upright as it rocked wildly. At last he collapsed over the oars, panting, letting the churning and foaming of the sea carry him through the wind and the rain.

Minutes passed.

In the distance, something floated up from the swell. A figure, more red than white. Bloody and broken, like a seagull savaged by a dog. It bobbed, face down in the water, the golden sun on its back torn and drenched in gore.

Grubb leaned over the side, and was sick.

Chapter Thirty-five

Tabitha was asleep in Captain Clagg's cabin. Newton had gone down below to sit with her and make sure that she got her rest. Neither of them had said a word since the battle.

On deck, the atmosphere was subdued. The fighting had been over quickly, but not all the smugglers had made it out alive. Some had met their deaths on militia sabres, or on Colonel Derringer's sword. Captain Clagg's young cabin boy Sam was among the dead. He had been down below when the *Incorruptible*'s guns opened fire, and the cannonballs had torn through the ship. The remaining smugglers were handling the *Sharkbane* as flawlessly as ever, but it was clear they were preoccupied. Even Frank and Paddy were keeping quiet out of respect.

Grubb leaned over the stern, watching the ship's wake spread out behind them. Some distance beyond came the *Incorruptible,* heavily damaged but still proudly flying the Cockatrice Company colours. It was under Cyrus Derringer's command now. Grubb had noticed the elf steering well clear of the watchmen in the aftermath of the fighting.

'Cheer up, matey,' said Clagg, ambling over. 'Give us a grin.'

Grubb smiled absently.

'You should be happy, matey. All over now.'

'I s'pose so.'

'I know so. Yer still alive, and that's what counts. You get a look at that sea demon?'

Grubb nodded.

'Scary, was it?'

'You could say that.'

'Didn't clap eyes on it meself, see, matey. Too busy with, er . . . taking care of me ship.'

Grubb realized that he hadn't seen Clagg at any point in the battle. The smuggler glanced around suspiciously and leaned over the stern, next to Grubb.

'While we're on our own, lad, I got a little proposition for yer. I could use a little rascal like you in me crew, see. Just so happens I've got a vacancy for a cabin boy, as I'm sure yer aware.'

How strange, thought Grubb. It was only three days ago that he'd dreamed of joining the smuggler's crew and heading off over the Ebony Ocean. But now the idea of leaving Port Fayt behind seemed wrong. Almost . . . ungrateful.

'Thanks,' he said. 'But I'm no smuggler.'

Clagg hawked and spat noisily into the sea.

'Well, offer's there if yer change yer mind.'

There was a silence, while both of them thought.

'What went wrong?' said Grubb.

'What's that?'

'With the wooden spoon. Something must have gone wrong.'

Clagg shrugged.

'Beats me, matey. Maybe she weren't as good a magician as she thought. Or that wooden spoon don't work on demons. Or, crazy old bat like that, maybe she just wanted to get herself drowned.'

'I don't know. Maybe.'

'Ain't no use worrying about it. She's gone the way of yer precious Thalin now, and good riddance is what I say.'

'Land ahoy,' came a shout from aloft.

Clagg rubbed his hands together.

'And not a moment too soon.' He grinned. 'I've been looking forward to this pageant o' yours. Grog all round, for the heroes of Port Fayt!'

The young fairy grasped the bars of its cage with tiny hands and grinned up at Newton. It was a New Worlder, with small, translucent wings, olive skin, shining eyes and pearly teeth.

'How much?'

'Twenty,' said the fairy seller optimistically.

'Try five.'

'Eighteen?'

'Five.'

'How about fifteen?'

Newton sighed.

'C'mon, Ned. You know it, I know it. He'd need to sprout gold wings before he'd be worth fifteen.'

The fairy seller grinned, revealing his rotten teeth.

'All right, fair's fair. Ten.'

'C'mon, mister,' said the fairy. 'That's cheap as brine, and I can fly faster than a rocket.'

Newton's hand hovered over his purse.

'Know a fairy, name of Slik?' he said softly.

'Oh, yes,' said the fairy, eyes wide. 'He's a dung-head, mister, if you'll 'scuse my saying. Tried to nick a whole flaming thimble o' sugar from my cousin once.'

'Oi,' barked the fairy seller, shaking the cage and making his captive yelp. 'Watch your mouth; that's Mr Newton's own personal fairy you're talking about.'

Newton clamped his hand on the man's arm.

'*Was* my fairy. Not any more.' He pulled open the purse. 'I like him. Ten ducats, is it?'

The fairy seller looked reluctant but nodded all the same, and tucked the money away inside his coat.

'What's your name then, mate?' asked Newton, as the fairy fluttered out of the cage and settled on his shoulder.

'Ty, mister. Pleased to meet you.'

'Pleased to meet you too, Ty.' He pulled a small bag of sugar from his pocket. 'My name's Captain Newton. Welcome to the Demon's Watch.'

Mer Way was overflowing with Fayters in fancy dress. The Grand Party had been impressive, but it was a mere tea party compared to the Pageant of the Sea. Newton and Ty passed an imp with his face painted green and wooden wings tied to his back – a dragon, though not much like the real thing. There was a magician with a big false beard, silver stars sewn onto her sackcloth robe. A mighty hero rattled as he passed, his sword made out of a broom handle, his armour out of plates strapped on with string.

They all ignored Newton, of course. But the truth was, he liked it that way. It was best to stay in the shadows, unseen and unknown. Always waiting, always watching.

The pageant seemed to bring out the best in Fayters. You could almost forget about the crooks and their shark pits, the double-dealing and the back-stabbing. Above the heads of the crowd he could make out the statue of the Navigator in Thalin Square, and the Maw, garlanded with flowers for the occasion. A troll child ran past, giggling and waving an outsized lollipop. Yes. Maybe this town was worth saving, after all.

'You heard the rumours, mister?' Ty was saying. 'Word is, old Governor Wyrmwood shot himself last night.'

'That so?' The rumours had it half right, at least. And it was probably better that way.

'Yes, sir, shot himself. With a gun,' he added helpfully. 'Skelmerdale's taken over, I heard.'

Newton winced. Skelmerdale was a nasty piece of work. A Cockatrice merchant who was rich as an emperor and always on the lookout for ways to get richer. Still, it was probably the best that could be hoped for. At least the new governor didn't have a crazy mother who belonged to the League of the Light.

'And he'll have his hands full,' Ty was saying. 'Because there's going to be a war. Yes, sir. With the League of the Light. Fayters might be celebrating tonight, but come tomorrow, the press gangs'll be out. You'll see, mister.'

'What makes you say that?'

'Maw's teeth, everybody's saying it! You need to keep your ears to the ground, mister.'

'The Maw has no teeth.'

'Huh?'

'The Maw has . . . Never mind. Press gangs.'

That was good news, at least. So Skelmerdale was worried. Maybe the old bilgebag would do Port Fayt proud after all. He was certainly moving fast. And just as well – the League had its eye on Fayt, Newton was sure of that. This business with Arabella Wyrmwood was only the beginning. From the way things were looking, it was only a matter of time before their warships crossed the Ebony Ocean.

'Captain Newton,' someone said, tapping his shoulder.

He turned, and was startled to see Colonel Derringer. The elf was still dressed in his black militia uniform, looking decidedly awkward and out of place amongst the fancy dress and party clothes of the crowds. Even Newton had put on a smart red jacket for the pageant, instead of his usual battered blue number.

'Evening, Colonel.'

Derringer was fiercely examining the ground, rocking on the heels of his boots and fingering the hilt of his sword.

'I thought I'd find you here,' he said.

'Hmm,' said Newton. The elf obviously had something he wanted to say, and was finding it very difficult. But Newton wasn't in the mood to make it easy for him. His leg was still smarting from the wound that Derringer's sword had inflicted. It was bandaged now, and the cut hadn't been serious, but still . . .

'This business with the Wyrmwoods,' Derringer blurted out. 'I, er, I believe I made a mistake.'

Newton was so surprised, he almost forgot to reply. Then he couldn't think what to say. Truth was, he'd made a mistake too, assuming it was Derringer who'd betrayed them to the witch. He'd been unfair.

'Umm . . . Don't worry about it.'

Derringer nodded, and stared at the ground again. At last he looked up, and Newton saw that the usual arrogance had returned to his face.

'This changes nothing though, understand? I'll be speaking to Governor Skelmerdale at the earliest opportunity about your watchmen. You can be sure of that.'

Newton nodded. This was more like what he was used to.

'You do what you think's best,' he said. 'In the meantime, enjoy the pageant.'

But Derringer had already turned on his heel and left, shoving past the partygoers.

'Who was that, mister?' asked Ty.

'That was Colonel Cyrus Derringer, commander of the Dockside Militia.'

'He a friend of yours?'

Newton thought about that for a long time.

'Well,' he said, at last. 'It's hard to say.'

A pair of gigantic fish bounded out of the crowd.

'Come on, grumpy guts, time to join the party!'

'Frank? Paddy?'

As one, the trolls pulled off their outsized fish heads and threw them on the ground, wiping sweat from their brows. Behind them came Old Jon and Hal, weaving through the crowded street. Old Jon had put a delicate blue wildflower in his buttonhole, but Hal didn't appear to have dressed up at all. Going by his expression, it looked as if he could think of a good ten or so places he'd rather be.

'Phew!' gasped Paddy. 'I feel like fish stew in that thing.'

'Now, come on, Newt,' said Frank, punching Newton's arm with a scaly silver fist. 'This is the biggest party of the year, remember? It's time you started having some fun. And that goes for you too, Hal.'

'Look at ol' Cap'n Cuttlefish,' hooted Paddy. 'Now there's a man who knows how to enjoy himself.'

Captain Clagg had climbed onto a passing float and was swaying unsteadily, belting out a song at the top of his voice. He paused every now and again to swig from a bottle, and fight off the driver.

Hal shook his head, as if he couldn't quite believe what he was seeing.

'If that's how to enjoy yourself, I think I'll pass, thank you very much.'

'Thalin's breeches, Hal. You might know a lot about magic, but I reckon me and Frank could teach you a thing or two about parties.'

'Tell you what,' said Frank, winking at Ty. 'How about a race to Ma's pie shop? Last one there buys dinner.'

'In a minute,' said Newton. 'There's a dwarf over there who's juggling with cutlasses.'

The twins turned to look, and Newton limped past

them as fast as his wounded leg would allow, with Ty clinging onto his collar.

'I'll have the eel pie,' he shouted back. 'With plenty of gravy!'

'What are you doing up there?'

Tabitha shrugged.

'Are you coming down, or shall I come up?'

She shrugged again.

Gripping the bag of fried octopus in his teeth, Grubb climbed clumsily onto a cart, and from there up onto the rooftop.

'Octopus?'

She shook her head, and then said, 'Well, all right.'

They munched quietly for a while, sitting hunched up, staring into the middle distance.

'You could close your mouth when you chew,' said Grubb.

In return he got a grunt. Cheering her up wasn't going to be that easy, apparently.

'My father used to bring octopus back from the docks,' he tried. 'Once a week, as a treat. He'd always pretend he'd forgotten, then bring it out just when me and Mother started to believe him.'

No reply.

It was quiet here, above the back streets. Mer Way

could be seen in the distance, lit by a thousand lanterns – a hazy, slow-moving ribbon of light and sound. There were just a few revellers in the street below, dressed to the nines and loaded to the gunwales with cheap grog. Grubb watched as a juggler dropped a lit torch and hopped around with his foot on fire, until a pair of spectators grabbed a butt of rainwater and tipped it over his head.

'What's that tune?' said Tabitha.

'Hmm?'

'That tune. The one you're humming.'

Grubb hadn't realized what he'd been doing.

'It's something my mother used to sing, back at home. When she was doing the dishes.'

'Doesn't it have any words?'

Grubb hesitated for a moment, then cleared his throat:

'*Scrub the dishes, scrub them clean,*
Cleaner than you've ever seen.'

The little song sounded strange without his mother's voice. Thin, and empty. But he sang it all the same. And even though it didn't sound right, it felt good.

'I like it,' said Tabitha, after he'd finished. 'It's nice.'

She popped the last morsel of octopus into her mouth, and licked the grease from her fingers.

There was another long pause.

'She's gone,' said Tabitha quietly. 'Arabella Wyrmwood. She's gone and it was nothing to do with me.'

Grubb glanced at her. She was clasping her knees tightly, still looking straight ahead.

'You wanted revenge?'

'Of course. What else?'

'But she was . . . mad. How can you take revenge on someone so crazy?'

'So what? The League of the Light, they're all crazy, every last one of them. But they're still dangerous scum. What about you? It was idiots like that who killed your parents, for the sky's sake.'

Funny how just the mention of it still made his heart feel like an anchor, weighing him down.

'Yes, I know. But—'

'But what? So that witch got what she deserved. Fine. But it wasn't us who stopped her. It was just bad luck, or chance, or whatever you want to call it.'

'Maybe you're right.'

Silence.

'I thought I would feel different,' said Tabitha at last, in a small voice. 'Once the witch was gone. I thought I could . . . not forget, but sort of . . . get away from it all. And I can't. I still feel the same when I think about them.'

'Lonely,' said Grubb.

'Lonely,' agreed Tabitha.

They sat for a while, looking out across the town.

'All those people,' said Grubb, 'carrying on as if everything's just fine. They don't have any idea a sea demon could have been rampaging through the town right now.'

'They'll know soon enough. Those militiamen won't be able to keep their gobs shut. The smugglers neither. Fayters won't care though. It'll just be a rumour that dies away within a week, you'll see.'

Grubb was pleased to see colour returning to Tabitha's cheeks. Of course, it was mainly because she was getting cross again. But that was better than being sad.

'And there'll be nothing in it for us, I can tell you that,' she went on. 'That's the Demon's Watch for you. We've spent the whole festival chasing after a deadly, powerful wand and a dangerous, crazy witch, and we might as well have been chasing after nothing at all.'

'Nothing,' said Grubb.

Tabitha turned to look at him.

There was something uncoiling in Grubb's mind.

He looked out over the rooftops, as memories whirled and surfaced . . .

How had he not seen it?

I can't detect a trace of his work.

'Joseph? What's wrong?'

You can't trust nobody in this town.

This is a leash, my dear, deluded friend. Do you understand what a person could do with this?

His stomach went cold.

'Oh, Thalin, you're right.'

'What do you mean, I'm right?' Tabitha asked grumpily. 'What's got into you?'

'What you said just now. All this time, right from the beginning, we've been chasing after nothing. Nothing at all. Just a wooden spoon.'

She looked at him as if he'd just told her he was a flying swordfish.

'What are you talking about?'

'The witch managed to call the Maw to the surface, but then she couldn't control it. So the wooden spoon didn't work, did it? Maybe that was because the spoon she used wasn't the wand that Captain Clagg smuggled in from the Old World. Maybe it was just an ordinary spoon.'

Tabitha was frowning.

'That doesn't make any sense.'

'But it does. It makes perfect sense. What if someone switched the magical spoon for an ordinary spoon, so they could keep the wand for themselves? Hal said that the best enchanters can lock magic into a wand, so it doesn't give off a magical trace until you cast a spell with it. So the witch wouldn't know she had a fake, until she actually tried to use it.'

'Well, who switched it then? The Snitch? It would be just like that maggot to pull a stunt like that.'

'No, it couldn't have been him. If he had the real spoon, he wouldn't have bothered bringing Captain Gore and his men to attack the pie shop.'

'Clagg, then?'

'I don't think so. Why would he come all the way over the Ebony Ocean to deliver a fake wand? Besides, he was terrified of that witch. I don't think he would have risked it.'

'So who, then? It couldn't have been a watchman.'

Grubb shook his head.

Do you understand how much it's worth?

It seemed so obvious.

'There's only one other person who could have made the switch.' He started to slide down from the roof. 'We'd better hurry. I just hope he's still in Port Fayt.'

Chapter Thirty-six

The ginger-haired man buttoned his shirt in front of the mirror, yellow eyes following every movement of his fingers.

'So this is it then?' said Slik, from the dresser. He shoved the handle of the wooden spoon with his toe. 'Doesn't look any different from the other one. Are you sure it's magic?'

The shapeshifter sighed and adjusted his lace jabot.

'Yes, I am sure. The fact that it doesn't look any different is precisely the point. If it did look different, it would hardly have been a very effective deception, would it?'

Slik sniffed and sat on the spoon, kicking his heels against it.

'If you say so. It still doesn't make any sense to me.'

'I can't say I'm surprised.'

Slik rolled his eyes. He was already thinking of finding a new employer, and he'd only been with this one for a day.

The cabin was dingy and cramped and smelled funny, but in a few hours the ship would weigh anchor, and Slik would be shot of this stinking town for good. It hadn't been easy to find a vessel that would set sail on the night of the Pageant of the Sea. But now, at last, he could relax. In the Old World, he could easily find another employer. There'd be plenty of opportunities for sugar there.

'So, Azurmouth, eh?' he said. 'What are we going there for?'

'Azurmouth is the greatest port in the Old World,' replied the shapeshifter, pulling on his waistcoat. 'And the spoon is worth ten thousand ducats, to the right buyer.'

Slik whistled.

The shapeshifter buttoned the waistcoat, straightened it and ran a comb through his tangled ginger hair.

'Understand one thing, fairy. If you are to accompany me to the Old World, you'll have to learn some manners. This crude provincial behaviour won't do at all.'

He sat down on the cabin's rickety chair, and bent down to pull on a shoe.

'Manners cost nothing, and besides, they're good for business. Nobody expects to be cheated by a gentleman. Like your Jeb, for instance.'

Slik was just about to reply, when someone put a hand over his mouth and grabbed him from behind.

The fairy made no reply.

'You see,' said the shapeshifter testily, 'this is precisely what I'm talking about.' He pulled on his other shoe. 'Manners, for the sky's sake. Pay attention when I'm speaking to you, if you please.'

'*Mmmmmf mmfff,*' said Slik.

The shapeshifter was fast. With practised ease, he whipped out a miniature pistol, stood up and kicked the chair backwards, straight into whoever was sneaking up on him. Except that the man who was sneaking up on him knew that trick, and was standing a little to the right.

'Game's up,' said Newton, as the chair clattered against the side of the cabin. His pistol clicked as he cocked it, right next to the shapeshifter's head.

'*Mmmmmf,*' said Slik again. Ty had him in a

headlock now, with one hand clamped over his captive's mouth.

The door opened and the rest of the Demon's Watch barged into the cabin.

The shapeshifter froze for an instant. Then, with a scraping, sucking sound, he was gone. His pistol clattered on the floor, and his clothes fell in a crumpled heap. A ginger cat leaped out of them, snatched the wooden spoon from the dresser and streaked towards the cabin door.

'Stop him,' roared Newton, but the cat was already through the watchmen's legs, sprinting out onto the deck, startling a pair of sailors who were rolling up a spare sail.

Grubb crouched, reaching for it. He felt its tail brush through his hand, but gripped at it too late and toppled over – just like the last time he'd tried to catch it. The cat vaulted onto a barrel a few feet away, put down the wooden spoon and sniggered nastily.

'So here we are again, mongrel,' said the cat. 'You, me, and your delightful falling-over routine. Last time you nearly broke your leg. Who knows, maybe it'll be your head this time.'

Newton stormed out of the cabin, followed by the rest of the Demon's Watch, weapons drawn.

'Don't shoot!' cried Grubb, scrambling to his feet. 'Nobody move.'

The watchmen stopped at once.

'I hope you know what you're doing,' said Newton.

'I hope so too,' said the cat, and it giggled.

Grubb had no idea what he was doing. But he did know that if the watchmen chased after it, the cat would escape straight away. It was too fast for any of them. He knew that from their chase over the rooftops.

He glanced at the gangplank to the quayside. The only way off the ship. It was old, wooden, covered in barnacles and barely wide enough for two. No rails, and nothing to secure it to the ship.

An idea began to form in his head.

The cat might be fast, but it was careless and arrogant, too. Even now, when it could get away so easily, it was sitting, waiting, enjoying his uncertainty. It would take any chance it could get to mock him . . .

Newton and the other watchmen were waiting too, still and silent, just like he'd told them. They trusted him. He really hoped he wasn't about to let them down.

'All right,' Grubb said loudly. He puffed up his chest, and did his best impression of Mr Lightly.

'All right, you little maggot. You can't escape me twice. I'll teach you some manners, you stupid, stinking FURBALL!'

Grubb lunged forward. The cat snatched up the spoon, jumped off the barrel, shot over the deck, hopped onto the gangplank and began to race down it. Grubb was no more than three strides short of the gangplank himself, when he tripped and hit the deck.

The cat heard him fall and paused, halfway to dry land, to turn and sneer at him.

Just as Grubb had hoped it would.

The cat's yellow eyes went wide. Its hair stood up. It dropped the wooden spoon.

Grubb hadn't tripped at all – he had dived to reach the end of the gangplank. Now he gripped the edge of it, summoned up all his strength and shoved it outwards.

With a scrape of wood against stone, the plank pivoted on the edge of the quayside. Then it swung slowly down into the sea, taking the cat with it.

'No!' yelped the cat, every trace of dignity gone. 'Mercy! Please! But I can't swi—'

There was a splash and a squawk, and the next moment the cat was soaked and flailing desperately in the water. The wooden spoon bobbed a short distance away, utterly forgotten.

Grubb had never known a cat look so terrified.

They used a long-handled fishing net to scoop out the wooden spoon and the waterlogged shapeshifter. Frank had found an old metal lobster cage to keep it in for the time being, and Paddy dumped it, dripping, inside. According to Hal, a shapeshifter needed hours to build up enough magic to change form. So, for now, this one was stuck being a cat. It sat, crouched and shivering, its fur plastered to its body and its yellow eyes glaring, unforgiving, at the mongrel boy who had tricked it.

Grubb couldn't help feeling a little bad. He knelt down next to the cage.

'It's all right,' he told it. 'Captain Newton isn't going to lock you up. He wanted to, but I told him how you looked after me when I fell off the roof. So you can stay on this ship, until you're back in the Old World. Then the crew will open the cage and let you go.'

'Count yourself lucky,' growled Paddy. He was carrying a bottle, thumb over the top, with Newton's old fairy inside. Slik sat hunched at the bottom, glaring out at the watchmen. 'This cove here's going to the Brig, so you got off lightly, understand? Just don't ever come back to Port Fayt.'

The cat curled up and ignored them. It hadn't said a word since they'd rescued it.

The cabin door opened and Hal stepped out onto the deck, his eyes shining.

'This is it,' he said quietly. He held out the wooden spoon, cradled in his hands like a newborn baby for all the watchmen to see. 'It's the real thing, just like Joseph said. A genuine leash. The most powerful I've ever seen.'

They all stared at the leash. Just a wooden spoon. And at the same time, not just a wooden spoon.

There was a hand on Grubb's shoulder, and he glanced up to find Newton frowning at him.

'You've got some explaining to do. How did you know this cat had the real wand?'

Grubb swallowed and opened his mouth to reply.

'Because,' said Tabitha, before he could get a word out, 'Arabella's one didn't work, did it? She couldn't control the Maw. So someone must have taken the real spoon, and switched it for a fake.'

'Um, yes,' said Grubb. 'Thanks, Tabs.'

'So the question was, who? And it had to be the shapeshifter. See, the fake spoon, the one that Hal examined, had no magical trace on it, of course – so Hal couldn't tell us what the wand was for. Joseph knew that it was supposed to be a leash, but only because the shapeshifter had said so, back in the shark pit. So how could the shapeshifter have known? The only way was if the *real* spoon *did* have a magical trace.'

'Blimey,' said Paddy. 'All pretty straightforward, then.'

'So after he stole the wooden spoon from Joseph on the night of the Grand Party, this joker took it to an expert, had it identified and decided to switch it for a fake. And it's that fake spoon that we've been chasing all over town and halfway across the Ebony Ocean.'

'Poor old Jeb the Snitch,' chuckled Frank. 'He paid Thalin-knows-how-many ducats and got a bit of useless kitchenware in return. It's like he always used to say . . . "You can't trust nobody in this town." '

The cat was staring at Grubb again.

'You,' it said at last. 'Mongrel.' Even soaked and locked up, it spoke as if it was a duke addressing a particularly inferior servant. 'You're not as stupid as you look. What's your name?'

Grubb was about to answer, but found he didn't know what to say.

Who was he?

Until a few days ago, he had always been Grubb. But to the watchmen, he was Joseph. His real name.

The name his parents had given him. He didn't want to give that up.

In the end, Newton answered for him.

'His name's Joseph Grubb,' he said. 'Of the Demon's Watch.'

Epilogue

'Ship ahoy!'

'Aha,' said Tuck, beaming. He'd always known he'd make a better captain than Gore, and now the old scumbag was dead, he finally had a chance to prove it. It was his time, at last.

'What you waiting for, boys?' he roared. 'Break out cutlasses. Raise skull and cleaver. We take this prize before we even reach Old World.'

The pirates raised a ragged cheer.

Tuck cupped his hands to shout up at the crow's nest.

'What colours she fly, Muggs?'

'Looks like the Golden Sun, Cap'n.'

'That's the League,' said the ship's new bosun, a nervous, weasel-like elf named Ringle. 'We want to be careful round that lot.'

'Stow it, Ringle. This the *Weeping Wound*, for sky's sake. We take any ship afloat. Eh, lads?'

There was another enthusiastic cheer.

'Ship ahoy!'

'We hear you first time, Muggs.'

'No no, I mean, another one.'

The pirates looked to their leader.

'Maybe we should leave it just this once, Cap'n,' said Ringle, in a whiny voice that Tuck found particularly irritating.

'Don't talk bilge. We take them both, so help me.'

The pirates cheered again, but this time it was noticeably subdued.

'*Gaaaargh*,' said Muggs, from the crow's nest.

'What you mean, "gaaaargh"?'

Tuck pulled out his spyglass and scanned the distant waters. There were the two vessels. Three vessels. Four, five . . . He adjusted the spyglass to get a clearer image, and his stomach went cold. From the shimmering horizon, ships were appearing. More ships than Tuck had seen in twenty years of piracy in all the waters of the world. Sails filled the sky, and above them, the white banners of the League of the

Light were proudly streaming out in the wind.

An armada.

Heading west.

Towards the *Weeping Wound*.

Towards Port Fayt.

HERE ENDS BOOK ONE

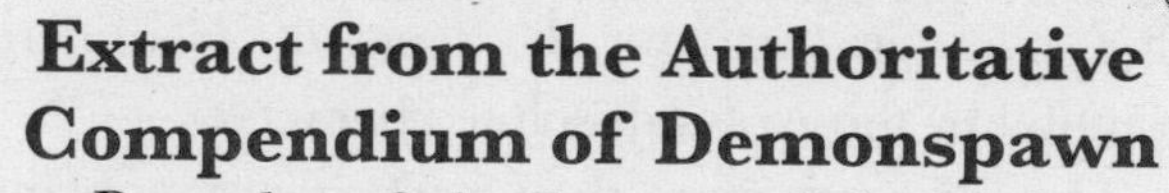

Extract from the Authoritative Compendium of Demonspawn

By order of the League of the Light

Compiled by Dr John Fortescue,
Dr William Silverbell and Dr Alfred Slaughton

This survey has been commissioned by the League of the Light, in order to illustrate the manifold degenerate creatures that currently plague both the Old World and the New. We, the authors of this survey, believe the Human to be the most noble creature of all, created by the very Seraphs themselves. Indeed, one might consider the Human to be the perfect form, of which all other creatures are mere perversions.

The Dwarf – Cantankerous and foreshortened, and in many cases possessed of prodigious facial hair on account of rapid follicle growth. In addition to its modest height, the Dwarf is generally stout and ill-favoured. Some conjecture that it is these factors which most contribute towards the Dwarf's notoriously foul temper. Otherwise Human in appearance, if not in temperament.

Not the most despicable of demonspawn by any means, yet still to be treated with suspicion and avoided wherever possible.

The Elf – Slender of form and very pale of skin; the

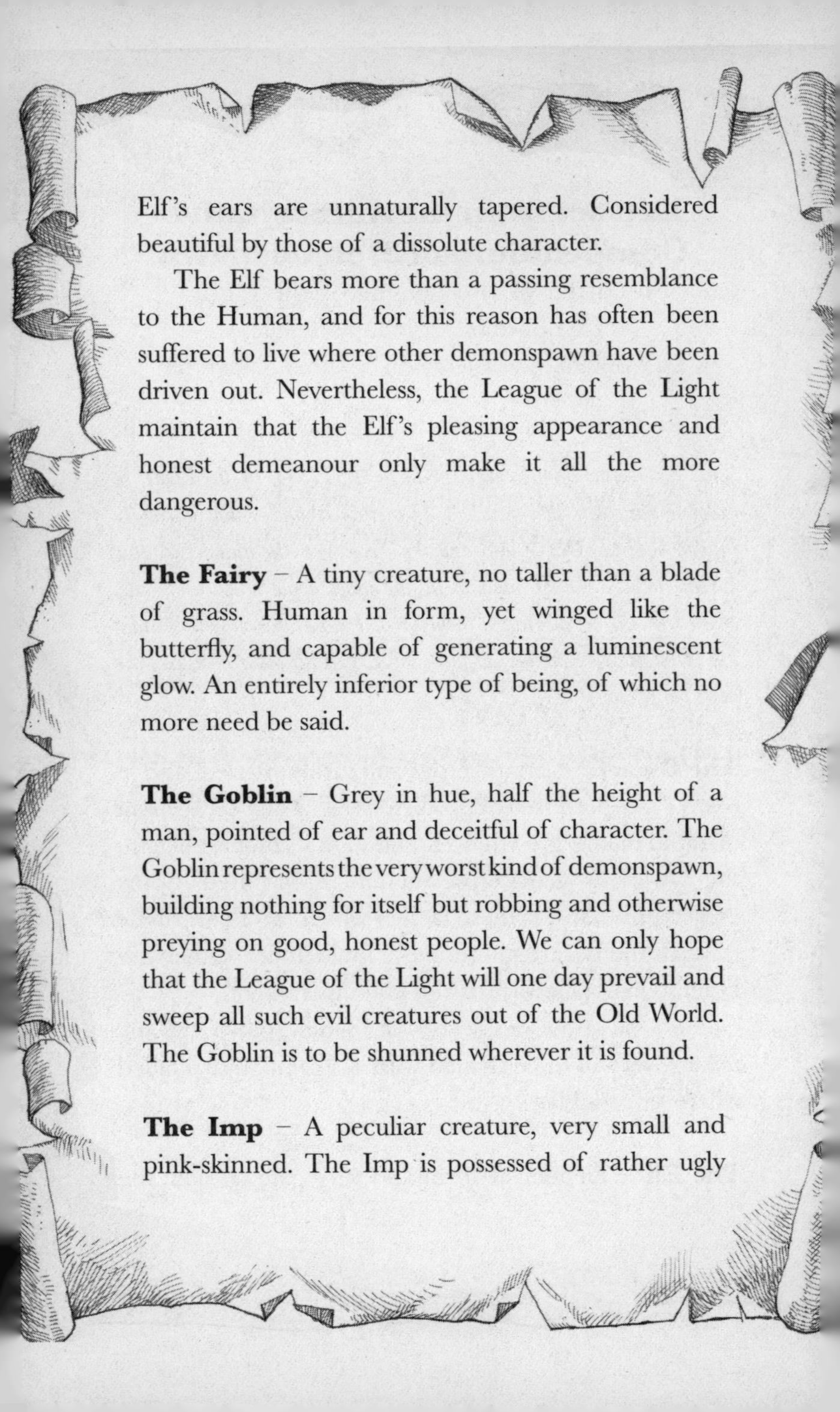

Elf's ears are unnaturally tapered. Considered beautiful by those of a dissolute character.

The Elf bears more than a passing resemblance to the Human, and for this reason has often been suffered to live where other demonspawn have been driven out. Nevertheless, the League of the Light maintain that the Elf's pleasing appearance and honest demeanour only make it all the more dangerous.

The Fairy – A tiny creature, no taller than a blade of grass. Human in form, yet winged like the butterfly, and capable of generating a luminescent glow. An entirely inferior type of being, of which no more need be said.

The Goblin – Grey in hue, half the height of a man, pointed of ear and deceitful of character. The Goblin represents the very worst kind of demonspawn, building nothing for itself but robbing and otherwise preying on good, honest people. We can only hope that the League of the Light will one day prevail and sweep all such evil creatures out of the Old World. The Goblin is to be shunned wherever it is found.

The Imp – A peculiar creature, very small and pink-skinned. The Imp is possessed of rather ugly

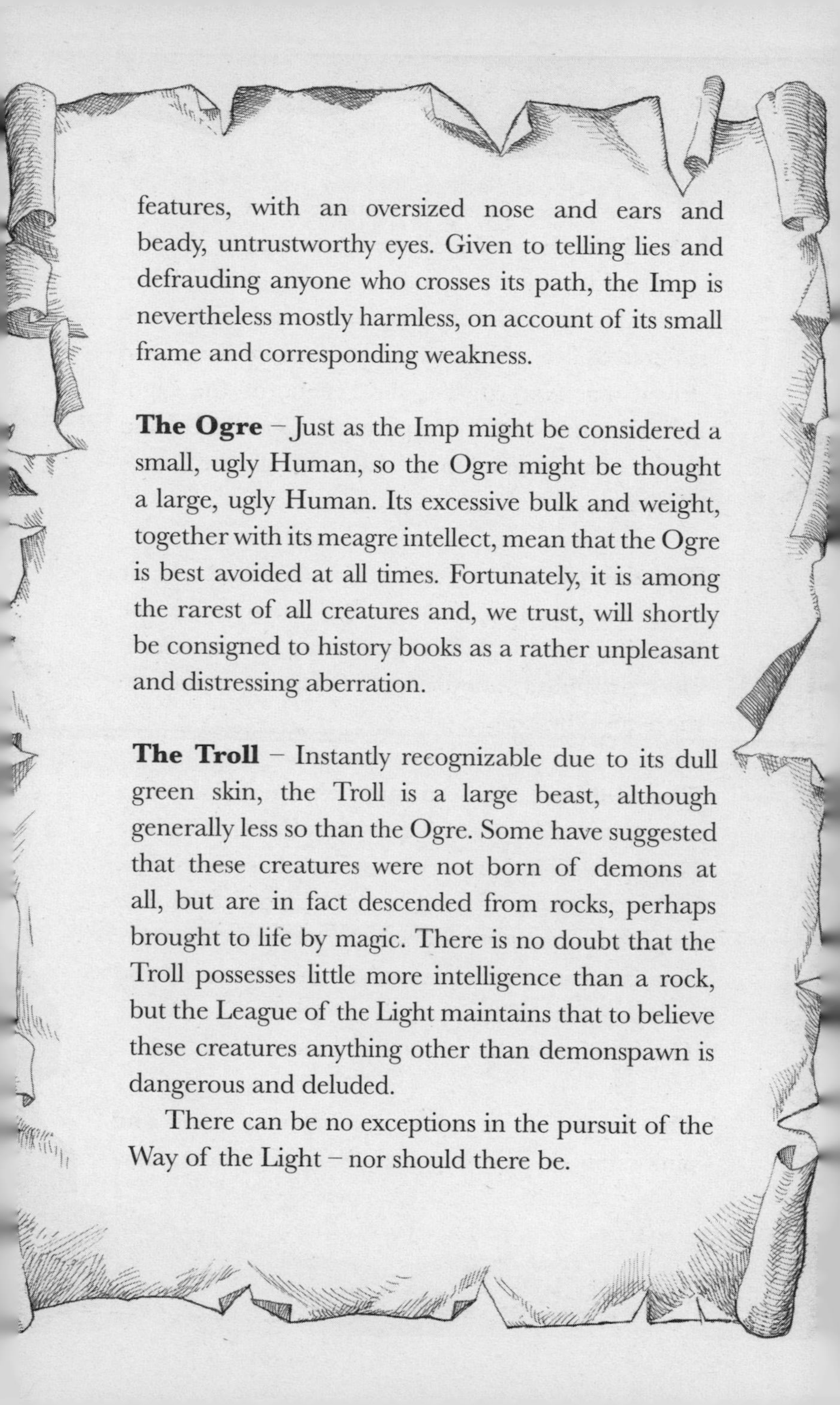

features, with an oversized nose and ears and beady, untrustworthy eyes. Given to telling lies and defrauding anyone who crosses its path, the Imp is nevertheless mostly harmless, on account of its small frame and corresponding weakness.

The Ogre – Just as the Imp might be considered a small, ugly Human, so the Ogre might be thought a large, ugly Human. Its excessive bulk and weight, together with its meagre intellect, mean that the Ogre is best avoided at all times. Fortunately, it is among the rarest of all creatures and, we trust, will shortly be consigned to history books as a rather unpleasant and distressing aberration.

The Troll – Instantly recognizable due to its dull green skin, the Troll is a large beast, although generally less so than the Ogre. Some have suggested that these creatures were not born of demons at all, but are in fact descended from rocks, perhaps brought to life by magic. There is no doubt that the Troll possesses little more intelligence than a rock, but the League of the Light maintains that to believe these creatures anything other than demonspawn is dangerous and deluded.

There can be no exceptions in the pursuit of the Way of the Light – nor should there be.

Acknowledgements

A big thank you to my agent, Jane Finigan, and to all at Lutyens & Rubinstein. To my friends and colleagues for their help and support in all kinds of ways, especially those who read and commented on the manuscript, and to Anne-Marie Doulton for invaluable advice early on ('you have to write the book first'). To the incredible team at DFB – my brilliant editor Simon Mason, Kirsten, Hannah, David and Tilda. And last but not least, to Mark, Verity and Katrina, whom I love, and who put up with a lot.

Conrad Mason was born in 1984. He studied classics at Cambridge University and now works in London as an editor of children's fiction. *The Demon's Watch* is his first novel.

You can visit him online at www.**conrad-mason**.com

BOOK 2 OF
THE TALES OF FAYT

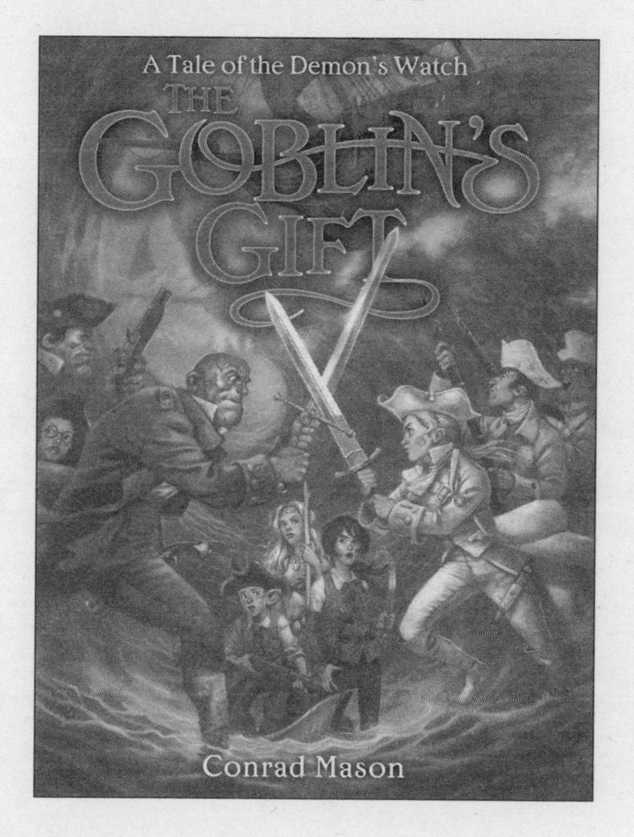

Read on for an exclusive extract . . .

It's not the pain that he enjoys.

It's the fear.

He straightens his glasses with a thumb and forefinger and inspects the creature squirming on the desk before him. It is pinned to a wooden block, wings pierced with Azurmouth steel so that it cannot escape from the darkened cabin.

A female fairy. Daemonium volans. *Demonspawn.*

There is a grotesque fascination in the way it struggles, tries to lift its wings against the steel of the pins, begs, pleads with him to let it go. Almost unbearably disgusting.

'I'll tell you anything,' it cries. 'Please. I promise.'

'Anything? Truly, you'd tell me anything?'

He is rewarded with a flicker of hope in the creature's eyes.

'Yes, sir. I've lived in Port Fayt all my life, sir. I've seen some things, I can tell you. Just give me a chance.'

He leans over the desk, one hand resting on a green marble paperweight, examining the way the creature's wings protrude through holes cut into the fabric of its dirty dress. So foul. So unnatural.

'But what could you possibly know that might help me?'

'I've seen their fleet, sir. The Fayter fleet. I can tell you about their men and their guns. I can tell you all about Governor Skelmerdale. I can tell you . . . I can . . .' Its voice peters out. The flicker of hope dies.

'Suppose you could. What difference would it make? Do you really suppose the Fayters stand a chance against us? No, my dear. I fear you are no use at all.'

'Kill me then. I'm not afraid.'

It has stopped struggling now and lies, tiny arms folded, glaring up at him. Its body glows faintly against the wooden block.

He raises his eyebrows. He had not expected this. Bravery, from such a despicable creature. He would not have thought it possible. And this bravery has driven away all trace of the fear. The fear that he so enjoys.

'I am impressed,' he admits. 'Most impressed.'

There is a knock at the door.

'Enter.'

Morning sunshine spills into the cabin as a white-jacketed marine ducks his head inside.

'Your honour, a vessel has been sighted to the west of our fleet. A wavecutter, flying no colours.'

The Duke of Garran considers for a moment, then nods.

'Very well. I will attend to it.'

He sweeps his hat from the desk, making the fairy flinch.

'Don't worry,' he tells it. 'You've shown me that you are brave. You're not afraid any more. That's good. Very good.'

Hope returns to the fairy's eyes. Delicious. And in one swift movement, the Duke of Garran lifts the marble paperweight and brings it down.

Once.

Twice.

Three times.

There is not even a scream.

He turns back to the marine.

'Send someone in here,' he says, 'to clean my desk.'

PART ONE
Armada

Chapter One

Joseph Grubb clung to the ratlines, gripping the ropes so tightly they burned his hands.

'What are you waiting for?' came Tabitha's voice from below.

He gritted his teeth and kept climbing, doing his best to block out everything except the regular motion: left foot, right hand; right foot, left hand. *Come on. You can do this.* Back in Fayt, he used to scramble up the stepladder in his uncle's pantry every day. Two weeks ago he'd even clambered onto the rooftops of the Marlinspike Quarter to chase a cat. And now he was climbing to the crow's nest of a wavecutter, swaying on a few bits of rope more than a hundred feet above the deck, so high that the people below looked like colourful beetles. So high that . . . He swallowed.

Not helping.

He paused again, panting, brow prickling with sweat. On his raised right arm a fresh tattoo was scored into his greyish-pink mongrel skin. A swirling blue shark – the mark of a watchman. It was still almost impossible to believe that this was what he was. But the proof was right there, in front of his eyes. The Demon's Watch. Protectors of Port Fayt. Scourge of all sea scum.

Scourge of Mrs Bootle's pies, more like.

The thought made him smile, and he started to climb again.

The crow's nest wasn't far now. As he moved, a spyglass bumped around inside the right pocket of his breeches, balancing out the bouncing of the cutlass on his left hip. Captain Newton had given it to him on the day he got his tattoo. The hand-guard was made of thick, solid brass, and the hilt had smooth oiled leather wrapped tightly around it. There was a small shark carved on the blade, and a word neatly lettered beneath it – GRUBB.

No doubt about it. His days as a tavern boy were well and truly over.

'Hey, tavern boy,' came a shout from below. Joseph chanced a look back over his shoulder. His stomach swam at the altitude, but on the deck he spotted the distant shape of Phineus Clagg – professional smuggler and captain of the *Sharkbane*. His hands were cupped around his mouth, and his long hair and dirty coat flapped in the breeze. 'We ain't got all day, yer know.'

Further down the ratlines, Tabitha's blue-haired head turned to shout at him. 'You want to climb up here? Oh wait, I forgot – you're too fat.'

Joseph didn't wait to hear the smuggler's reply. He closed his eyes and kept going. *Left foot, right hand; right foot, left hand*. The higher he got, the more the breeze buffeted him, forcing him to grip the ropes tighter still. But he couldn't stop now. If he did, Tabitha would never let him forget it.

He opened his eyes and at once they began to water in the wind. One last effort . . . *Right foot, left hand* . . . And finally he was there, hauling himself up through the gap and collapsing onto the platform of the crow's nest. He lay there for a moment, gasping for breath, while Tabitha clambered up after him.

'What's wrong?' she asked, slapping him on the back. 'Don't tell me you're scared of heights!' She was trying to sound casual but Joseph didn't believe it for one second. She crouched on the platform, her eyes wide, her face tinged with green.

'You have to admit, we *are* quite high up.'

Tabitha opened her mouth to argue, then flashed him a smile.

'I s'pose you could say that.'

Joseph grinned back at her. Tabitha acted tough, but she was friendly too. Most of the time. She was always asking him about his old life working for his uncle at the Legless Mermaid, and about the time before, when his parents were alive. She didn't talk about her own much, but for some reason she seemed to enjoy hearing Joseph tell stories about his home with the green front door. He enjoyed it too. It was good to have someone he could share the memories with.

Tabitha nodded out to sea. 'What are you waiting for?'

He scrambled to his feet and grabbed hold of the rail at the front of the crow's nest, trying to ignore the fact that on three other sides there was nothing but a sheer drop down to the deck. The view laid out before him did nothing to calm his churning stomach.

In the distance, Illon rose from the sparkling waters of the Ebony Ocean – the easternmost of the Middle Islands; a hazy green hump like the back of a sea serpent. Its largest bay was cluttered with vessels, anchored with their sails furled, white banners fluttering from every masthead. There were wavecutters and frigates on the fringes, and beyond, towards the heart of the fleet, lay the real battleships – galleons and men-of-war.

In the centre was a ship that could only belong to the Duke of Garran. It towered above the others like a wooden castle, its banner so vast that, even from this distance, Joseph could make out the Golden Sun embroidered on it. It was the biggest ship he had ever seen. But then, this was the biggest fleet he'd ever seen too.

He drew out the spyglass and held it to one eye. He could see movement on board some of the nearest vessels – League marines in their white battle-dress, bayonets gleaming. All humans, of course. It sent a shudder down his spine. The League of the Light had come from the Old World for one purpose alone – to destroy Port Fayt and everyone who lived there. Elves, trolls, fairies . . . and mongrels, naturally. Being half human wouldn't save Joseph when the other half of him was goblin.

Tabitha snatched the spyglass away from him.

'Let me have a look,' she said. 'We're supposed to be gathering information, not just gawping. That's the whole point of this expedition, remember? So we can get back to Fayt and figure out how to beat these dungheads.'

Joseph cast a sidelong glance at her as she sighted down the spyglass, blue hair tied back in a ponytail so the wind wouldn't blow it in her face. Like him she wore a watchman's coat, but with a bandolier of throwing knives slung over her shoulder. *Most* of the time she was friendly. But sometimes Joseph thought she liked those knives better than any real person. Tabitha was the first girl he'd ever met properly. Maybe they were just different from boys.

'No,' said Tabitha.

'Pardon?'

She was lowering the telescope, still staring out to sea. Her face had become greener, and her eyes even wider than before. 'No, no, no. Look!'

Joseph turned back to the League armada. It took him a few seconds to see it, but when he did his blood ran cold. The three closest vessels were moving away from the main fleet, heading towards the *Sharkbane*. They looked like frigates. Fighting ships. Fast ones.

'They've spotted us,' said Tabitha. She leaned over the side of the crow's nest and bawled at the top of her voice, 'Turn about! Three League frigates are closing on us!'

Joseph swallowed. 'Does this mean . . . ?'

Tabitha sighed, louder than was necessary. 'Yes, it means we're climbing down again. You first. I don't want you throwing up on me.'

By the time they got down, Phineus Clagg was at the wheel. Joseph had to lean against the tilt of the deck as the *Sharkbane* came about, faster than he would have thought possible for a ship of her size. He and Tabitha hurried towards the stern, dodging smugglers tugging on ropes and shouting out instructions. Hal and the Bootle twins had already gathered around the wheel. All of the Demon's Watch were on board except Newt and Old Jon, who had both stayed behind in Port Fayt.

'Can we outrun them?' asked Hal, adjusting his glasses and peering across the water. He looked anxious. But then, he often did. Before he'd joined the Watch, Joseph had never imagined that a magician could be so . . . jumpy.

'*Can we outrun them?*' Clagg mimicked. 'Course we can, spectacles. Ain't nothing to worry about. This is the *Sharkbane*. The fastest—'

'– ship in the Ebony Ocean,' chorused Frank and Paddy, the troll twins.

'We know,' said Paddy.

'You've mentioned it once or twice before,' added Frank.

Tabitha sprinted up the steps to the poop deck and inspected the League vessels with her spyglass.

'They're gaining on us,' she shouted. 'Those frigates are going faster than a greased fairy.'

'Ain't possible,' said Clagg. He took a long swig from his bottle of firewater and stuffed a fresh lump of tobacco into his mouth, his lazy left eye flicking nervously around the deck. The smuggler hadn't exactly jumped at the chance of helping out the watchmen, but a few ducats and a dangerous look from Newton had been enough to persuade him. He was probably starting to regret it now.

Joseph climbed the steps to join Tabitha. He almost gasped out loud when he saw the frigates. They were much closer than he'd expected, moving steadily, as if unaffected by the waves. In front of every vessel the air shimmered like a mirage, but the ocean was as calm as a glass of water.

'Magic,' he murmured. 'They've got magicians on board.' Spell-casting was banned in Port Fayt – unless you had a warrant, like Hal did – but that made no difference to the League.

Hal appeared next to them. He took the spyglass from Tabitha and examined the enemy ships.

'Ah,' he said at last. 'I fear you may be right. It's elementary brinecraft, applied on a much larger scale than is usually attempted. They're exerting willpower on the waves, reducing tidal movements that would ordinarily disrupt the passage of the vessel. Also I imagine they're performing some sort of aeolian manipulation to increase the flow of wind to the sails. It's rather extraordinary. I've not seen anything like it since—'

'That's fascinating,' cut in Tabitha, 'but maybe we should *do* something about it?'

Joseph leaned over the railing of the poop deck. 'Can we go any faster, Mr Clagg?'

'That's *Captain* Clagg, matey,' replied the smuggler. He was frowning at the ocean ahead, chewing on the tobacco, his hair and coat flung back by the breeze. 'And no, not without a better wind.'

'Thank Thalin we hired the fastest ship in the Ebony Ocean, eh?' said Paddy, clapping an enormous green hand on the smuggler's back. 'Fastest except for those three frigates, anyway.'

'They're cheating! Stinking magic . . . Ruins all the fun, if you ask me.'

'Hal,' said Tabitha. 'If they're speeding up their ships with magic, why can't you do the same for the *Sharkbane*?'

Hal shook his head. 'I'm flattered, but it's out of the question. Spells that powerful require a team of trained magicians working together, focusing their minds as one. I couldn't do it on my own.'

Frank drew his enormous cutlass and swung it in a practice stroke.

'In that case,' he said, 'we'd best get ready for a fight.'